"She's the queen of witty dialogue and sexy scenes!"

—*New York Times* bestselling author Rachel Van Dyken

## PRAISE FOR
## THE CENTRAL PARK PACT SERIES

### *Passion on Park Avenue*

"I couldn't put it down! Not only is the friendship between Naomi, Claire, and Audrey refreshing and inspirational, the chemistry between Naomi and Oliver is off the charts! I love a sassy heroine and a funny hero, and Layne delivers both. Witty banter and an electric connection between Naomi and Oliver kept me turning the pages late into the night. Lauren Layne knocks this one right out of Park Avenue!"

—Samantha Young, *New York Times* bestselling author of
*Fight or Flight*

"Chic and clever! *Passion on Park Avenue* comes to life like a sexy, comedic movie on the page."

—Tessa Bailey, *New York Times* bestselling author

"Strong characters and relatable situations elevate Layne's big-hearted contemporary. . . . This vivid enemies-to-lovers romance digs into class differences, emotional baggage, and the reality of dealing with aging parents."

—*Publishers Weekly* (starred review)

"Featuring wine in coffee mugs, dinner parties with ulterior motives, and Naomi and Oliver being (almost) caught with their pants down, this is perfect for readers who love the dishy women's fiction of Candace Bushnell."

—*Booklist*

# PRAISE FOR
# THE WEDDING BELLES SERIES

"Enchanting and chock-full of all the witty repartee we have come to joyfully anticipate . . . an absolute delight."

—*Hypable*

"Go, grab the entire series, you won't regret it."

—*Caffeinated Reviewer*

## *To Love and to Cherish*

"Not only the fabulous culmination of a slow-burn love story, but the conclusion of a world I was delighted to visit for several books. These characters will stay with me for a while and I already miss them."

—*All About Romance*

"Another fabulous addition to Layne's backlist and it's one that I'll reread again and again because Logan is full of yum! I definitely recommend this book."

—*Book Binge*

## *For Better or Worse*

"I loved this book and can easily recommend you add it to your #needtoread. I am smiling like a lunatic while writing this and re-membering Heather and Josh's journey. I laughed, cheered, cried, sighed, and almost swooned while reading *For Better or Worse*, and any book that can make me feel this wide spectrum of emotions is a book that qualifies as one of my favorite reads."

—*All About Romance*

"A love story that is carefree, real, and packed with emotion any reader can relate with!!! TRULY FANTASTIC!!"

—*Addicted To Romance*

"I highly recommend *For Better or Worse*. The second in a series, it can be read as a stand-alone, but I say start with the first because it's just as good. They've got the funny bickering that I love, and even as her stories have a light touch with cute flirty, they delve deep into the characters."

—*Harlequin Junkie* (Top Pick)

## To Have and to Hold

"Completely endearing characters."

—*Harlequin Junkie* (Top Pick)

"Super entertaining, sweet, and sexy and it leaves you smiling big-time at the end."

—*About That Story*

"A character-driven and sizzling romance!"

—*Fresh Fiction*

## From This Day Forward

"Layne packs as much into this sexually charged and emotionally intense novella as most authors do in a full novel. . . . The heat between [Leah and Jason] is enough to melt steel, and the emotional connection and psychological struggles will keep readers engaged."

—*Publishers Weekly*

# Love on Lexington Avenue

## LAUREN LAYNE

**G**

Gallery Books

New York   London   Toronto   Sydney   New Delhi

# G

Gallery Books
An Imprint of Simon & Schuster, Inc.
1230 Avenue of the Americas
New York, NY 10020

First Gallery Books trade paperback edition September 2019

GALLERY BOOKS and colophon are registered trademarks of Simon & Schuster, Inc.

For information about special discounts for bulk purchases, please contact Simon & Schuster Special Sales at 1-866-506-1949 or business@simonandschuster.com.

The Simon & Schuster Speakers Bureau can bring authors to your live event. For more information or to book an event, contact the Simon & Schuster Speakers Bureau at 1-866-248-3049 or visit our website at www.simonspeakers.com.

Interior design by Davina Mock-Maniscalco

Manufactured in the United States of America

10   9   8   7   6   5   4   3   2   1

Library of Congress Cataloging-in-Publication Data
Names: Layne, Lauren, author.
Title: Love on Lexington Avenue / Lauren Layne.
Description: First Gallery Books trade paperback edition. | New York :
    Gallery Books, 2019. | "Gallery ORIGINAL FICTION TRADE." | Description
    based on print version record and CIP data provided by publisher.
Identifiers: LCCN 2019003708 (print) | LCCN 2019007363 (ebook) |
    ISBN 9781501191619 (ebook) | ISBN 9781501191602 (trade pbk. : alk paper)
Classification: LCC PS3612.A9597 (ebook) | LCC PS3612.A9597 L69 2019
    (print) | DDC 813/.6—dc23
LC record available at https://lccn.loc.gov/2019003708

ISBN 978-1-5011-9160-2
ISBN 978-1-5011-9161-9 (ebook)

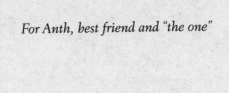

For Anth, best friend and "the one"

# Love on Lexington Avenue

# *Prologue*

*I*t would have been downright tacky to say so out loud, but anyone who was anyone in New York City knew that the funeral of Brayden Daniel Hayes was *the* social event of the summer.

Not because Brayden was at the top of Manhattan's A-list.

He'd been more on the periphery, the type of guy who was in the solar system but was a forgettable moon, orbiting around someone else's more impressive planet. Brayden had money, but not *big* money. He'd been on the attractive side of average, but still average. Well-liked, but not adored.

For most of his relatively short adult life, Brayden Hayes had been solidly in the *oh yeah, that guy* category of society. The type who came and went through life without causing much of a blip.

Except, of course, if the way one left said life was an accidental drowning.

At the age of thirty-five.

With two empty bottles of sauvignon blanc rolling around one's sailboat. To say nothing of the rumors of what he'd been doing before he'd set sail. Or *who* he'd been doing.

That kind of death could catapult just about anyone to *Page Six* for the season.

And so, on a sunny afternoon in July, Manhattan's elite sat in Central Presbyterian Church on Park and Sixty-Fourth, their expressions the perfect masks of somber respect, even as they quietly exaggerated their closeness to the deceased.

*Did you hear? He'd just accepted my dinner party invitation the day before they found him.*

*I should have known something was up. When we caught up just last week, he wasn't at all himself.*

*He and I dated once, years ago. I can't help but think what might have been . . .*

Others had never met the man, and so merely gossiped amongst themselves, wondering if the rumors were true that his body had been found naked. If it was true that it was an NYU undergrad who'd called the Coast Guard when he hadn't met her at the dock as they'd planned.

But at the heart of all the hissed whispers beneath black hats and somber suits was one delicious, looming question mark.

*Where was Claire Hayes?*

As it turned out, not *everyone* was at Brayden's funeral.

In the front pew of the church, where Brayden's family sat stoically listening to placid words of a life ended too soon, a prime front-row seat stayed conspicuously, shockingly vacant.

Even as the theories on *why* reached a fever pitch, three women who'd only just met sat a mere few blocks away on a bench in Central Park, having two vital things in common:

1. Matching Louboutins.
2. A very intimate connection to Brayden Hayes.

And so, as strangers who'd barely known the man began filing out of the church, murmuring plans of mimosas and imminent returns to Hamptons vacation homes, these three women who knew him better than anyone were making a very different sort of plan altogether.

The wife.

The girlfriend.

The mistress.

They had a pact. To never, *ever* let one another fall for a womanizer like Brayden Hayes again.

*Chapter One*

*I*t all started with a cupcake.

Well, the cupcake and the cards.

Claire Hayes stared down at the lone cupcake, with its single pathetic candle and wondered why she'd bothered. Some things didn't need acknowledgment, much less celebration. And as far as Claire was concerned, thirty-fifth birthdays were one of them.

Particularly the thirty-fifth birthday of a widow who was woefully short on optimism, whose metabolism was getting increasingly lazy, and who was celebrating said birthday alone.

At least the alone part had been her choice.

Claire's parents had offered to come back from their retirement home in Florida to take her out to dinner, but she'd nixed that. She loved Helen and George Burchett to pieces, but the last thing Claire needed right now was her dad's constant muttering.

*I swear, Princess, if Brayden hadn't been such an idiot as to fall off that boat, I'd kill him myself.*

Nor her mother's well-meaning but exhaustive concern over

the state of Claire's reproductive organs. *Did I tell you that Annmarie's daughter froze her eggs? She thought it was prudent, and she's only thirty-two . . .*

So, no. Claire's parents had not been what she'd needed on this particular birthday. And though she felt guilty admitting it, she hadn't been up for seeing any of her friends, either. Partially, because friends—the real kind—were hard to come by these days. Her once thriving social circle had all but dried up after Brayden's death.

Some of that was on them. They'd apparently decided a widow at a cocktail party was a downer, and the invitations had stopped rolling in just as abruptly as the sympathy flowers.

But a little of her current isolation from her old social group was on Claire.

Even the well-intentioned friends, the ones who cared more about her than the gossip, hadn't understood. Not what it was like to lose a spouse so young, and certainly not what it was like to lose a spouse who'd turned out to be downright odious.

But there were two people who got it. Two friends who understood her in a way Claire's old social set never could. In fact, Naomi Powell and Audrey Tate had been the only people with whom Claire would have considered ringing in thirty-five.

They'd have been here in a heartbeat, and her husband's girl-friend and mistress, more than anyone, would have understood the melancholy tone of this particular "celebration."

And yet, some nagging part of Claire wondered if they would truly all-the-way understand.

Naomi Powell may not have known that Brayden was married any more than Claire had known that Brayden was cheating, but that didn't change the fact Naomi had been the hot, adventurous mistress. The Jessica Rabbit type of seductress that men were drawn to when they weren't satisfied at home. Men like Brayden, apparently.

Audrey might have understood a little more. Naomi had thought of Brayden as a fling, but Audrey Tate had loved Brayden, had confessed to Claire that she'd hoped—even assumed—she'd marry him some day, unknowing that the title of Brayden Hayes's wife was already in use. The sheer pain of the betrayal, Audrey understood.

It was the way Audrey and Claire had emerged from Brayden's betrayal where they were different. Audrey, with all the hopeful optimism of a woman in her twenties, was still convinced that Prince Charming was out there.

Claire? Not so much. Sometimes a toad was just a toad, no matter how properly he was kissed.

Her lone birthday candle now dripping green wax all over vanilla frosting, Claire blew it out with an irritable puff and turned to the *other* harbinger of her birthday blues:

The stack of birthday cards.

She'd thought the smattering of text messages and emails that had been trickling in all day had been depressing enough. Most of them had simply said Happy Birthday, resulting in balloons exploding all over her iPhone. Others had contained a chipper Happy BDay, Girl! from women she hadn't heard from since her *last* birthday.

But *these*—the cards that had been appearing in her mailbox for a few days now—they felt like they were from a different lifetime. Claire hadn't even realized people under the age of sixty still sent paper cards, but alongside the expected cards from some distant relatives, there were plenty of cards from people Claire's age.

They were well-intentioned, she knew that. They were meant

to let her know someone was thinking of her, but part of her, the new bitter, jaded part that had emerged since Brayden's death, couldn't help but wonder . . .

Had these so-called friends sent paper cards because they were a one-way communication? As a way of acknowledging her birthday without having to interact with all of her tainted, depressing *widowness*?

They were all expensive, as was the way of the Upper East Side elite. Glitter and rich, heavy card stock abounded. Personalized heartfelt messages did not.

> *Cheers to another year, Claire.*
> *Best wishes, Claire!*
> *Enjoy your big day!*

She swallowed, fighting a wave of despondence at the realization that these generic birthday messages were the grownup version of "Have a great summer!" scrawled in a high school yearbook.

When had she become that woman nobody thought about until her birthday popped up on their calendar? *Oh yeah, her. Poor thing. Better send a card . . .*

Claire shoved away the cards and resumed glaring at the cupcake. She plucked the candle out of it and sucked the frosting end.

*So. This is thirty-five.*

Claire's only consolation was that thirty-five couldn't possibly be worse than thirty-four. A year ago, she'd still been dealing with the aftermath of planning her husband's funeral. Not great. The fact that she hadn't attended the funeral she'd planned? Worse. Much worse.

Claire had made it as far as the top of the steps of the church. Even as her brain had dictated she play the role of grieving widow, her heart had commanded something else:

*Screw him.*

Screw Brayden, and the mockery he'd made of her marriage.

And so she'd run. Figuratively. More accurately, she'd teetered as fast as her stilettos would carry her. And so, while family and friends had gathered to say farewell to Brayden, Claire had been sitting on a bench in Central Park.

Ironically, it had been that day, in that spot, as she'd sat both hating and missing Brayden, that she'd met Audrey and Naomi. It had been there that the three women had made a pact not to fall for another man like Brayden.

But what Claire hadn't said that day—what she still hadn't told them—was that she had no intention of falling for another man. *Period*. She'd done the big white wedding. She'd promised to love and cherish. And damn it, she'd *honored* those vows. No one had told her that it would be one-sided. Nobody told her that lurking beneath the veneer of a relationship, hiding under the label of "love," was a whole steaming pile of crap.

Did that make her bitter? Ab.So.Lutely.

And she was just fine with bitter.

Claire swiped her finger along the side of the cupcake, scooping up some of the frosting that the wax hadn't gotten to. The familiar flavor of vanilla rolled over her tongue. She scowled. Of course it was vanilla. It had long been her favorite flavor. Of cake, ice cream, coffee.

Vanilla frosting, vanilla cupcake . . .

*Vanilla life.*

She narrowed her eyes at the cupcake, irrationally angry at the baked good for not being exciting. She could have gone with

Naomi's favorite: red velvet with cream cheese frosting, flecked with spicy little flecks of cinnamon. Or Audrey's: double-chocolate everything, all the time, the richer, the better.

Claire gave a rueful smile when she realized that the trio's respective favorite cupcakes paralleled their looks. Naomi's red velvet matched her vibrant red hair. Audrey's chocolate fetish perfectly matched her silky dark hair.

And Claire . . . vanilla.

She lifted a hand to her shoulder-length blond hair. Not platinum; not really gold, either; just a flat, WASP-pale yellow. Shoving the plate aside in annoyance, Claire stood, and desperate for something to distract her, she went to the kitchen counter, determined to lose herself in her latest obsession:

Her house renovation.

For three years, Claire had been itching to overhaul her New York City home. Location-wise, she was living the dream. A three-bedroom brownstone on Seventy-Third and Lexington Avenue was about as elite a Manhattan address as you could get. She and Brayden had inherited the property from Brayden's grandmother.

The problem was, it looked like Brayden's grandmother still lived here.

And while Claire and Brayden never truly felt the pinch of money pains, they hadn't had an unlimited bank account in the way of a lot of their peers. Brayden had been more preoccupied with *looking* like they had money than actually having it. Most of his salary had gone to extravagant gifts, designer labels, expensive dinners at the trendiest restaurants, whatever it took to play the part of upper-crust New York.

He'd encouraged Claire to do the same; to buy the Givenchy and Chanel, to sip the most expensive champagne when out with her friends, but never to invite those same friends back home.

Brayden's income had been generous by most people's standards, but they weren't *rich* rich. Not enough to live the high life when out and about, and have money to put back into their house.

As a result, Claire's home looked old. Not in the distinguished Vanderbilt way, but in the tired way, *I wonder if there's a lava lamp upstairs* sort of way. There wasn't. But Claire was betting the carpet was the same as when lava lamps had been in vogue.

It was the kitchen she hated most. Small and cramped, more of a hallway than an actual room, with awful beige laminate cabinets, a Formica counter, and a stove far older than Claire. The rest of the house wasn't *quite* as bad, but it needed some work. For starters, Claire would like to have words with whoever had decided to put dark yellow carpet throughout the entire downstairs. And she was pretty sure whoever had picked the dark red-and-green floral wallpaper had been color-blind, if not all the way blind.

The woodwork was too dark and the outdated furniture too light, resulting in a mismatch of styles. The modern white sofa that belonged in a trendy Swedish nightclub was horribly out of place in a room that looked like it should be in a Gothic horror movie.

*But not anymore*, Claire thought, as she began shifting through her pile of paint swatches, tiles, and wood samples. After months of planning and allocating funds from Brayden's life insurance, tomorrow kicked off her official plunge into renovation.

Even though she knew her home would be a work zone for several months, she welcomed it. She couldn't wait for hammering and drilling and muttered swearing. Sure, it was turmoil, but Claire needed it. Craved it.

And yet . . .

She narrowed her eyes at the samples she'd chosen for the kitchen. Cherrywood cabinets and floor to match. Contrasting white granite countertops. Stainless-steel sink. A muted eggshell paint color for the walls. Just a couple of days ago, Claire had been thrilled with the choices. They'd seemed timeless. Elegant without being stuffy. Modern without being trendy.

But now, through the lens of that damn cupcake, all she could see was . . . vanilla. Every single sample, every color, every texture was precisely what was expected.

Slowly, Claire began shuffling through her color selections and textile samples for the other rooms of the house. Her motions became increasingly more frantic as her brain registered what her eyes were seeing.

White. Off-white. Soft white. Snow white. Simply white. Ultra white. Warm white. Paper white. Cream. Beige. Eggshell. Ecru. Cream. Ivory. Oatmeal. Powder. Coconut. Snow. Bone. Linen. Lace. Porcelain. Dove.

For the love of God, one was *actually* called vanilla.

The worst part wasn't the blandness, though that wasn't great. The worst part was the gut-level knowledge that this pile of blah was exactly what everyone expected of her. It's what she expected of herself.

Claire had always thought of herself as steady. Had prided herself in her reliability, but what if there was a dark underbelly to that constancy.

What if instead she'd fallen into a pit of *boring*? And worse? What if she didn't have the foggiest clue how to climb back out again?

Panicked now, Claire snatched her cell phone off the counter.

"Claire?" Audrey's voice sounded puzzled when she picked up. "Are you okay?"

Translation: *Why are you calling instead of texting like usual?*

Claire took a deep breath. "I bought a cupcake today. Guess what flavor it is?"

"Oh, it's a cupcake emergency," Audrey said with such understanding that Claire knew she'd called the right person. Naomi would have rolled with the direction of the conversation, too, but Claire knew that Naomi's nights were spent cuddled up with her sexy boyfriend, and cupcake phone calls might be slightly less welcome.

"Hmm, okay, you bought it for yourself?" Audrey was musing. "Then it's definitely vanilla."

Claire's heart sank. "Yeah. Yeah, it's a vanilla cupcake."

"I'm confused," Audrey said slowly. "I feel like I both passed and failed a quiz at the same time."

"No, it's not you," Claire said rubbing her forehead. "Out of curiosity, what is the zaniest cupcake flavor you can think of?"

"Well . . . Magnolia has this absolutely decadent flourless chocolate cupcake that's—"

"Not chocolate," Claire interrupted. "I mean, it can have chocolate *in* it. But I don't want the standard flavors. I'm talking about a cupcake that breaks all the rules."

"Do cupcakes even have rules? Are you at a bakery having a decision crisis, or is something else going on here?"

*Something else.*

Though she didn't blame her friend for the confusion. Claire wasn't the type of person to call at nine at night with a dessert-related emergency.

For that matter, Claire wasn't the type to have *any* emergency. She was a problem solver. She was the one other people called when they needed help, advice, or just a listening ear. The friend who could tell you how to get red wine out of silk or who would gently but firmly tell you that no, a bob wouldn't really suit your face shape.

In her marriage, she'd been the rock, the one who'd made Brayden a drink at the end of the day and then patiently listened as he unloaded about his brainless coworkers, his small-minded boss, the barista who'd gotten his order wrong.

The roles had rarely reversed, and Claire had never minded—or even noticed, really. Not until Brayden had died. Not until, on the heels of that death, Claire had learned that the stable foundation upon which she'd built her entire life hadn't been nearly as steady as she'd imagined.

Because Brayden hadn't just *died*. He'd left the world naked and drunk and falling off a boat while a twenty-year-old college student waited for him on the dock so they could do exactly what it was that cheating men and carefree twenty-something girls did together.

His autopsy had revealed that he'd hit his head and was unconscious when he went into the water, unaware that he was drowning. Unaware that his quietly dedicated wife once again would be tasked with cleaning up the mess and picking up the pieces.

And she had. She'd gone through all the stages of grief. She'd shed her tears, vented her anger, talked through her confusion.

She'd put her life back together, damn it.

So why did she feel so *flat*?

"Claire?" Audrey said tentatively.

Claire's attention snapped back to her friend. "It's my birthday today."

"What?" Audrey's voice was borderline outraged. "How could you not—"

"I wanted to celebrate alone," Claire said quickly. At least she'd thought she had. "It's just that . . . well, I was sitting here, feeling a little sorry for myself, and thinking about how eight new wrinkles popped up last night. And I was looking down at this little plain vanilla cupcake. And the thing is, Audrey, I picked that flavor. I went to the bakery with the intention of buying myself a birthday treat, and out of all the options, that's what I selected. I think it's the only one I saw. And now, I don't know. I'm just wondering . . . am I boring, Audrey?"

*Am I boring, and is that why Brayden went to find someone* not *boring? Someone like you?*

She didn't say it out loud, but she suspected Audrey heard the unspoken words, because her friend was quiet for a long time.

"Strawberry lemonade," Audrey said.

"What?"

"Molly's Cupcakes on Bleeker. They've got a bunch of fun flavors, but I was there last week, and strawberry lemonade is one of their summer features. It's not wild. It's a traditional flavor pairing, but it's unexpected for cupcakes and it totally works. It's sweet and tart and it sticks with you. It's memorable."

"Strawberry lemonade," Claire said thoughtfully. "I like strawberries. And lemonade."

"See! You're not boring! You're strawberry lemonade! Do you want to head down there right now? I can come over, we'll grab a cab . . ."

Claire laughed. "I love the enthusiasm, but I think my days of going down to the Village on a Tuesday night are behind me. Especially considering I have a contractor coming by at seven tomorrow morning to give me a quote for the renovation."

Audrey let out a tiny sigh of resignation. "Yeah, okay. This weekend maybe?"

Ordinarily, Claire would have nodded in agreement, relieved that her friend didn't push. But hearing the complete lack of surprise in Audrey's voice at Claire's refusal affirmed Claire's worst fears.

She wasn't just boring. She was *predictably* boring.

Claire's gaze flitted over the pile of generic birthday cards. The pale, lonely cupcake. The pile of uninspired swatches and neutral samples that indicated even her house renovation, a process that by its very nature signaled change, would somehow end up . . . the same. Her house would be more modern, yes, but if she stayed the course of white and off-white, it would be what everyone expected of her. *Vanilla*.

An urge washed over Claire, strong and unfamiliar, and as a lifelong rule follower, it took her a moment to register what she was feeling: rebellion.

She wanted to surprise people. She wanted to surprise *herself*.

"Actually, Aud?" She told her friend. "About that cupcake date. Let's do it."

"Now?" Audrey asked in surprise.

"I'll be at your place in twenty. We can share a cab."

"Yes! You're sure though?"

"Absolutely," Claire said. "I'll see you in a few."

Claire started to head toward the stairs to change her clothes but backtracked to the kitchen.

And tossed the vanilla cupcake in the trash.

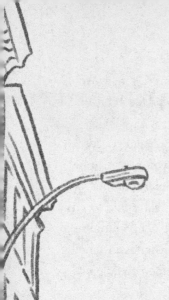

# Chapter Two

*A*t exactly six fifty-eight the following morning, Scott Turner slammed the door of his pickup closed, not really caring if he woke up any of the residents who lived on Seventy-Third Street. In fact, rather perversely, he hoped he did wake them up.

It wasn't that he hated Upper East Siders. He just hated *all* people until he got his morning coffee. He hated especially that his rancid mood was his own damn fault. He'd been the one to agree to consider this job. He'd been the one who'd suggested the early morning meeting.

It had seemed like a good idea at the time. To get anything done in August in New York City, early mornings were crucial unless you wanted to sweat your way through the day. Hell, it was already sticky, and they hadn't even rounded the bend on 7:00 a.m.

But when Scott made the appointment with Claire Hayes, he hadn't been factoring in a delayed flight from Seattle the night before, which had then prohibited him from restocking coffee.

To say that Scott was having regrets about doing his friend

Oliver a favor was an understatement, but if this Claire Hayes woman had air-conditioning and coffee, all would be forgiven. Mostly.

As expected, Claire Hayes's brownstone looked like every other house on the block, and he supposed that was meant to be the charm of it. In Manhattan, where the sheer number of bodies on a relatively small strip of land forced real estate to go up, literally, high-rise apartment buildings and condominiums were a dime a dozen. It was these stately brownstones in fancy historic neighborhoods that the city's elite creamed their pants over.

In almost any other part of the country, these unassuming town houses served as starter homes for new couples and families. The training wheels of home ownership until one could afford the actual house, with a proper yard, a garage, room for the kids, etc. Not so on the Upper East Side of Manhattan, where skinny structures went for eight figures, easily. Even the outdated ones got seven-figure offers just for the property value and bragging rights.

Scott wasn't sure which category he was dealing with. Oliver had just said this Claire woman wanted a major reno. For all he knew, that meant replacing last year's kitchen counters. In his experience, wealthy housewives weren't known for perspective. Their emergency was someone else's average weekday.

Scott jogged up the steps, egged on as much by the hope of coffee as he was by the desire to get this damn assessment over with so he could politely turn her down and move on to a project that lit his fire.

As with the early morning, it was his own damn fault that he was in this position in the first place. Scott had told Oliver he'd wanted a break from the corporate stuff, though he'd neglected to mention that changing a snobby widow's towel rack from silver to copper wasn't exactly what he had in mind.

He wanted a true fixer-upper, not a glorified decorating gig for a rich woman who would probably want to replace original hardwood with some bamboo nonsense. But Oliver was on the short list of people that Scott would do just about anything for, and so he'd agreed to at least see Claire Hayes's project before turning her down.

Even as he had no intention of agreeing to the project, Scott's trained eye took in the details of the front porch as he knocked. Dilapidated would be a nice word for it. And he didn't even bother with the fussy brass knocker that looked like a good door slam would send it to its death.

Instead, he rapped his knuckles against the wood, as much to test its solidity as to actually knock. Old, he realized. Really old. In fact, the front door was in the same condition as the knocker. *Tired*. Fading paint, warped wood, ugly, outdated frosted glass panes. Even the doorknobs were bad.

"Jesus," he muttered, running a finger over some fugly shape carved into the wood at waist level. "Are these supposed to be leaves?"

The door opened, leaving his hand extended awkwardly, finger now pointing at . . . well, the woman's crotch. Unembarrassed, Scott's hand dropped back to his side as his eyes traveled back up the woman's body. Boring gray slacks, boring blue blouse . . .

His eyes slammed into hers, and he was abruptly jolted out of his boredom. Not because her face was particularly interesting. All her features were right where they were supposed to be. Small nose, full mouth, angular jaw.

The *eyes* though. They were worth a second look.

He supposed hazel was the official label, but they were a hell of a lot more interesting than that. Green at the centers, gold at the outer edges. Scott had always been fascinated by things that changed the more you looked at them. Prisms. Sunsets. Clouds. The night sky.

He mentally added Claire Hayes's eyes to the list.

Too bad the rest of her was so Stepford Wife.

"You must be Scott," she said with a smile that did nothing to light those magnificent eyes, her hand extending to his.

"Must be." He shook her hand, pleasantly surprised by the strong handshake, even as he looked beyond her to the inside of the brownstone, wanting to move this along.

Claire seemed to sense it, because she forwent any more small talk, moving aside to let him in. Scott stepped into the foyer and immediately felt it. *The rush*. That feeling he got when he'd stepped into a space that was so far from reaching its potential, it was almost physically painful.

He whistled as he did a cursory scan of his immediate area. He took in the dark foyer, the cramped sitting area just off the front door, the staircase that was as narrow as it was ugly. Even without moving his feet, he could tell that this project was no minor face-lift.

"That bad?" Claire said, watching his face.

"It's a phoenix," he muttered, proceeding farther into the home without being invited.

"A what?" She followed him as he ran a finger along the ugly metallic wallpaper in the hallway.

"A phoenix. It's what I call a space that's so damned ugly, the only way to fix it is to burn it to the ground and rebuild. Figuratively speaking, of course."

"Of course," she murmured politely.

Scott stepped into the kitchen. "God."

"Yeah. It's my least favorite part," she said.

"Seventy-four," he said, taking in the Formica everything, the chipped tile floor, the impractically shallow sink.

"What?"

"Nineteen seventy-four. That's the last time this place was updated, though the building's much older than that."

"Yeah, I think that's about right," she said, after a pause. "How'd you know?"

"My job to know." He started to back out of the kitchen to explore the rest of the downstairs, then came back into the kitchen, pointing at the coffeepot. "That work?"

She followed his point, then looked back at him, giving him a bland look. "You think I keep a broken coffeepot on my counter?"

"How'm I supposed to know? Your knocker's a summer storm away from blowing off."

"My . . ."

"Front door knocker," he clarified, doing what he thought was a damn admirable job of not letting his gaze drop to her breasts. "Not knocker knockers."

He expected her to blush or at least look flustered. He perversely hoped for it, for which he blamed the lack of coffee. He didn't get a blush. Hell, he didn't get any sort of reaction. Claire Hayes merely gave him another of those bland, unruffled looks, before going to the god-awful cabinet and pulling out two mugs. "Cream? Sugar? Vanilla coffee creamer?"

"Just black. Thank you." He mentally applauded himself for not lunging at the cup. "I'll be less rude once I get some caffeine in me."

*Maybe*. It was a fifty-fifty shot. Scott didn't consider himself an asshole, but he also knew he wasn't the poster child of pretty manners, or pretty anything for that matter.

Claire didn't acknowledge his commentary on his rudeness. She simply handed him the mug, then pulled a container of coffee creamer from the fridge and added a liberal amount to her mug. She pulled out a spoon and stirred the liquid from dark brown to a pale tan color.

He gave a slight shake of his head at the crime of diluting the caffeine.

"So, I know you haven't seen the whole house yet, but what do you think?" she asked, cupping both hands around the mug and lifting it to her face. She didn't take a sip, just watched him over the top, the steam adding another layer of mystery to those strange green-gold eyes.

Scott met her gaze directly. "It's god-awful. But you already know that."

She lowered her mug and tilted her head, studying him the way one would a zoo animal.

"What?" he asked, a little surprised to realize that he was genuinely interested in what she was thinking.

"I was under the impression that you and Oliver are good friends."

"We are."

"Huh." She took a sip of her coffee, and damn it, he was all the way interested now.

"That surprises you?" he asked, sipping his own coffee. It was good. Really good.

"Well, yes. Oliver has impeccable manners. You, not so much."

Scott shrugged. "What did you expect me to say, that the house has *character*? I don't speak in niceties, Ms. Hayes, so if you're looking for gentle euphemisms on what needs to be done, I'm not your guy."

And he wanted to be her guy, as it related to this project. This home needed him.

"I suppose it's refreshing. In its way," Claire said, apropos of nothing, as though he hadn't spoken.

"Sorry?"

Claire waved a hand over him. "The basic blue jeans. The flannel over T-shirt that I haven't seen since *Gilmore Girls* was on the air. A jawline that's . . ." She tilted her head and studied him. "Four days past a shave?"

He ran a palm over his stubble. Four days seemed about right. "Good eye."

She shrugged. "You date kitchens; I date men's grooming. Seven years of marriage will do that for you."

*Right.* He'd been so eager to get this meeting over with, he'd forgotten that Claire Hayes was a relatively recent widow. "Sorry about that," he said gruffly. "Heard he was a real asshole."

Over the past year, Scott had gotten to know Oliver's girlfriend, Naomi, who'd filled him in on some of the dirty details of how she'd met Claire the day of her husband's funeral. It pissed him off. He didn't put stock in relationships, but he damn well expected people who did enter them not to cheat.

She laughed into her coffee. "Are you sorry because he died, or because he was a real asshole?"

Scott shrugged again. "You tell me. I didn't know the guy."

Claire set her mug aside. "To be clear, Mr. Turner, if we decide to work together, discussion of my deceased husband is off-limits."

"Fine by me." He preferred it, actually.

She nodded in acknowledgment. "So. Are you interested? I know it's small compared to what you normally do. And I'll tell you right now that I have some money set aside, but I know this is no minor undertaking, and I have no idea how much it'll cost, or if I can afford it. Depending on the quote you come back with, I may have to phase out the renovation."

He nodded, already knowing he'd fit the project to her budget, not the other way around. Even before he'd been financially secure, Scott had never made his decisions based on the money. It all came down to instinct, and he'd known the moment he'd walked in the door that this was the challenge he wanted. The chance to build a home, his way, not some sterile, elaborate showpiece whose primary purpose was to get a write-up in *Architectural Digest*.

"Let's forget the budget for now," he said, helping himself to more coffee. Scott held up the pot, silently offering a top-off, but she shook her head.

He turned toward her, leaning back against the counter, which he noted was a full two inches too low. Either it had been designed for someone exceptionally short or, more likely, whoever had built the house hadn't given a crap about detail.

"What's your vision?" Scott asked her.

She gave a small smile, the first one he'd seen yet, though it was still guarded. "How much time do you have?"

He tried not to wince. "So, you've got specifics in mind?"

Scott had been hoping for the opposite. That she wanted someone else to make the decisions. *Him*. He wanted to make the decisions for this place.

"Lots."

He sighed. "Let's see them."

She hesitated, and his interest piqued. Based on the excitement he'd heard in her voice a moment ago, he'd have assumed she'd come at him ready with paint swatches and Pinterest boards.

Not that he minded the lack of the latter. Pinterest was his and every contractor's worst enemy. Actually, scratch that. Pinterest was bad, but it was the damn house-flipping shows that were the *real* nightmare. Gone were the days when customers maybe had some vague opinion about the paint color for their bedroom but more or less trusted the contractors to take care of the rest. Now, people had rooms planned down to the square inch, wanting things like skylights on the ground floor.

The trouble was, most people didn't have any vision. It was why he was so good at his job. Not only did he have vision, but for all his hermit ways, he also knew people. At least as it related to what they wanted out of their residence or office building or commercial project. That was what he was good at. Building what people didn't even know they wanted.

"I'm still sort of . . . deciding," she said, sounding hesitant in a way he guessed wasn't typical for her.

"Explain," he said bluntly. If they were going to work together, he needed to know up front if Claire Hayes was a loose cannon who wanted to turn her living room into an aviary or her master closet into a panic room.

"What's your favorite cupcake?"

He stared at her. "Sorry?"

She laughed, looking surprised both by her own question and the laughter that followed. "Never mind. Let's just say that I'm still working out the details on what exactly I want, but I know I don't want boring."

"I don't do boring."

"Do you do strawberry lemonade?"

Scott rubbed the back of his neck. *Hell.* Oliver and Naomi

had conveniently forgotten to mention that Claire Hayes was off her rocker.

"What's that have to do with the reno?" he asked.

"I'm still working on it," she repeated. "But you can get started without knowing the details, right? Ripping up carpet, tearing off wallpaper, that sort of thing?"

He could. But he wasn't sure he wanted to. Not if he was going to end up building a Candy Land house for a woman who was talking about cupcakes and strawberries.

"High-level vision," he pressed.

"I already told you. Strawberry lemonade. You know, little touches of pink. Unexpected . . . delights."

"Oh God," he grumbled.

"A man who doesn't like pink," she said drolly. "How very original."

"Pink doesn't belong in houses."

"Maybe not your house. *I'm* the one who will live here."

Scott took another drink of the coffee. It really was very good. Too bad he was going to have to say no to the job. *Pink.* For God's sake.

She studied him with those spooky hazel eyes of hers, looking oddly disappointed in him. "Haven't you ever looked at your life and realized you were just . . . tired of it? Or yourself?"

Scott hesitated, wanting to say no. He wanted to say that only the self-indulgent had the time and energy to sit around assessing one's life direction and then talking to strangers about it. But the truth was . . . he *did* get it.

Wasn't it the very reason he was standing in this eyesore of a kitchen in the first place? Because he needed a change? Because he had the sense the life he'd built so carefully to his own specifications was no longer doing it for him?

Scott scratched his cheek, a little surprised to realize that maybe he and this widowed housewife might understand each other more than he expected.

"I'll do it."

She looked skeptical. "Really? Even with the threat of pink? And you haven't seen the whole place. It's three bedrooms, three baths—"

"Sounds good. Starting tomorrow okay?"

"*What?* No! I haven't even figured out—"

"We'll figure it out later," he said, draining the coffee and setting his mug in the sink. "That's half the fun."

"That doesn't sound fun *at all.*"

He smiled a little at her honesty and headed back toward the front door. "We start at seven tomorrow, and every weekday thereafter. Weekends optional, depending on both our schedules. I'll try to start on the lesser-used rooms first, try to upset your life as little as possible, though fair warning, it'll be loud, and it'll be messy. I work mostly alone, except when I need an extra pair of hands for the big stuff. You'll be without a kitchen for a couple of weeks, because that thing is the worst, but I'm quicker than most, and I'm damn good."

"Mr. Turner—"

"Scott," he said. "We're about to live in each other's back pocket, so first names are a must. And last thing. *No pink.*"

Her eyes narrowed in warning. "Sorry, I must be confused. I thought this was *my* home."

He nodded, rocked back on his boots. "Absolutely it is. Which is why I can assure you that you will regret making it look like Pepto exploded in here."

She gave him a withering look. "A little credit, please. I'm not entirely without taste."

"Well, what the hell am I supposed to think when you say things like strawberry lemonade. I have no idea what the hell that means. And I don't think you do, either."

"No. I don't," she snapped. "But I'm going to figure it out with or without you. Isn't that *half the fun*? And yes, it will mean some pink. *Or*," she added when he grimaced, "I can find someone else."

"Someone else will be a yes-man," he argued.

"That sounds *great*," she said enthusiastically.

He ran his tongue over his teeth, considering. The project wouldn't be easy. The client definitely wouldn't. And yet . . .

He scanned the space once more. Truly, *truly* awful.

Scott looked back at her. "I'll be here at seven a.m. tomorrow. We can talk money and timeline. How do you feel about dogs?"

"Dogs?"

Scott hesitated, knowing it was unprofessional, but then decided he didn't care. "I travel a lot and don't get to see my dog as much as I'd like. I was thinking—hoping—I could bring Bob with me."

"Oh." A faint line appeared between her eyebrows, and she appeared to be deliberating his question very carefully. "I guess that'd be okay."

He felt a surge of relief that he'd have at least a few weeks to spend with his too-often-left-behind dog. "Thank you."

"You're welcome," she said primly, reaching around him to open the front door. "Until tomorrow."

He stepped out onto the porch, turned back. "When you say pink, you at least mean a discreet mauve, right?"

"Goodbye, Mr. Turner."

He turned away. "Strawberry lemonade my ass."

The front door slammed behind him, and he grinned at the metallic *ting* of the follow-up sound. He'd been spot on, as usual. That brass knocker really *was* a good door slam away from its demise.

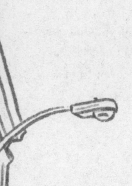

# Chapter Three

*I* didn't even know places like this existed," Audrey said, glancing around in awe.

"What, hardware stores?" Naomi Powell asked, holding one of the metal objects she'd accumulated from her tour of the store up to Audrey's ear, as though assessing the bolt for earring potential. Knowing Naomi, she probably *was* assessing it for earring potential. Naomi wasn't a jewelry designer, per say, but as founder of Maxcessory, a subscription accessory service, she was always on the lookout for the next big thing.

"Are they all like this?" Audrey asked, looking adorably out of place in her lace dress and platform sandals.

"Actually, I think this is a relatively small version of a hardware store," Claire said as she picked up yet another swatch of paint colors and added it to her stack. "Home Depots are even more massive anywhere outside of Manhattan."

Both her friends gave her a curious look at her expertise, and Claire shrugged. "I took an Uber out to a Jersey hardware store when I first started thinking about the renovation."

"Jersey," Audrey mused, as though it were a foreign country and not just a few miles to the west.

"Real talk," Naomi said, looking at Audrey. "When was the last time you left Manhattan?"

"Last month," Audrey retorted, clearly proud to shake up Naomi's assumption that the Upper East Side princess never left her own neighborhood.

"Really?" Claire glanced over in surprise.

Not that Claire herself could claim to be any more adventurous most days. She'd been born and raised in the Connecticut suburbs, but the city had gotten under her skin in a permanent kind of way almost immediately. She couldn't imagine calling anywhere other than Manhattan home.

But Audrey Tate didn't just live in Manhattan, she *was* Manhattan. A society princess through and through. Not only that, she'd literally made a career out of it. Audrey was an "influencer," which Claire fully admitted to never having heard of before meeting Audrey. For that matter, she still wasn't entirely sure she got it, but as far as she could tell, companies paid the gorgeous, charismatic Audrey to feature their handbags, shoes, beauty products, sports bras, *anything*, on her blog and Instagram.

"I did, too, leave Manhattan," Audrey insisted, her tone smug. "I was in the Hamptons for two weeks last month."

Naomi snorted. "Doesn't count."

"It does, too!" Audrey protested. "Claire?"

"No, dear." Claire patted her arm, then she put the swatches in her bag. "Not really."

Audrey frowned stubbornly. "Naomi asked if I'd left Manhattan. I have."

"Fine, we'll give you that one on a technicality," Naomi said, scooping up the assortment of metal bits and bobs in two hands. "Who wants to help me put these back in their right spots?"

Audrey squinted at the assortment of stuff. "I couldn't tell you what a single one of those things is."

Claire just shrugged. She'd learned her way around the home improvement store in recent months, but her expertise was mostly limited to tile samples and paint swatches.

"All right, Plan B," Naomi said, scanning the store until she found who she was looking for. Fixing a bright smile on her face, Naomi strode purposefully toward an employee. Claire recognized the fifty-something guy. He was crusty, irritable, and condescending, especially to women.

But not *all* women, apparently.

Claire watched in bemusement as Naomi not only coaxed a smile from the man, but a full-on laugh. Claire felt an unexpected jolt of envy at how effortlessly dynamic her friend was. She bet Naomi didn't get generic birthday cards. She bet Naomi didn't default to beige everything.

Claire watched as the Home Depot guy blushed. *Blushed!*

"How does she do that?" Claire mused.

Audrey glanced up from her phone. "How does who do what?"

Claire nodded toward Naomi. "I've been in this store at least a dozen times, and I haven't so much as gotten a civil word from that man. He's known Naomi all of thirty seconds and is practically eating out of her hand, even though she's just handed him an hour's worth of work in putting all that crap away."

"She's got a gift," Audrey said distractedly.

"Yes, but what *is* the gift?" Claire pressed.

Her friend finally registered that Claire was actually asking, and it wasn't just a rhetorical question. "Well." Audrey glanced over at Naomi and then back. "It's her confidence, I suppose. That's like, eighty percent of the art of flirting."

"Flirting," Claire repeated, testing the word out. She hadn't voiced or given much thought to the concept of flirting in . . . years. And not just because she'd been a married woman, but because come to think of it, Claire wasn't sure she'd *ever* really mastered flirting.

"Yes, flirting," Audrey said with a little laugh. "You know, eye contact, lingering smiles, banter."

"But she's with Oliver."

Audrey smiled kindly. "Sure, but flirting's not always about romancing someone."

"Then what's it about? How does one decide with whom to flirt?"

"With whom—what—" Audrey broke off when she saw Naomi approaching, "Oh thank God. Backup."

"On what?" Naomi demanded.

"Trying to explain to Claire the nature of flirting."

Naomi shook her head. "Pointless endeavor. Flirting's not an explainable thing. It's more of an art than a science. It just happens."

That wasn't a good enough answer for Claire. There had to be a reason why men smiled and laughed with Naomi—and Audrey, for that matter—whereas Claire generally only warranted bland smiles or polite indifference.

Yes, her friends were gorgeous. Naomi was the sort of woman people looked twice at, and not just because of her bright blue eyes, dark red hair, and toned runner's body. But it was her energy that drew people in. The way she seemed to own every room she walked into and dared people to ignore her.

And Audrey was beautiful in her own right with long shiny

brown hair and wide Bambi brown eyes, but that wasn't why people flocked to her. It was her sweetness. Not saccharine sweetness, but a genuine goodness that people wanted to be around.

What did Claire have?

She lacked Naomi's boldness and Audrey's effortless charm.

She was polite, sure. Likable, hopefully. Traits she'd always thought were enviable, but now she wasn't so sure. Where had that gotten her?

She was widowed. Alone. Bored.

She had no career, no romantic prospects—not that she wanted those—no hobbies. Nobody looked twice at her, and she never looked twice at anyone else.

Claire was more sure than ever that she was due for a change. The spontaneous cupcake date with Audrey on her birthday had been a good start, but it was *only* the start. She wanted more of that. More of doing whatever she wanted *just because*.

"What's going on with you?" Naomi demanded, giving Claire an assessing look. "You're all up in your head." She waved a finger around Claire's head as she said it.

"Too long a story for a hardware store."

Naomi studied her a moment longer, then nodded, pointing at Claire's purse. "You get what you need?"

Claire nodded. She'd picked up just about every paint swatch she could find in the pink/rose/mauve category. Partially because she was warming to the idea of pink accents in her newly renovated home, partially because it pleased her to imagine Scott Turner's face when he saw her haul.

"Perfect! It's time for your belated birthday lunch. Which is on me since I was left out of the actual birthday festivities. Cupcakes without me. The betrayal burns my very soul."

"We texted. Twice," Audrey said in defense. "You didn't respond."

Naomi inspected her manicure. "Oliver and I were busy."

The slightly satisfied look on her face said exactly what they were busy with.

"Oh?" Claire said innocently. "Netflix or . . ."

"Or Netflix and chill?" Audrey said in a sly tone.

Claire looked at Audrey. "What does that mean?"

"Do not answer that question," Naomi said, pointing a finger at Audrey. "Come on. Lunch."

Naomi charged out of the store, never breaking stride in her five-inch Jimmy Choos. Claire and Audrey exchanged a bemused glance and followed. It was pointless to argue with a determined Naomi.

Fifteen minutes later, the three women were seated at a trendy French bistro as a server opened a bottle of champagne and poured three glasses. When he moved away, Naomi lifted a glass in a toast. "To our birthday girl. How does thirty-five feel?"

"Well," Claire said, taking a sip. "So far, better than thirty-four. I no longer have a husband to cheat on me."

"Dark," Naomi said approvingly. "Very dark, and I like it. Now, fill me in, what did I miss when you got cupcakes without me?"

"You mean when you were having sex with Oliver?" Claire countered.

Audrey leaned in. "By the way, *that's* what Netflix and chill means."

Claire frowned. "Why not just say sex?"

"See, that's why you can't flirt, dear. You're too wonderfully literal and straightforward."

"It doesn't feel wonderful," Claire muttered. "It feels boring."

She looked at Naomi. "Did you know that my favorite kind of cupcake is vanilla? Was vanilla," she corrected quickly.

"Oh, not this again," Audrey said, slumping slightly in her chair.

"Sure," Naomi said. "What's wrong with vanilla?"

"I've just been wondering what it says about me that my favorite cupcake is flavorless, colorless."

"They have a color. They're sort of yellowish. Beige. And they have a flavor. *Vanilla*. Better yet, it's a flavor everybody likes."

"Well, I've decided I don't want to be *beige* anymore," Claire said. "And I don't want to be universally liked. I want to be . . . interesting."

Naomi frowned. "You *are* interesting. And what do you mean *you* don't want to be beige. You are not your cupcake flavor, Claire."

*Aren't I?*

The past couple of months flitted by in a sad, drab little montage. Her generic birthday cards. The flavorless cupcakes. Her Pinterest boards and renovation project folder overflowing with whites and beiges. The realization that she apparently didn't even know what flirting was, much less know how to do it.

"Claire?" Audrey nudged, worry in her voice.

Claire smiled. "Don't worry. I promise this isn't some sort of midlife crisis where I'm going to go get a pixie cut that doesn't suit my face or decide to start collecting tattoos that I'll regret in a month. I'm just realizing I'm in a tiny rut is all."

"A vanilla rut?"

"Basically." Claire let her shoulders rise in a shrug before dropping them again. "I'm just so aware that my only identity these days is widow. And even more alarming, even before Brayden died, my only identity was wife. Before that it was girlfriend. Before that . . . I don't know. I guess I just have this weird sense that I've lost sight of who I am. If I ever even knew."

Naomi opened her mouth, but before she could reply, the server approached the table. Feeling unexpectedly vulnerable, Claire welcomed the interruption, placing her order before her friends could tell the waiter to come back later. "I'll have the mixed green salad, and I'll add the scallops to that, please."

"Same, but add salmon for me," Audrey said.

"Croque Madame. With fries," Naomi ordered.

Claire handed her menu to the server, but when he reached out to take it, Claire's fingers didn't release it, realizing she'd just ordered a salad. Of course she had. Because she *always* ordered the salad.

"Actually, I'll take the Croque Madame as well," she told the waiter, finally releasing the menu.

"Fries?" he asked, scribbling the correction in his notebook.

"Why not."

The server moved away, and both her friends were studying her.

"What was that?" Naomi demanded. "I feel like something just happened."

"Yes. I changed my food order," Claire said, sipping her champagne.

"Yes, to fries. You never get fries. And you love salad."

"Nobody loves salad, but not all of us are running fiends," Claire said pointedly at the exceptionally fit Naomi.

"Plus, she's burning all sorts of calories having sex," Audrey grumbled.

Naomi gave another of those secret, smug smiles as she took a demure sip of her champagne.

Audrey sighed. "And it's *good* sex, too. You can tell by her face."

"Oh, it's not my face that knows it's good. Well, actually—"

"Nope," Claire cut in. "I love you; I love Oliver; I do *not* want details."

"I do," Audrey said morosely.

"You know, I'd feel worse for you if you were even trying to have sex," Naomi said, giving Audrey's arm a playful flick. "When was the last time you went on a date? Or you?" She glanced at Claire.

"It's not that I don't want to date," Audrey protested. "I just haven't felt the spark. I don't want to date for the sake of dating."

"Why not?" Naomi asked. "It's fun."

"Is it?" Claire interjected.

Naomi gave her a look.

"No, I'm really asking," Claire said with a laugh. "Other than the awful blind date you sent me on a few months back, I haven't dated anyone since Brayden. I guess I've never understood the point of dating just for the 'fun' of it."

"Is that why you were interrogating Audrey on the nature of flirting?" Naomi asked.

"Sort of. Seeing you with that guy in the hardware store—"

"Good Lord, sweetie, you can't date *that* guy," Naomi interrupted, aghast. "Not only was his breath appalling, but even more prohibitively, someone apparently has managed to look past his egg breath to marry the guy. He was wearing a ring."

"I don't want to date *that* guy," Claire said in exasperation. "I was just marveling at the way you marched right up to him and effortlessly charmed the pants off him."

"Huh," Naomi said. "I can't figure out if I've just been insulted or if there's a compliment in there."

"A compliment," Claire reassured her. "I love the way that

you don't overthink things. Neither of you do," she added, with a glance at Audrey.

"Well, that's not always a good thing," Audrey pointed out. "Maybe had we thought through things just a *little* bit more, we wouldn't have ended up all falling for the same guy."

"That's why we have our pact," Naomi said. "Impulse control, as it relates to the opposite sex."

Claire thoughtfully tapped her nails against her champagne flute. "What if I said I wanted your help with *less* impulse control?"

Audrey reached over and set the back of her fingers to Claire's forehead. "Hmm, nope. No fever. Wait. Is that what the cupcake binge was about? And you wanting to go grab pizza after?"

"I missed cupcakes *and* pizza?" Naomi said.

"Sex," Claire and Audrey reminded her at the same time.

"Fine," Naomi muttered. "So, what are we dealing with here? A food revolution? You've decided to banish salads and embrace fries, cupcakes, and pizza to get out of your rut? Please say yes."

"I'm not really sure yet," Claire admitted. "I just know something needs to change, and I have to start somewhere. Why not with cupcakes and French fries?"

"And your house," Audrey reminded her.

Naomi tapped the table excitedly with her palm. "Oh! That reminds me, I never got the lowdown on Scott."

"Who's Scott?" Audrey asked.

"My contractor," Claire said wrinkling her nose.

"You hired him!" Naomi said, pleased.

"I think so?" Claire said.

"What do you mean you think so?"

"Well, he never really told me how much he was charging me, just said we'd figure it out later."

"Yeah, that's Scott for you," Naomi said. "Super fly by the seat of his pants."

"You might have also mentioned he's a little abrasive," Claire said.

"Abrasive?" Naomi titled her head. "He's more just . . ."

"Rude, condescending, and opinionated?"

"Maybe a little," Naomi admitted. "He's good at his job, and he knows it. And has no issues saying it."

"Sounds like someone I know," Claire said with a smile.

Naomi blew her a kiss, knowing full well that she *was* good at her job and, like Scott, had no qualms saying so.

"Is he hot?" Audrey chimed in.

"No," Claire said, just as Naomi said, "Yes."

"Oh, come on," Naomi protested. "I may be in love with Oliver, but even I can see Scott's got his own appeal. He wears a bomber jacket when it's not a million degrees out, and let me tell you, it looks good."

Claire shrugged. "Well, yesterday he showed up wearing *flannel*. And it did not look good."

"Hmm," Audrey said, tapping a fingernail to her chin. "See, I feel like I could totally work with the flannel. Lumberjack is super in right now."

"What about an ego so big it barely made it through my front door?" Claire asked. "Is that super in?"

"Always," her friends said in unison.

"It even has a name," Audrey said. "Alpha."

"Well, trendy or not, alpha lumberjack is not my thing. But as long as he goes along with my house plan, he can wear whatever he wants," Claire said, setting her napkin in her lap as the server brought their food. "And he skips haircuts more often than he should."

She dove into the fries and closed her eyes for a moment in bliss. No doubt about it. Spontaneity tasted way better than lettuce.

"Okay, what is the house plan?" Audrey said, picking up her fork.

"The house plan is there is *no* plan," Claire said gleefully.

"Wait, seriously? You've been working on this for months, if not years. You've got that enormous pile of samples and crap."

"All in the garbage," Claire said. "I'm starting fresh, bringing in whatever idea I feel like at the moment. If that's a disco ball tomorrow and a built-in stripper pole next week, I'm rolling with it. And your boy Scott will have to roll with it, too," she told Naomi defiantly.

"I cannot wait to see this go down," Naomi said, taking a bite of her cheese-laden sandwich. "When does Scott start?"

"He's there now."

True to his word, Scott had shown up at Claire's home at seven that morning. She'd been ready with coffee, figuring it was the least she could do, though she regretted the kind gesture when he'd rolled his eyes upon hearing about her Home Depot errand.

"Actually," Claire said, reaching down and pulling out some of the swatches from her bag. "You ladies can help me with my first impulse while we eat."

"Ooh, *pretty*," Audrey said, reaching out and running a finger over a lavender-tinted paint swatch. Her gaze scanned the assortment of pinks as Claire set them on the table, then grinned. "Strawberry lemonade! For your home."

Claire smiled. "Yup. I mean, I don't want it looking like a gin-

gerbread house or anything, but I don't want to default to the expected neutrals."

"Like a Barbie dream house!" Audrey explained, already
reaching for the brightest color options.

Claire gave Naomi a wide-eyed *Help!* look.

"We've got this," Naomi said reassuringly, shoving a subtler
set of colors into Audrey's hand. "I'm thinking we're going for
fresh and feminine, right?"

Claire nodded, grateful her friend understood the vision.
Fresh, to shake off the stale feeling a year of mourning had left
her with. Feminine, because even with her new impulse project,
there was one thing she wasn't leaving up to whim and spontaneity:

She had no intention of sharing her home—or her life—with
a man.

Ever again.

## Chapter Four

*C*laire returned home from her time with Naomi and Audrey feeling both a little mellow from the champagne and revived by the companionship.

Claire had always been a girl's girl. Throughout high school and college, she'd prided herself in her ability to navigate among the cliques and have multiple friend groups. She'd been the "mom" in every group. Levelheaded and thoughtful, Claire was the one who always had ChapStick, a bobby pin, and breath mints. The one who'd handed out water at frat parties and held her friends' hair when they'd ignored her water and ended up puking their guts out. She was the one who'd dispensed advice that perfectly straddled tough love and gentle.

When she'd married Brayden, she'd been extremely conscious of not letting her girlfriends fall by the wayside. Of course, it had helped that nearly all of her friends had similarly been married or in serious relationships. It had been great. For a while. Claire's social calendar had alternated between wine and book club nights with the girls while the guys had poker nights and golf trips, and couple-centric dinner parties.

And then Brayden had died, and everything had just . . . changed.

Not at first. At first it had been . . . okay. Or as *okay* as the death of a cheating spouse could possibly be. When the news broke, Claire had been inundated with support, both the well-meaning and nosy varieties. She'd received more flowers than she had surfaces to put them on and had enough bagels delivered to fuel the carbo-load for all of the New York marathon runners.

Eventually, though, the invitations had stopped. While she still heard from her college best friends with baby updates and the occasional check-ins, Carrie and Melissa didn't live in New York. Text messages, phone calls, even FaceTime didn't make up for an in-person shoulder to lean on, and those had become scarce after Brayden's death.

Her Manhattan friends, the group she'd once been the center of, had slowly disappeared. Claire knew it wasn't malicious. She'd been in their shoes. When Kristen Seymour and her husband had separated, Claire had tried to include Kristen just as before, but eventually her friend had somehow sort of slipped away. Just like Claire had.

And if she were being honest, Claire couldn't be entirely sure she hadn't brought some of it upon herself. Had she pulled back? Changed? Or was it that her newfound cynicism just didn't fit in around married couples?

Regardless, she wasn't sure she would have survived this past year without Naomi and Audrey. Whether it was because of their shared experience with Brayden or just three women finding each other at exactly the right time, Audrey and Naomi felt more like sisters than friends, and had from the very beginning.

Case in point, Naomi was with Oliver now, but unlike Claire's other coupled-up friends, Naomi hadn't drifted away. If anything, their friendship had become more rock-solid since Naomi and Oliver had gotten together, plus there was an added bonus of Claire now counting Oliver as a good friend.

Claire was hanging up her keys on the hook by the front door when she heard a thump from upstairs, followed by a muttered masculine curse. She paused, half thinking about going upstairs to see if Scott was okay, but deciding better of it. If she went dashing after him at every crash and bump, it was going to be a long few months. It was *already* going to be a long few months, she realized as she eyed the pencil markings all along the walls on her way to the kitchen. Most were numbers, although the wall to her left simply had an unceremonious X.

Claire had just poured herself a glass of water and was in the process of setting the paint swatches she and the girls had settled on next to her tile samples when Scott came into the kitchen.

She glanced up briefly, then did a double take. The flannel he'd arrived in yesterday morning was nowhere to be seen, and instead the man wore only a white T-shirt with his jeans. A very fitted white T-shirt.

He was more muscular than she'd expected. Yesterday she'd thought him lean, and he was. But seeing the way his arms filled out the sleeves of his shirt, it was obvious he was also strong. Not in a gym rat way, but in a masculine, *I put this body to good use* sort of way.

The lumberjack comparison was increasingly apt. As was the alpha part.

"What?" he asked gruffly, going to her cupboard and helping himself to a glass of water.

Claire realized her gaze had been lingering a little too long.

She blamed it on the champagne and looked back down at her paint swatches, pretending indifference. "Nothing."

He finished his water in three gulps, then set the glass down on the counter next to the stack of mail on her counter. Unabashed, he used a single finger to move the top item of mail aside, then another.

"You had a birthday."

"Obviously."

He leaned back against the counter and studied her. "How old are you?"

"No wonder you don't have a girlfriend," she mused without looking up.

His eyebrows lifted. "Who says I don't?"

"Um, everything about you?" If he wasn't going to be polite, why should she bother?

"It's not like I asked your weight," he said, clearly trying to provoke her.

"You know," she said, still not glancing up, "for a man who seems determined to give off unsociable, taciturn vibes, you sure are chatty."

"Just trying to figure you out, since we're stuck with each other for the foreseeable future."

*Good luck with that. I haven't even figured myself out.*

Claire shifted in her chair to face him. "Don't worry, I have good news. I've already got a read on you. Let me guess. You have no sisters, your mother subscribed to the boys-will-be-boys model, and you have no serious relationship to show for it?"

"Right, wrong, wrong," he replied without hesitation.

He turned and unzipped the small cooler he'd brought with him, giving Claire's brain a chance to catch up as he pulled a sandwich out of a Ziploc and took a bite.

"No sisters, awesome mom, and . . . serious girlfriend?" She amended her guess, wondering if Naomi had been wrong about his commitment-phobe status.

"No sisters, no mom, and one fiancée."

Claire blinked rapidly. Naomi had gotten it *really* wrong.

"When's the wedding?" she asked.

"What?" He balled up the Ziploc and shoved it back into the cooler as he polished off the last bite. "Oh. No. Former fiancée."

"Ah."

He gave her a knowing look. "Go ahead. Say it."

"Say what?"

He turned back toward her, crossing his arms. "That you're not surprised."

Claire frowned, not loving that he was more perceptive than he seemed.

"I'm sorry your relationship didn't work out." Her voice sounded stiff, even to her own ears.

"I'm not."

"You're not . . . sorry that your relationship ended?"

"Nope." There was a curtness to his tone, and Claire found herself intrigued in spite of herself. However, she'd only known the guy a little over twenty-four hours. She couldn't very well go prying into the most painful parts of his past.

Not that he was likely to tell her what she wanted to know. Despite his assertion that he wanted to "figure her out," he seemed the type of man to use as few words as possible, and she doubted he'd waste them on her.

Still, she was curious enough that she made a mental note to ask Naomi later. If Oliver and Scott went way back, Naomi was likely to at least know something about the mysterious fiancée.

"What're those?" Scott asked, nodding at her paint swatches, the topic of their personal lives apparently finished alongside his sandwich.

Claire gave him a sweet smile. "My color choices."

He grunted. "You're still on that banana cream pie thing?"

"It's strawberry lemonade cupcake, and if anything, my vision's becoming clearer." *For now.*

"My vision's becoming clearer, too." He jerked his head to the right. "That needs to go."

She glanced in the general direction, having no idea what he was talking about. "Are your other clients mind readers? Because I lack that skill."

"The wall," he snapped. "We need to tear it down."

"Don't we sort of need it?"

He walked toward it, knocked on the portion closest to the arched entryway to the kitchen. "Beam's right here, and that's the only load-bearing part. The rest is just a throwback to when galley kitchens were in style. We can turn the support beam into a pillar, open the whole thing up."

"Can we paint the pillar hot pink? Ooh, we could add glitter!"

Scott's incredulous look was far too delicious for Claire to tell him she was kidding. It was surprisingly fun to try and goad a reaction out of her stubbornly implacable contractor. Claire deliberately picked up the brightest, most awful bubble gum shade of pink she could find among her swatches.

She held it up in the general direction he'd indicated, squinting as though she were pretending to imagine the pink as a pillar.

"Unbelievable," he muttered. "Do not be surprised if that paint swatch goes missing. For good."

She smiled and, having had her fun, set the ugly paint color back on the table and got down to business. "Okay, lay it on me. How bad does the upstairs look?"

"Depends," he said with a shrug. "You've got some options based on what you're looking for. The two guest rooms are small and share a wall. It'd be easy to tear it down, make a bigger space. But most people would probably opt to leave it as is. Two small rooms, and the bigger master."

"Really?" She was surprised. She'd been toying with the idea of making it one big room herself. The two guest rooms as they were now were barely large enough to fit a double bed and a dresser.

Scott was looking at her ceiling, distracted by—and apparently displeased with—the overhead lighting. "Yeah," he finally replied, looking back at her. "This part of town especially, people like to keep their extra bedrooms open. You know. Nursery. Kids' rooms."

"Oh jeez," she said, sitting back. "Not you *and* my mother."

He stared at her. "Did you just compare me to your mother?"

"Why is it," she continued, "that every woman of childbearing age is expected to be beholden to her uterus?"

"Whoa. Hey." He held up his hands, looking slightly panicked. "I have absolutely zero interest in your uterus."

"Me neither," Claire said firmly. "And I've got no use for a nursery."

He shifted, looking a little uncomfortable. "You don't have to decide right now. I can start with other stuff, figure out what to do with the guest rooms later."

"I don't care what order you do things in, but I'm not going to change my mind about wanting a nursery."

He looked at her for a while. "What if husband number two has a different opinion? Once I'm done with this project, I'm not going to come build a baby room for you when you get married again."

"Gosh, you mean you and I will have to part ways at the end of this? *Devastating.* And there's not going to be a husband number two. I'm not getting married again."

"Fine by me. But women opt to have kids without husbands all the time."

She made an exasperated sound. "What is it with you and my reproductive system?"

He winced. "Right. Sorry."

Claire nodded, relieved to drop the subject, even though she should be used to it. Up until a couple of years ago, Claire had automatically tensed when she'd said that she didn't want to have children, and braced for the usual responses.

*Oh, but you'd make such a great mom!*

*You'll change your mind.*

*It's different when they're your own.*

*You may think that now when you're young and healthy, but who's going to take care of you when you're old?*

For a long time, she'd told herself those people were well-meaning, but in recent years she found the assumptions downright insulting. She wasn't a clueless kid who didn't know her own mind; she was an adult woman who'd always known that kids weren't part of the picture.

"Do you *want* kids?" she asked, half curious, half wanting to steer the conversation away from her ovaries.

"Nope. I'm good with Bob."

"Bob?"

"My dog."

"Oh right. Where is he? I thought you were going to bring him with you."

"Already had the pet sitter booked for today. Bob'll tag along tomorrow, if that's still cool."

"Sure, of course."

To be honest, Claire wasn't entirely sure how cool it was. She'd never had a dog. Her dad had been allergic, or so he'd claimed when Claire had gone through the typical *I want a puppy for Christmas* phase between the ages of six and eight. After high school, she'd moved straight from her parents' house to college, from college to living with Brayden, and her husband had most assuredly not been a dog person.

"What kind of dog?" she asked.

Scott shrugged. "A mix. Lab mostly, the vet thinks maybe some beagle in there. Funny looking dog, but loyal as they come."

It was a telling statement, and there was something extra in his tone when he said the word *loyal* that Claire recognized on a gut level. Claire would have bet a million dollars in that instant that she knew exactly what had gone down with that former fiancée of his. *Cheating*.

When their gazes caught, almost on accident, Claire was even more sure. She may have only met the guy yesterday, and she definitely didn't like him. But in that single moment, she knew him as well as she knew anyone, and she knew exactly what he'd meant.

*Dogs were loyal in a way that people weren't.*

## Chapter Five

*B*e cool, okay?" Scott said to his dog as he stepped onto Claire's porch and pushed open the front door.

It was a pointless request. Scott's dog was as extroverted as Scott was introverted. The second the door opened, Bob shot forward, sensing a new friend to be won over. Shaking his head in resignation, Scott followed the mutt inside, hoping Claire was true to her word and that she was cool with dogs.

A second later, he got a verbal cue on just how *cool* she was.

At Claire's startled shriek, Scott stepped into the small sitting room off the foyer, watching as Claire frantically tried to keep an upholstered yellow chair between herself and Bob. She gave him a panicked look. "What is that, a dinosaur?"

"Yes, Claire, it's a dinosaur," Scott said, grabbing Bob's collar just as the dog lunged at the frightened woman. He knew the pup just wanted to say hi. Claire apparently did not.

"Bob. Sit."

The dog did so reluctantly, and Scott rubbed Bob's head as

he gave Claire an exasperated look. "I thought you said you were cool with dogs."

She continued to study the dog with apprehension. "I wasn't expecting him to be so huge."

Bob actually *was* huge in a disproportionate, clumsy kind of way. The long skinny legs didn't quite look like they should support the enormous barrel-shaped body, and the slightly too small head did make Bob look a bit like, well . . . maybe she wasn't that far off on the dinosaur thing.

"Her," Scott corrected. "Bob's a girl."

"You named a girl dog Bob?"

Scott hadn't named the dog at all. The people at the shelter had said that was her name, bestowed by the former asshole owner who'd given her up and apparently hadn't bothered to check the sex. But he had better things to do with his time than correct a snobby Manhattan widow's misassumptions.

"If you were scared of big dogs, you should have told me. I'd have left her at home."

"No, she's fine. We'll be fine." She gave Bob a pointed look. "Won't we?"

Bob wagged her tail happily, having the good sense to look charming. Or at least, Bob's version of charming.

Scott frowned, noticing the chair she was still hiding behind was in the center of the room, not next to the window beside its ugly twin. "Rearranging?"

"What? Oh." She pointed at the painting on the wall. "You said you were starting on this room today. I was going to take that down so it wouldn't be in the way."

"Where's your stepladder?"

"A stepladder! Why didn't I think of that?" she said in a sing-song, pretending to twirl her hair.

"Sarcasm noted. You don't have a stepladder."

"I do not."

"What did your husband use to do things around the house?"

She snorted. "You obviously never met Brayden. Or anyone who lives on this street."

Scott gave a disdainful grunt. He knew work came in all kinds. Some wore suits and used their brains; others wore a tool belt and used their hands. But he had a hell of a time respecting a man who, he was betting, didn't know a Phillips from a flathead.

He was also having a hard time reconciling the idea of Claire with someone so . . . useless. Much less someone who had screwed around on her. From what he'd seen of her over the past few days, she was efficient, self-reliant, and had minimal BS tolerance. He'd offered to help her open a pickle jar she was wrestling with and gotten a near snarl in response.

Then again, Scott supposed he wasn't one to judge based on the choice of one's romantic partner. A much younger, dumber version of himself had invested his emotions in a woman who hadn't deserved them. Since then, he'd learned that life was simpler if you didn't get attached to any thing, any place, and certainly not any person. He made an exception for Bob.

Scott frowned. He hadn't thought about Meredith in months. Maybe years. She'd popped into his mind twice in the last week, first when he told Claire he'd been engaged and again at the thought of Claire's husband. Irritated with himself and, irrationally, with Claire, he jerked his chin toward the painting on the wall. "I've got a couple of guys coming over later to move everything. They can take care of the art."

"Oh. Well, you didn't mention that," she said primly, starting to drag the chair back across the room. The chair was ugly, but it was substantial, and he stepped forward to help. His hand brushed over hers as he reached out to take over the task. He was annoyed he noticed the contact. Even more annoyed that she didn't.

Instead, her attention returned to the dog. More curious than trepidatious now. "I really didn't expect her to be so big."

"I told you yesterday she was a Lab."

"I haven't spent much time with dogs. I didn't realize Labs were the size of camels."

She reached out a hand toward the dog, then stopped a full foot from the dog's face, palm up, the way one might offer a horse a carrot.

Bob gave Scott a puzzled look. *What the hell do I do with this?*

When Claire's hand dropped back to her side without making contact, Scott sighed and stepped forward.

"Here," he said crouching beside the dog to hold Bob in place. "Give me your hand."

"No, thanks. I'm good."

Ignoring this, Scott reached out, snagged her smaller hand in his. Again registering the contact, again hating that he did so. The last thing he needed was to be physically aware of a widow for God's sake. Not to mention, she was a friend of Oliver's. Scott never apologized for his one-night-stand lifestyle, but he also made it a point to treat the people closest to him—and the people closest to them—as off-limits.

He held her hand still just long enough for Bob to sniff it and give her fingers a friendly lick. When that didn't freak her out, Scott released her hand, smiling a little as she gave Bob's head a pat, the way a little kid might with a tentative tap, tap, tap.

"Good dinosaur," she said, growing more confident in her pats.

Bob, bless her, seemed to sense the woman's wariness and kept her butt planted on the ground, tongue to herself, despite her barely contained enthusiasm at finally getting some love from Claire.

Scott watched the woman carefully, relieved to note that she looked more wary than scared. "You always been scared of dogs?"

"I didn't realize I was," she admitted. "I've never had one and haven't spent much time around them. Especially not big ones like Bob."

"It's the big guys who are the most gentle," he said, patting Bob's back.

"Big girls," Claire corrected. "You said she's a lady. Named Bob. I think she needs a pink bow. So people know."

"Nope," Scott said, standing. "We're not doing that."

"I didn't say we were. I said *I* was."

Recognizing a pointless argument when he saw one, he changed the subject. "When the guys come over later, you want us to put the ugly painting with the rest of the furniture in the spare bedroom? Or hang it somewhere else? Say, the trash can?"

"The painting's not ugly."

He looked at the painting of an extremely mediocre, drab landscape of the countryside with copious shades of brown, then looked back at her.

"Okay, it's a little ugly," she admitted.

"So why do you have it?"

She opened her mouth, then shut it, frowning as she gave the painting an assessing look. "I don't know. It was here when Brayden and I moved in. He inherited the place from his grandmother. I guess it never really occurred to me that I don't have to keep it."

Bob wiggled up to Scott's side and nudged his hand for a pet. Scott obliged the dog while studying the woman. He couldn't quite figure her out. She gave off stubborn *I don't care what anyone thinks* vibes one minute, and people-pleasing rule follower ones the next. She'd told him to bring his dog over, yet she was apparently terrified of dogs. Her makeup was muted, her clothes unimaginative neutrals, and yet she wanted a pink house. She wouldn't let him help open a damn pickle jar, but he was welcome to drag a chair across the room.

"I guess, for now, put it with the rest of his stuff," Claire said distractedly, still staring at the painting.

*His* stuff. The husband's.

Scott had combed over every inch of the house during his assessment, and though Claire was fairly neat and minimal, one of the upstairs bedrooms was a noticeable exception. It looked like a hoarder's haven, filled nearly floor to ceiling with haphazardly packed moving boxes, stacks of books, skis, luggage. Even if he hadn't noted that the assortment of stuff was distinctly masculine, the fact that the door was kept closed—always—told him exactly whose stuff it was.

"You ever think of getting rid of it?"

"What?" she snapped, her gaze coming around to his.

He nodded in the general direction of the stairs. "It's not like he's coming back for it."

Her hazel gaze flickered with an emotion, but it was gone before he could identify it. Pain? Anger? Denial? Still, he couldn't bring himself to feel guilty for his remark. The woman was too darn interesting to be hung up on a ghost. Especially one who, from what he'd heard, had been the world's worst husband.

"I know he's not coming back," she said testily. "I've been through all my stages of grief."

"Then why the hell do you have a veritable museum devoted to the guy up there?"

"Oh, I'm sorry. I didn't realize when I hired you that you were also available for unsolicited advice on my life."

Scott held up his hands. "Fair enough. I'll add the painting to the shrine."

Her expression twisted angrily, but instead of replying, she lifted her chin and walked past him, the click of her heels muted by the ugly carpet that covered most of the damn house. The muffled click of her heels grew louder again as she walked past once more, this time toward the front door, purse over her shoulder.

"Where you going?" He shouldn't be curious. But he was.

She halted and turned, giving him an icy look. "None of your business. And neither," she said, pointing emphatically up the stairs in the direction of the Brayden Hayes memorial, "is that."

Scott winced as she punctuated her point with a slam of the front door, and looked down at the dog who gave him a baleful look. "She's right. It's definitely not our business. *She's* not our business."

But damn. He was intrigued all the same.

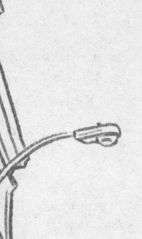

# Chapter Six

*W*hen Claire's anger hadn't abated after several blocks of an attempted "cooldown" walk, she blamed it on the sweltering ninety-degree weather and ducked into a Starbucks near Park Avenue, as much for the AC as for the beverage.

She was still seething as she waited in line. What the hell did a man who, best she could tell, had the emotional sensitivity of a piece of cardboard think he was doing giving her advice on how to adjust to life as a widow? On an intellectual level, she'd known that Scott would see the room where she'd stuffed all of Brayden's belongings in the days following the funeral. She'd even acknowledged that he'd be able to figure out to whom the stuff belonged.

She hadn't, however, thought it through *emotionally*. She hadn't been prepared for how it would feel to know that someone else knew what she could barely admit to herself.

That some stupid part of her, probably the young, naive girl that had fallen in love with Brayden all those years ago, wasn't ready to say goodbye.

*It's not like he's coming back.*

"Oh really?" she muttered snidely under her breath. "He's not?"

She knew Brayden was gone. She knew he wasn't the man she'd thought she'd married. In all honesty, Claire wasn't even sure she was sad anymore. And she was not mad, either.

So why couldn't she get rid of his stuff?

"Ma'am?"

Claire realized she'd zoned out, and the barista was ready to take her order. She stepped forward and ordered her favorite guilty pleasure on hot days. "Grande vanilla Frappuccino, please."

"Wait," she blurted out, realizing what she'd just done. Again with the vanilla. "Not that, I don't want that." *I am not vanilla.*

The barista gave her an impatient look.

"I'll have . . ." She scanned the menu above his head. "A strawberry Frappuccino. Is that good?"

"Yeah." He scribbled the revised order on the cup with a Sharpie.

"What about strawberry lemonade? Is that a Frappuccino flavor?" she asked hopefully.

"Nope," the barista said, clearly having no time for Claire's existential crisis. "You want any food?"

"No. Thanks." Claire paid for the drink and made her way toward the mob of people waiting for their orders. Her anger had eased slightly, if nothing else because it pleased her to picture Scott's face when she walked in the door with a frothy *pink* beverage.

"Claire?"

She turned toward the familiar masculine voice, a smile already breaking over her face. "Oliver!"

She hugged Naomi's boyfriend. Oliver Cunningham had been a casual social acquaintance when she and Brayden were married, but since he'd started dating Naomi, she'd come to count the handsome Oliver as a good friend. As usual, he wore a suit, paired with a light blue tie that matched his eyes. It was hard to believe that perfectly groomed, impeccably mannered Oliver could possibly be friends with the rough and surly Scott.

"What brings you to this part of town?" she asked, since Oliver and Naomi lived downtown, and his office was on the West Side.

"Visiting my parents' friends at the old stomping ground. My former neighbor just a had a hip replacement, so I took over some flowers and a basket of pears that my assistant informed me people like."

"Nice touch. You really are one of the good guys. And I always forget you used to live just around the corner from me."

"Well, that's reassuring," he said with a grin. "Sometimes I worry everything about me still screams Upper East Side as clearly as if I had my zip code tattooed on my forehead."

"Oh, everything about you does still scream that," she said, patting his arm. "Once a Park Avenue prince, always a Park Avenue prince, though you wear it well."

"You want to grab a table?" he asked. "It's been too long since we've caught up. You kick off the renovation?"

"Yup, as of this week it's officially begun. So far so good, though your contractor buddy and I aren't getting along nearly so well."

He grinned. "That's what I want to hear about."

"Ah, so you *did* know what you were getting me into," she teased with a smile, stepping forward to retrieve her drink as the barista called her name.

"That is one pink beverage," Oliver marveled as she returned to his side. "Is it good?"

"I've never had it before," she said, as she pushed the green straw into the frothy Frappuccino and took a sip. "Oh! It *is* good!"

Better, perhaps, than her trusty vanilla. Or maybe it was merely the change that tasted good.

"Table opening up by the window," she said, gesturing with her drink.

"Go. I'll be along with my boring brown beverage as soon as it's up."

Claire swooped in on the table and was just using a couple of napkins to clear off cranberry scone crumbs when Oliver joined her. He swiped her drink from the table and took a sip.

"It's good, right?" she asked, sitting across from him.

"It's something. I'd offer you my double espresso, but I'm afraid you'd find it a bit dull."

"I never did understand people who don't put sweetener, or at least cream, in their coffee. Isn't that the whole point?"

"You and Naomi. I swear her coffee to creamer ratio is nearly one-to-one these days. And I think us black coffee drinkers would argue that it is you who misses the point of, um, *coffee*?"

She sighed and shook her head. "You and Scott."

"Ah yes," he said, leaning back, and his presence was as commanding in a small wooden chair at a bustling Starbucks as it was in a boardroom. Oliver was an architect who'd started his own firm, but she could have just as easily seen him at the head of a conference room table if he'd followed in the footsteps of his well-known businessman father.

"Is he really that bad?" he asked.

"No," she said on a sigh. "I can handle him. It wouldn't be so bad if he wasn't going to be practically living at my house for the next month or so. If we kill each other, it's on your head."

Oliver laughed. "Scott does know how to alienate people when he's on a project. Though I thought you were made of stronger stuff, Hayes." His smile slipped slightly. "I'm sorry. I've never really asked. Did you . . . Are you . . . Did you change back to your maiden name?"

"I thought about it," she admitted. "I asked myself if I really wanted to continue sharing the name of a man who apparently forgot to mention we were in an open marriage. But I don't feel like Claire Burchett anymore. For better or worse, and there was admittedly a lot of worse, I'm Claire Hayes now."

"Perhaps one day you'll be Claire something else," Oliver said softly. "Or is that too old-fashioned of me?"

She gave a rueful smile. "You mean if I got married again? It's not the name-changing part I'd be averse to so much as the marriage itself."

"Ah." He took a sip of his drink.

Claire leaned forward. "I'm an Upper East Sider, too. I know a noncommittal disagreement when I hear one."

"I don't disagree," he said carefully. "But Naomi felt that way, too. You saw how hard I had to work to win over that woman."

"I did," Claire said with a smile. "It was better than any movie. But I don't have an Oliver desperately in love with me."

"And if you did?"

She shook her head. "Still not on the marriage track."

"Fair enough," he said easily. "What about the dating track?"

"I'm thirty-five. The men who want to date me are either looking for marriage or a fling."

"And?"

"And, I don't want to get married," she said, puzzled that the usually sharp Oliver wasn't following.

"And?" he pressed again, eyebrows lifting.

"Oooh." Claire laughed as she realized it was *she* who hadn't been following. "Oliver Cunningham, are you suggesting I date men with the intention of using them for a booty call?"

"As a gentleman, I couldn't possibly," he said with a boyish grin. "As a friend, I will point out that just because you're not looking for anything long-term doesn't mean you have to cut yourself off from male companionship."

"Does Naomi know you offer this sort of advice?"

"Absolutely not," Oliver said, looking slightly panicked. "And I doubt she'd be thrilled. I know you three women have that pact."

"You say it like it's a dirty word."

He hesitated for a moment, taking a sip of coffee. "I think it's good that you three made that pact. I'm glad it brought you together, and I'm certainly glad that you're looking out for each other. I wouldn't want to see any of you be hurt by someone like Brayden again."

"But?"

"But, I worry that the pact could potentially backfire—end up being too restrictive. There's being careful with your heart, and then there's becoming jaded."

"You don't want me to become a cynical old crone."

She smiled, but he didn't smile back. "No, Claire. I don't want you to become lonely."

Her smile disappeared as the word seemed to hit her squarely in the throat. It was a word—an emotion—she hadn't really let herself consider since Brayden's death, and yet she knew, she sensed that it was lurking around every corner. On an emotional level, and yes, to the point Oliver was dancing around, on a physical level. Brayden was dead. She wasn't. And her body knew it.

"Also, sex is fun," he said, as though reading her mind, and lightened the mood with a grin.

"Yeah, well." She took a sip of the Frappuccino. "Trust me, I have zero game."

"I'm an adult male who loves jigsaw puzzles, and I got a hot billionaire girlfriend."

"Nerds are in right now," Claire argued. "And even if they weren't, you're ridiculously charming. I don't even know how to flirt."

Oliver downed the rest of his coffee and checked his watch before standing. "Well then. Might I suggest a tried-and-true approach for learning a new skill?"

Claire groaned, knowing what he was going to say even before he said the word.

"Practice."

---

Having parted ways with Oliver, Claire took a leisurely walk home, less fired up than she was when she'd left the house. Granted, she still felt the urge to scream when she thought of Scott, but the joy of talking with a good friend had taken the edge off her anger. And if she were honest, the male company in particular had been pleasant. Not in a romantic or sexual way—she thought of Oliver like a brother. But there was no denying that spending time with the opposite sex felt . . . different.

Nice.

Which, annoyingly, sort of proved Oliver's point. If Claire

wasn't careful, she *was* going to end up lonely. And as for the rather cheeky suggestion of a booty call, Claire was rather intrigued by the idea, even as she felt completely out of her element just considering it.

Walking up the steps to her brownstone, Claire heard the boisterous sound of male voices, even before she opened the door.

"Oh!" she said, taking a startled step back, as a gray-haired man with a ponytail crossed her foyer, single-handedly maneuvering one of her sitting room chairs up the staircase.

A happy bark had her bracing for Bob's greeting, and she was relieved when the dog went easy on her, sitting patiently by her feet for a pet rather than jumping up on her as she feared.

"Hi, girl," she said, rubbing the dog's ear tentatively, enjoying how soft it was. "How's it going in here?"

She stepped forward as she asked, poking her head into the sitting room. Her first thought was how much bigger it looked when it wasn't dwarfed by too-large furniture.

Her second thought?

*Oh, mama.*

Claire had never been the type to ogle a man, but then she'd never seen a man who looked like this one. She had the epitome of man candy in her home.

He wasn't particularly tall—an inch or two shorter than Scott, who was on the other side of the room doing something with a tool and an end table, and who Claire purposely ignored.

But what the fantasy man lacked in height he made up for in sheer brawn. His biceps were tanned and filled out his Yankees shirt to perfection. His dark hair was cut short, his teeth white and even against his tanned skin. He was also clean-shaven, not a hint of five-o'clock shadow in sight.

Simply put, he was the personification of a boy-toy fantasy. The type of man that would be cast as the "young hot stud" with whom the middle-aged divorcée has a steamy vacation fling.

He must have felt the weight of her stare—or sensed her drool—because he grinned her way with a polite nod. "Ma'am."

"Hi," she said, her voice a little breathy, like the shy freshman who'd just earned a wink from the senior homecoming king.

Scott glanced up, eyes narrowed as he studied Claire for a moment. She saw his gaze drop to the pink beverage still in her hand before rolling his eyes.

Turning back to the younger guy, Claire's hand lifted almost against her will, as she gave a ridiculous little finger waggle of a wave.

Worse and worse.

She was grateful he'd already turned away from her and missed the awkward gesture. Scott, however, was still watching her, a puzzled *What the hell am I looking at here?* expression on his face.

Ignoring him, Claire ordered herself back to the kitchen and opened the fridge. She eyed a package of mixed greens, debated making a salad for lunch. She shut the refrigerator without taking anything out. She didn't want salad. She wanted . . . damn it, Oliver. She wanted sex. Or at least the prospect of it.

Maybe she'd just check on the movers, see if they needed anything . . .

The gray-haired guy with the ponytail had returned, only to leave the room once more with the other chair in hand. Scott was nowhere to be seen, but dark and hunky was still in the sitting room, unscrewing a lightbulb.

*You can screw my lightbulb.*

No, too obvious.

*Light my fire?*

Too awful.

Still oblivious to her staring, or too kind to embarrass her by noticing, the man bent down and began adding some sort of protective tape to the underside of the glass of her coffee table.

The muscles of his forearms flexed slightly, and—

"Seriously?" said a male voice close to her ear. "He's not a day over twenty-five."

Claire jumped in surprise, though she refused to feel guilty as she pulled out of sight and glared at Scott.

"*Really*," she said, pulling him farther down the hallway so as not to be overhead. "And I'm sure every woman you've hooked up with has been in your age range, right? Thirty-two and above?"

His eyes narrowed slightly, then he shrugged. "Point taken. Still, you're practically drooling."

"I was just looking," she said, refusing to be embarrassed. "He's very . . ."

"Young?"

"Hot," she corrected. "He is *hot*."

"Dean also has a job to do. Stay out of the way," Scott said, before brushing past her and going to join the movers.

Dean. She could work with that.

She was tempted to return to the kitchen. Scott, while an ass, was right. Dean was too young for her; he was here working for Scott . . .

And yet Oliver's reminder that there was only one way to learn a new skill wouldn't stop running around on repeat in her brain.

"Oh hell, why not," she muttered to herself.

New Claire gave in to whims, and right now, she wanted to dust off her stale flirting skills.

Ignoring Scott's high-handed order to stay out of the way, she strode into the sitting room, adding a little waggle to her stride, hoping it was sultry and didn't look like she was drunk. The disgust on Scott's face told her she wasn't terribly successful.

Practice.

She walked straight to where Dean was crouched by the table. "Hi, I'm Claire, owner of the ugly furniture you're so kindly moving. Can I get you anything? Water?"

*My loins?*

He stood slowly, giving Claire a boyish smile. "No, thank you, ma'am."

"Claire," she corrected, feeling a little fluttery at the rather perfect smile. "'Ma'am' makes me feel old."

She ignored the knowing look Scott gave her from across the room. *Compared to him, you are old.*

Instead, she tried to channel confident, sensual woman. Like Naomi and the guy at the home improvement store. Like Audrey and anyone.

"Claire, then," Dean said, grinning again. "Good to meet you."

Oh *God*, he had a chin dimple. Was he even real?

"Do you work with Scott often?" she asked, scrambling for something to say.

Dean lifted his broad shoulders. "Nah, he's not in town much. I like to be available when he calls, but this is really just a side gig for extra cash."

"Oh yeah? What's your main gig?" She immediately dropped her hand to her side when she realized she'd been on her way to *literally* twirling her hair. God, she was even more out of practice with flirting than she'd realized.

"Acting. Well, modeling mostly, but when I get my big break . . ."

This time it was harder to ignore Scott's knowing look, but she determinedly kept her eyes on Dean. "What sort of acting do you do?" she asked, noting that there were no signs of tattoos peeking out from beneath his T-shirt. She wondered if that applied to the rest of him. She rather hoped so. She'd never understood tattoos, and it seemed a shame to mark up all that perfection.

Scott deliberately stepped into Claire's view behind Dean's back and made a quick swipe of his thumb on the side of his mouth, as though indicating that she should wipe up her drool.

"Commercials so far," Dean said, oblivious to Scott's antics. "But I've been an extra a few times on primetime. You may have seen me . . ."

He named a few procedural dramas that Claire had heard of but never seen, and she wracked her brain for something dazzling to say.

Scott interrupted before she got inspired. "Hey, Dean, I feel like an ass. I just realized I never asked . . . how the hell is your wife? Newlywed life treating you well?"

Claire's eyes went wide, and she glanced from Scott, back to Dean, praying that Scott had made some sort of mistake . . .

"It's good!" Dean said with a happy smile. "Even better now that we've moved into a bigger apartment. Juliana's having a great time decorating. Wouldn't mind picking your brain on what to do with our kitchen though; we're trying to find ways to modernize it without too much expense . . ."

*Oh God. Oh God, oh God, oh God.*

She'd just gotten a tiny glimpse of what Audrey and Naomi must have felt knowing they'd been flirting with a married man without realizing it.

It was horrifying.

*Beyond.*

Claire slowly backed out of the room as Dean and Scott began talking about garbage disposals. Her pride was stinging hard. Flirting with a younger man was one thing. Flirting *badly* was slightly embarrassing. Flirting badly with a married younger man?

"Kill me," she said out loud, walking back toward the kitchen.

Worst of all, Scott had seen it. No, wait. That wasn't the worst thing. The worst thing was that Scott had known Dean was married and let her go out on that limb anyway. It was wrong to feel betrayed. Even more stupid to feel stung, but she did, just a little.

She knew the guy was gruff and a little rough around the edges. She somehow hadn't expected him to be *mean*.

Bob joined her in the kitchen as she pulled out a rotisserie chicken and began pulling off pieces for her salad.

"Your father's an ass; you know that, right?" Claire asked the dog.

Bob's butt was planted on the floor, her tail wagging furiously in what Claire was pretty sure was agreement. "Yeah," Claire said, as she broke off a big chunk of meat and fed it to the dog. "You totally know that."

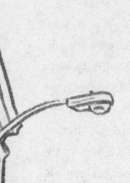

## Chapter Seven

*I*t wasn't one of his favorite pastimes, but Scott could admit when he'd been an ass. Today had been one of those days. Scott had known the second he'd seen Claire gawking at Dean what was going on. He'd hired Dean enough times to know the sort of response the bronzed, beefy kid elicited from women.

Somehow, though, Scott had been surprised—and annoyed— to see that Dean's brawn had had its usual effect on Claire Hayes. The woman seemed far too levelheaded to drool over a gym rat who was a good guy but had the conversational skills of a saltine.

And yet, she had. She'd found Dean *hot*, her word, and for some perverse reason, the whole situation had gotten under Scott's skin. Enough so that he'd avoided taking the high road and letting her know Dean's marital status. Instead, he'd let her flutter and titter around the kid.

Scott wasn't proud of it. Especially since his motives for not telling her had seemed to come awfully close to jealousy. She could not have made it clearer that touching Scott that morning hadn't done it for her.

And then a twenty-something beefcake rolled in, and she'd practically swooned.

Scott liked Dean well enough. The kid was more reliable than most and didn't drive Scott up the wall. But the thought of Claire with a slightly dim model seemed all sorts of wrong, even as he knew it was hypocritical. Scott had hooked up with plenty of twenty-something aspiring actresses himself, many of whom had been eloquent and informed and others who knew very few words beyond *like*.

But that was him. He was practiced at this sort of thing, knew exactly how to extricate himself from the bedroom after the main event without anyone getting hurt. Claire, on the other hand; he was betting she didn't have the first clue about how to have a relationship with a man without getting her emotions involved. She was a woman who had an entire room of her dead husband's belongings upstairs; her emotions were definitely a mess, whether she realized it or not.

He rubbed at his chest, acknowledging the slight tightness that had been there ever since she'd stormed out of the house earlier. The things he'd said to her about Brayden had been overstepping in a big way. They'd been borderline cruel, and while he knew he could be blunt, *mean* didn't sit right with him.

He should have apologized the second she came back into the house with that stupid pink beverage. Instead, he'd let her throw herself at Dean. Scott cursed softly as he replayed the horrified embarrassment on her cheeks when she'd learned Dean was married, the pink cheeks of humiliation that he could have spared her.

*Damn it.*

It was half past six by the time Scott wrapped for the day, closer to seven by the time he ran his errand and made it back to her place. Claire looked up in surprise when she saw him standing in her kitchen entryway. "Oh! I thought you'd left for the day."

"Left, yes. But not for the day. You thought I'd left Bob?"

She glanced to her right, where Bob sat adoringly staring at whatever Claire was stirring on the stove. He didn't blame the dog. It smelled delicious.

Claire gave a slight frown. "I guess I forgot Bob had to go home."

"You two have come a long way since earlier," he observed.

"We called a truce," Claire replied. "I agreed to share my chicken earlier, and she agreed not to kill me in a vicious dog mauling."

"Yes, because that was definitely a risk," he replied dryly.

Claire tilted her head. "What do you think about calling her Bobsie? It's more feminine."

"Veto."

"Yeah, but you owe me," Claire said, giving him a dark look as she stirred. "I realize we aren't friends, but that was straight up mean today. You could have told me he was freaking *married*."

"I know."

She didn't look up from the stove until he stepped forward, his apology gift extended. She stared at it in confusion. "What's this?"

"Peace offering."

Claire set her wooden spoon on a plate beside the stove and, turning around fully, reached for the bottle of wine. "It's *pink*."

"Yeah, well." He shoved his hands into his jeans, feeling atypically embarrassed. "You seem to be a fan of the color in your home. I thought you might like your wine that way, too."

She looked up at him. "You bought rosé? My brain can't even comprehend that."

"I admit it was a first for me. I can't promise it's any good, but the guy at the wine shop around the corner insisted it was the best he had."

Claire held up the bottle. "He's right. I've had it, and it's excellent. It's also expensive."

Scott shrugged. "Good thing I'm loaded then."

She let out a startled laugh at his blunt announcement.

"You are . . ." She studied him, looking for the right words. "Not like other people."

"I'll take that as a compliment."

"Well, don't," she mused, looking back at the wine. "I'm not entirely sure I like you."

He smiled, enjoying her bluntness, especially because he expected it wasn't typical of her. Claire Hayes struck him as the type of woman who had an endless supply of polite banalities at the tip of her tongue for every situation, and yet she didn't bother using them with him.

A fact that strangely pleased him.

She continued to study the wine, a frown on her face.

"Everything all right?"

Claire met his eyes. "You're undercharging me."

*Yes.* "How do you figure?"

She held up the wine bottle. "This isn't just expensive, it's *very* expensive. Which makes me think you weren't joking just now when you claimed to be loaded. And yet, based on the contract I signed yesterday, you underbid every single other contractor I talked to by *a lot*, and none of them have your expertise."

"Was there a compliment in there somehow, or . . ."

She set the bottle on the counter, refusing to be deterred. "I don't want you doing me favors."

"Noted."

Claire merely looked at him, her hazel gaze steady and patient. Waiting for an explanation.

Scott was no stranger to stubborn staring contests, though usually they were for the opposite reason—a client hoping to wear him down to a lower price.

Scott always won those staring contests, but not this one.

He sighed and relented. "Fine. I undercharged you."

"Because I'm a poor little widow?"

"I'm not that nice," he said bluntly. "But then, you seem to have figured that out already."

Her lips twitched in a half smile. "Then why?"

Knowing she wanted the honest answer, Scott gave it to her. "Most of my clients are enormous corporations with nearly limitless budgets. If I charged you what I normally charge, you couldn't afford it."

"No, probably not," she agreed. "So why not just politely decline my little house renovation and move on?"

"I intended to."

She blinked, and he felt a surge of satisfaction that he'd been able to catch this unshakable woman off guard, even in a small way.

"What changed your mind?"

He crossed his arms and shifted his feet, feeling slightly uncomfortable with the direction of the conversation. He didn't know how to explain to people that his work was as much *feeling* as it was numbers and supplies and good, old-fashioned elbow grease.

"The front door knocker," he evaded. "It was just so god-awful, I knew I wouldn't be able to sleep at night knowing one of those was still in existence."

"You're a terrible liar, Mr. Turner," she said with a slight smile, turning back to the stove.

He didn't deny it. He was a terrible liar—he didn't have much use for lying, and thus didn't have much practice. Still, he didn't know whether he was surprised or disappointed that she was apparently going to let him off the hook. That she wasn't going to press him to explain that he'd simply stepped into the home and felt it—the sense that he needed to put his mark on this place.

Or the fact that as much as he loved to travel, he'd jumped at the excuse to sleep in his own bed, in his own city. To eat something other than microwave dinners and room service. To see his freaking dog.

So, no. He didn't need Claire's money.

What he needed was a chance to catch his breath. To remember what it felt like to enjoy life instead of just going through the motions. He wasn't exactly sure how or why an unremarkable brownstone off of Lexington Avenue was the answer, but somehow . . . it was.

Scott told Claire none of this.

Instead, he pointed at an ugly pink tile on her counter. "No. Hell no."

She turned around, her gaze following the direction of his finger, and gave a slow, satisfied smile. "Oh, this?" She picked up the tile and held it up for inspection. "I picked this out just for you. I was thinking it could be the floor *and* the walls of the powder room."

"Good God. You can't—"

She laughed, delighted by his expression, before tossing the tile sample aside. "*That* was *exactly* what I was hoping for when I picked it up today."

He sagged a little in relief. He knew this wasn't his home, but he didn't know if he could bring himself to place the ugly 1950s-style tile in anyone's home. "So we're not going with that?"

"No." She opened a drawer and pulled out a white marble sample. "I haven't figured out the walls yet, but I'm crushing pretty hard on this for the floors. I just have to figure out if I can afford it. You may be giving me a discount for mysterious reasons, but suppliers are not cheap."

He was already reaching for the tile, relieved that the woman wasn't entirely without taste.

"Is it too white?" she asked, sounding unexpectedly vulnerable.

"Too white?"

"I told myself I didn't want to go blah, and I figure white is as blah as it gets. And yet, I keep coming back to that one."

"What were the other options, pink sequins? Magenta-stained wood?"

She gave him a quelling look as she pulled a corkscrew out of the drawer and reached for the wine bottle.

"There's white, and then there's *white*," Scott told her.

"Clears it right up. Thank you."

He ran a finger around the edge of the marble, trying to figure out how to explain. Wondering why he even wanted to. Typically, he told his clients what they wanted, and they nodded and agreed, or they found another contractor. This project was different. She was different. Though *how*, he was still figuring out.

"When you talk about *blah* white, you're talking about using white as the absence of color. A drab blank canvas with no personality, no vision. It's how most people use white in a home.

They tell themselves they're selecting neutral, but really they just lack the guts to commit to one thing, so they choose something that will go with everything."

He glanced up and found her listening with rapt attention.

"Other whites," he said, continuing to rotate the piece of marble with his finger, "like this one, are deliberate whites. See the strands of silver? The glimmer? The vibrant richness of the white? You didn't choose this because it goes with everything. You chose it because it *is* the thing. That's the difference."

Neither of them said anything for a long moment, and Scott was fully braced for her to make a polite excuse to get him out the door. Scott didn't try to express himself often; he knew he wasn't good at it . . .

Claire held up the wine bottle. "If I open this, will you have a glass, or does that threaten your manhood?"

He exhaled slightly in relief, strangely pleased that she wanted him to stay.

She misunderstood his lack of response and shrugged. "Sorry, I don't have any beer in the fridge, but I've got some red wine and a couple of other liquor bottles up there." She pointed to the cupboard above the fridge. "Brayden liked whisky, you're welcome to help yourself. Unless that stuff expires."

He reached out, took the bottle from her. "I think I'll take my chances with the pink wine over a dead man's booze."

"You can stay for dinner. If you want. It's just chili, but it's pretty good if you're okay with spice."

He felt another of those unfamiliar surges of pleasure at the invitation, though he kept his tone indifferent. "Okay. Might as well, since I'm not sure I could drag Bob away just yet."

"Me and Bobsie have bonded, haven't we, sweetheart?" She

crouched down to pet the dog with both hands, and he searched for wineglasses.

"If I get a dog." she said, rubbing Bob's ears, "I'm getting a big dog just like this one."

"Says the woman who thought she was a dinosaur. And you say that now, but you haven't had to pick up her poops yet." He poured two glasses of wine, a generous one for her, smaller for him. He had to drive and wasn't at all sure he'd even like the pale pink liquid.

Claire winced at the poop mention as she stood and accepted the glass he held up. "I'd forgotten that part of owning a dog in Manhattan."

She started to take a drink, then lowered her glass and looked at him. "I just realized I don't know where you live. Manhattan?"

He nodded. "And Brooklyn."

"*And?*"

"I've got a place over on Sixtieth and Eleventh Avenue, but I kept my place in Bushwick. I keep meaning to rent one out, but I can never decide which."

That was only part of the truth. The *whole* truth was that not having options made him itchy. Picking a place seemed like the first step to settling down, and that's not something he wanted. Hadn't wanted in a long time.

"Huh. I'd never have pegged you for a Manhattan guy."

"Yeah, well. My neighborhood and your neighborhood are not the same Manhattan."

"True," she said, sipping the wine. "Which does Bob like better?"

Scott shrugged. "I've got a little yard in Brooklyn, so probably that one. But Manhattan means a shorter commute from your place, so at the moment, I think she likes that one."

"She'll be coming with you every day now," Claire said matter-of-factly.

"I guess." He sipped the wine tentatively.

"Well?"

He looked at the glass. "I don't know that I'd buy it for myself, but it's not as bad as I was expecting."

"Most people expect rosé to be sickly sweet, but it doesn't have to be. This one reminds me of strawberries and lemon."

He lifted his eyebrows. "Strawberry lemonade."

"Right! I didn't think of that." Her spontaneous laugh thawed something deep inside him, but he immediately put that shit on lockdown and scowled.

It was a wasted frown. She was looking at the stove. "Hmm, now that I think about it, the wine doesn't at all go with the chili. But I suppose after the day I've had, I'll take any alcohol in lieu of a proper pairing."

"What was wrong with your day?" He winced as soon as he asked it, belatedly remembering the reason he was here in the first place, with his pink wine peace offering.

She scoffed and picked up the wooden spoon, giving the sauce a stir. "Did you not see me awkwardly try to seduce a married man half my age?"

"Not half your age," he amended. "And *that* was seduction?"

"Hey," she snapped, though there was a good-natured joking to it. "I was married for years and have been widowed for one. Give me a break."

"It'll come back to you," he said. "Plus, bonus, it's easier for women."

"How's that?"

He took a sip of wine. "Breasts."

Claire snorted. "That may be true of twenty-year-old boobs. Thirty-five-year-old boobs, not so much."

*I can assure you, your thirty-five-year-old boobs are fine.*

More than fine. Claire's body was neither skinny nor particularly generous, just appealingly feminine.

"Trust me, it's just a matter of putting yourself out there," Scott said, clearing his throat. "You know, just maybe not with one of my guys. Especially not the married ones."

She flinched. "I'm horrified. Knowing how much it hurt to find out my husband had been with other women, I can't believe I even tried to make a move on a married guy."

*Shit.* He felt even worse now for not telling her. It hadn't just been embarrassment for Claire, it had been a reminder of what she'd been through.

He should have brought two bottles of wine.

"So how do you do it?" she asked, washing her hands. Scott noted the way the flimsy faucet sprayed every which way. He made a mental note that the whole sink had to go; the thing was ancient and awful.

"Do what?"

"You're all about the casual sex, right? How do you find your partners?"

"Well, for starters, I don't call them partners," he said with a slight smile.

"Okay, this is good. Tell me more."

"Isn't this a conversation to have with your friends?" he asked skeptically, taking another sip of wine. "Not a contractor you've known for three days?"

"Maybe. But it's like I said earlier, your stance is . . . refreshing. I can't imagine having this conversation with some of my girlfriends."

"What about Naomi, and who was your husband's other side piece? Aubrey?"

"Audrey. And I love those women to death, but I'm not entirely sure how supportive they'd be of my most recent . . . endeavor."

"What endeavor is that, exactly? I confess I don't speak fluent *woman* and only have half a clue what you were yelling at me about earlier."

"I wasn't yelling. But to answer your question, I guess I'm after . . . casual sex. Or at least the possibility of casual sex?"

"With a married wannabe model?"

"I didn't know he was married, because someone forgot to mention it."

He grinned. "I didn't forget."

"I *knew* it," she grumbled. "You *did* do it on purpose."

"I did," he admitted. "And I'm not proud of it." He took a deep breath and released it. "And I'm sorry. For the thing with Dean, and for the things I said about Brayden earlier. It's not my place to tell you what to do with your husband's stuff. Or when."

She was silent for a long moment before looking up and meeting his eyes. "Thank you. And, forgiven."

He tilted his head, surprised. "Just like that?" In his experience, women liked to hold on to their mad for at least an hour.

She sipped her wine. "Well, I mean, don't do it again. But if I survived my husband cheating on me many times, I can certainly ignore your acting like a boar."

"Well, thanks," he said, still feeling ill at ease. "Believe it or not, I don't get off on watching women feel embarrassed."

"What do you get off on?"

Scott choked on his wine. "Jesus."

"Oh, calm down," she said practically. "I'm not acting as an interested party. But Oliver said something today—"

"You saw Oliver?"

*Jesus.* Surely he wasn't *jealous*. Of his best friend. He knew Oliver was with Naomi, that he and Claire were just friends, and yet . . . he *also* knew that Oliver and Claire were the same. They both had the same polished manners, the same genteel way of speaking. They were alike in a way he would never be like Claire.

"Yeah, I ran into him at Starbucks. I always forget what a small town Manhattan can be. Anyway, he got me thinking that just because I never want to get married again doesn't mean I have to be a nun."

"And you're telling me, because—"

"Well. Rumor has it you're sort of a no-strings-attached guy. I'm wondering how that works."

She took a sip of her wine, and then pulled a spoon out of the drawer and took a taste of the chili. Her head waggled from side to side as though she were contemplating something, and then she pulled out another spoon, held it out. "Here. Taste. Does this need more salt?"

He didn't want to talk about salt. He wanted to know more about this no-strings-attached sex thing, and how he fit into it. But he also sensed it wasn't something he could rush her on, so Scott went to her side, taking the spoon and tasting the chili. "A bit, yeah."

He watched as she sprinkled some salt into the pot, a little surprised by how non-weird it was to be standing in the kitchen of a woman he'd just met, talking about sex and seasoning and the philosophy of the color white.

"Did Oliver tell you we had a pact?" she asked, glancing his way. "Me, Audrey, and Naomi?"

He searched his memory. "Sounds vaguely familiar. Remind me."

She placed her wooden spoon on the spoon rest and leaned against the counter. "The day of Brayden's funeral, the day we all first met, we were all . . . hurting. Not only because he'd died, but because we'd been so blind. And we—well, Naomi—had the idea to make sure we never fall for the same bullshit again. Never let ourselves be so charmed by a guy that we can't see him for what he really is."

"I can't decide if that's smart or cynical."

Claire shrugged. "Both, I think."

"Why tell me?"

She studied him over her wineglass. "Just trying to figure out where you fall on the bachelor scale. Snake or one of the good ones."

"Verdict?"

"Both, I think," she repeated with a smile.

"I'm not sure I've shown you much of the good side," he said, not at all sure why he felt the need to defend himself.

"You haven't," she confirmed, making him wince in regret. "But Oliver's a good judge of character. And he likes you. And Bob likes you, and in my experience, dogs are good judges of character, too."

"I thought you said you hadn't had much experience with dogs."

"Really? You want to argue with me on this?"

No. No he did not. They were making progress, and he was strangely pleased she didn't *completely* hate his guts.

Scott had no intention of making any kind of move on Claire Hayes. All her talk of no-strings sex aside, she was not a woman to be bedded and left, and Scott always left. But maybe they could be friends. Of sorts.

"So you're trying to figure out what, exactly?" he asked, taking another sip of wine, finding it was growing on him. "How to have sex?"

She leveled a peeved glare at him. "I know how to have sex. I was *married*."

*To an ass.*

"Sure," he granted. "But relationship sex is different from sex for sex's sake."

"It is?" Then she winced. "I can't believe I'm having this conversation in my kitchen, over chili, with my contractor."

"Don't think of me as your contractor until tomorrow morning. For now, think of me as a friend of a friend."

"All right." She took a deep breath, as though gathering her courage. "Friend of friend, will you set me up on a blind sex date?"

He mentally applauded himself for not laughing. "A blind sex date?"

"You know. A booty call. A one-night stand."

Scott shook his head. "You can't be set up by a third party for a one-night stand."

"Why not?"

"Because it gets weird for everyone. It's the same reason you and I will never sleep together. We care about Oliver and Naomi too much to put them in an awkward place, having to know that we've seen each other naked but aren't a couple."

She pursed her lips. "I would never sleep with you for many reasons, but . . . that's surprisingly wise. Okay then, *expert*. How'd you find your one-night stands? Dating app?"

"Nope. The old-fashioned way."

"Mail order?"

He laughed, enjoying her off-beat sense of humor. "Bars. Good, old-fashioned, belly up to the bar, have a drink, buy a drink for the girl, have a few more, take her home . . ."

"That actually works?" she asked skeptically.

"Does for me."

"All right then," she said, turning to face him full on. "Be my wingman."

"No."

"Just one time," she said, stepping toward him, hazel eyes pleading. "I just need to see how this all works in action."

"So you want me to help you have sex?"

He said it to irritate her and was surprised when she nodded. "Yes."

"You do realize that goes against every male instinct, right? Setting a beautiful woman up with another man?"

"Flattery looks terrible on you," she murmured as she pulled down two bowls. "And you don't have to set me up. Just show me this bar scene you're talking about, keep me away from the married men."

He studied her, looking for traces of vulnerability, but saw only a woman who knew what she wanted.

He also knew what he wanted. He hadn't a moment ago, but that's the way it went with him. He acted on instinct, figured the messy stuff out later.

"I'll do it on one condition," Scott said.

"Name it," she said.

"Let me design your kitchen my way. No peeking until it's done. And no pink."

He didn't know why this was important, but instinct told him it was vital, even if he didn't know why yet.

Her eyes narrowed as she considered him. "And you'll take me out, show me how to get a guy I won't ever have to see again after one night. Someone who, if I forget to shave my legs, I never have to come face-to-face with?"

He extended a hand. "Tomorrow night. Leg shaving optional. I'll pick you up at nine o'clock."

"*Nine?*"

"This isn't dinner and a show, Claire. It's a different scene entirely. So, what do you say? Trust me with your kitchen?"

She sighed and put her hand in his. "All right, wingman. Let's do this."

# Chapter Eight

*C*laire was just finishing putting on her mascara the next evening when she jumped in surprise at the sound of Scott's voice calling up the stairs.

"Claire? I let myself in. Down here whenever you're ready."

She shook her head in bemusement as she wiped the accidental swipe of mascara off her brow bone. It was hard to remember that a week ago she hadn't even known Scott Turner. Now he had a key to her house, creative control over her kitchen renovation, and she was about to spend Saturday night with the guy.

It should feel like the twilight zone, and instead it felt . . . She gazed distractedly down at the mascara wand for a moment in puzzlement. Instead, it felt exactly right.

Why was that?

The man was basically a stranger, and yet he didn't *feel* like a stranger. Perhaps because Scott Turner had zero artifice about him. He was blunt, a little callous, and could be downright rude.

It was refreshing as heck. After being married to a two-timing, no *three*-timing—probably more—snake, Scott's candor was refreshing and . . . *safe*, somehow.

Scott was exactly as he seemed to be. No false advertising. No ghosts. No hidden facets. She liked that. She was even starting to like *him*, when he wasn't ticking her off.

Done with her makeup, she slipped on her favorite black stilettos, the ones that managed to be comfortable and make her legs look amazing, if she did say so herself, and walked down the stairs. Following the sound of her TV, she walked into the kitchen and found Scott watching a baseball game.

"Well?" she said, just a tiny bit smugly when he didn't turn. She was oddly eager to see his face when he realized she knew her way around a contour kit and had a rather impressive push-up bra in her arsenal.

He glanced over, then did a double take. And *not* the good kind. "What is that?"

Claire felt her face fall. "What do you mean?"

"Are you going to a funeral?"

She immediately retracted all her thoughts about his candor being refreshing and gave him a withering look. "Is that *really* the thing you want to say to a widow?"

Though now that she thought about it, was this the dress she'd worn to Brayden's funeral? Still, she stood by her choice. "It's a little black dress," she argued. "It's classic and works for every occasion. Everyone knows that."

"Not this occasion. What else you got?"

"You mean, do I have a gold lamé hooker dress in my closet?"

"Do I look like the type of man who would know what gold lamé is?"

No. No, he did not. He looked exactly the same as he did

every day. There was no sign of flannel, but he wasn't exactly dressed up for a night on the town, either. He wore dark jeans, a gray T-shirt, scuffed boots, and a leather jacket. There weren't a whole lot of leather jackets spotted in this neighborhood, and she was surprised to realize she didn't hate it.

He apparently had decided the occasion hadn't merited a shave, as his usual scruff was approaching full-on beard status.

Scott gave her an amused look. "Are you done staring? Do I pass muster?"

"If you think I have a matching leather jacket upstairs, you're going to be disappointed. This is my best option. Trust me."

He sighed and turned off the TV as he stood. "Come on."

Claire curiously followed him back up the stairs. Since he knew her house as well as she did these days, he went straight to her bedroom, directly to the closet.

"I don't suppose you've figured out a way to make the closet bigger?" she asked hopefully, as he opened the doors.

"Not unless you want to get rid of the tub and shrink your bathroom," he said, crossing his arms and surveying her wardrobe. "I'm good, but even I can't pull space out of my ass. Is this everything you own?"

"I keep my formal dresses in the guest bedroom, but otherwise, this is it."

He glanced over at her, a very unflattering frown plastered on his face as he gave her a once-over. "The shoes are fine. I guess."

"The shoes are Manolo Blahniks," she protested. "They're more than *fine*."

"You got anything . . . you know . . . strappier?" He looked over the shoe rack as he said it, then pulled a high-heeled nude sandal with an ankle strap from the shelf and shoved the pair at her. "Here. These are better."

"These don't go with the dress."

"That's good, because you're not wearing the dress." He riffled through the hangers until he found two pairs of jeans. He held both out to her. "Which of these is tighter?"

She pointed to the darker pair, a cropped pair of PAIGEs she wasn't sure she'd ever worn. She didn't even know if they still fit. "Probably those, but—"

He draped the denim over her shoulder, then moved on to her shirts, pushing through them with rough impatience. "Do you have any tops that don't belong at a PTA meeting?"

"Sorry, we can't all look like we're grunge-cool, straight out of the nineties, with a dash of farmer."

He rewarded her with a grin, but then gave up on the closet and went to her dresser, pulling open the top two drawers, going still for a moment when he realized he was looking at her bras and panties. Claire crossed her arms, shoes dangling from one finger, refusing to be embarrassed that her contractor was looking at her unmentionables.

With a single finger he lifted a thong. "Please tell me you're wearing one of these right now."

"Well, if you do your job right, it'll be some other man's job to find out," she said, rather pleased with her quick retort.

Scott looked unimpressed. He turned back to the dresser, dropping the thong and closing the top two drawers, then opening the two below. He reached into the drawer where she kept her pajamas and general lounge-around-the-house clothes.

"What about this?"

She looked at the clothing in question. "That would be one of Brayden's undershirts that shrunk in the wash. I wear it to watch TV and do laundry."

It was also just about the only thing of Brayden's that hadn't been closed up in *the* room.

Scott gave the folded tank a quick shake to see it more fully, and Claire waited expectantly for him to realize what she already knew. The tank was thin and shrunken enough to be formfitting. He glanced back at her—chest region, specifically.

"What bra are you wearing?"

"I'm not answering that."

"Black or white?"

"Why are those the only two options?"

He opened her bra drawer again and gave her a telling look.

"Right," she muttered. There really *were* just two options, with the majority being shades of white. Vanilla once again.

She made a mental note to give her lingerie a strawberry lemonade overhaul. They made pink bras, right? She'd been ordering hers online from the same store for years; maybe it was time to see what else was out there.

An impatient Scott marched toward her and unceremoniously slid a finger into the neck of her sleeveless dress. His gaze locked on hers for a split second as his fingertip dragged across her skin, then he looked away, pulling the bra strap all the way out from beneath her dress so he could see it.

"Black," he said, the strap snapping back into place against her shoulder. "Perfect. Wear this." He shoved the tank top at her.

Claire looked down at the jeans, undershirt, and nude sandals, three items of clothing that she'd never have put together in her life. Every instinct wanted to protest, but then she remembered that her instincts weren't to be trusted. Her instincts were what had landed her in a sham of a marriage, followed by a pathetic year of wallowing.

She headed to the bathroom to change, muttering, "You'd better be right about this, wingman."

---

An hour later, it became irritatingly clear that Scott *had* been right. She'd gotten more looks from guys while wearing an undershirt in a dive bar than she had in her Givenchy dress at the Met Gala a few years ago.

Still, while she couldn't deny that the lingering, appreciative once-overs were an enormous ego boost, so far there'd hadn't been any action to back up the looks.

"Why are none of them coming over?" she asked, leaning toward Scott so he could hear her over the weekend soundtrack of people with a few drinks in them and an undercurrent of Journey hits coming from tinny speakers.

Scott tipped his beer back without glancing her way. "Me."

"What?"

He glanced her way. "They think you're with me."

"They . . . *Oooh*," she said, feeling stupid for not realizing that sitting as they were side-by-side after spending a solid fifteen minutes bickering about whether or not she should ask the bartender if they served champagne, they probably looked like a couple.

"I guess I didn't think that through when I asked a guy to be my wingman. That's why no women have approached you, right?" She wasn't blind. Scott had gotten every bit as many lingering looks as Claire had. Probably more.

And though she still stood by her affinity for clean-cut guys in tailor-made suits, she had to admit that, objectively, she could see the appeal. Scott was entirely in his element here, and it showed with the easy way he moved, the confidence with which he did everything from ordering his beer to pulling out the bar stool for her.

And somehow the awful fluorescent light of this somewhat dingy but undeniably popular dive bar on Ninety-Eighth and Madison seemed to suit him.

Scott nodded once in response to her question.

"Sorry." She winced. "Didn't mean to crash your game."

He smiled a little. "I'll manage. Besides, tonight's about you."

"Right." She rubbed her hands together. "Me getting some."

He laughed, a good-natured real laugh that had her smiling back. "Don't call it that. Not if you actually *want* to get some."

She sighed, her hands falling to her lap. "This is hopeless."

"Don't underestimate your wingman. Hey, Dave," he called louder to get the backward-cap-wearing bartender's attention. "My sister's glass is empty."

It took Claire a moment to realize that Scott was talking about her. A moment later to realize that he'd deliberately said it louder than necessary so that the people nearest them heard it, too.

The bartender nodded and, pulling one of those jumbo-size bottles of wine out of the ice rack under the bar, filled her glass to the brim. The wine was mediocre, but she'd take whatever liquid courage she could get.

"All right, *sis*," Scott said, lowering his voice. "Anyone here fit your hoity-toity criteria?"

"Well, it's not exactly my kind of place," she admitted. "But there is a guy a few seats to your left— No, don't look!" she said, panicked, putting her hand on his arm. "Give it a minute. But he's at your ten o'clock, blue suit, no tie. A little wrinkled, but like maybe he just got off a flight."

Scott took his time glancing over, subtler than she'd have expected.

"Business traveler," he agreed when he turned back. "Probably lives in one of the new high-rises in the area. You sure? He's kind of . . . bro." He pronounced it *brah* with an effected "cool guy" voice. "Like the guy who organized all his frat's parties and actually liked it."

"What's wrong with that? I was in a sorority."

"Shocking," Scott said. "All right, fine. Let's roll with the *brah*. He give you any looks, or is he too busy replaying his lacrosse glory days in his head?"

"We've made eye contact once," she admitted, unable to keep the giddiness out of her voice. Who knew that being on the prowl was actually kind of . . . fun.

"Whoa, eye contact? Slow down there, tiger, keep your clothes on."

"Don't make fun. I'm new at this."

"I know." He smiled, and Claire noticed for the first that his eyes crinkled when he smiled—a real smile—and it was surprisingly attractive.

*Just the light, Claire*, she reminded herself. *Fluorescent lighting just weirdly works for him.*

"All right," Scott said, swallowing the rest of his beer and pushing back his stool. "Let's hope he caught my *this is my sister* announcement."

"Wait!" She reached out and grabbed the front of his shirt, fisting it her fingers. "You can't leave me here!"

"Easy," he murmured, gently untangling her fingers from his shirt. "Try to remember that I'm your brother. Clingy shirt grabbing is not going to sell the sibling vibe."

"Right, okay." She pulled her hand back. "But you still can't leave me here!" she repeated.

"I'm just going to shoot some pool," he said, nodding in

thanks as Dave passed another beer across the bar without being asked.

"But I don't know how to play pool."

"We'll tackle that another night—guys love to teach women how to play pool; you'll have a dozen dying to bend you over the table. Just stay put."

"What am I supposed to do? I can't just sit here doing *nothing*."

"You bring your phone?" he asked.

"Of course."

"Scroll through Pinterest or whatever. The more bored you look, the better. Look at pink kitchens, that should help."

"This plan sucks. It's rude to be on your phone in a restaurant," Claire protested.

Scott leaned forward. "Look around."

She did and saw what he saw. Nearly everyone had their phone out, even the ones in groups.

"I don't particularly love the glued-to-the-screen vibe, either," he muttered. "But it'll be a good security blanket for you until you're ready for the next level."

"What's the next level?"

"Sitting *without* your phone, perfectly content to be alone in a bar."

"Is there a level beyond that?" Claire asked curiously.

Scott leaned in farther, speaking directly into her ear. "Sitting alone. No phone. And looking directly at a man as you let him know with your eyes what you want to do to him."

Claire's heart caught in her throat. She was exceptionally aware of Scott's closeness, the warmth of his breath against the side of her face. He lingered for a second too long, but when he stepped back, the moment—if it even was one—was broken.

Claire felt a surge of relief. Being attracted to her contractor was not part of the plan.

"I'll go with the cell phone plan," she said on a rush.

He nodded knowingly. "Thought you might." His eyes found hers. "You good?"

"Yeah!"

Scott lifted his eyebrows at her too-chipper tone.

"Okay, maybe a little nervous," she admitted.

"Relax." He nodded toward the pool tables. "I'll be right over there. Or give Dave a look if things get weird. We go way back; he's a good guy."

"Got it. I'm good. I can do this," she said, rubbing sweaty hands on her jeans and feeling like an inexperienced college girl, and not at all like an adult woman who'd been married.

"Yeah. You can." Scott ambled away. Claire tracked his movements, noticed she wasn't the only one, as several other women seemed to take note of the fact that Scott was suddenly fair game.

She forced her attention away from Scott and pulled out her iPhone to scroll through Pinterest. Even if he hadn't suggested it, it'd been her time-killing go-to since she'd started the renovation planning on the house. She reluctantly archived her Kitchen board, realizing she no longer needed that since she'd traded her how-to-have-casual-sex training for creative control.

Strangely, she didn't mind. It was one less thing to worry about, and she trusted Scott's judgment, even if it meant that her kitchen was one area that wouldn't get the strawberry lemonade touch. She could accessorize with pink later, when he was out of the picture. Pink stand mixer. Pink Le Creuset. Pink napkins. Pink—

"Anyone sitting here?"

Claire jumped at the voice, then did a double take when she realized the speaker was none other than *Brah*.

*Holy crap, it worked.*

"Ah, no! No. Sit." She patted the seat vacated by Scott, then winced, worried she'd seemed too eager.

She glanced Scott's way, but he was talking to a tall blond woman with a crop top that revealed a very toned, twenty-something belly. He wasn't smiling, but if the girl's obvious lean-in was any indication, she was very into the scowling, smoldering vibes Scott was putting out.

"So, which one of you's from out of town?"

"Hmm?" Claire turned back to rumpled-suit guy. He was even more attractive up close, though his eyes looked just a little unfocused, making her think he was probably a couple of drinks ahead of her.

He tilted his head back in the direction of Scott. "Your brother. I've got a sister myself. Love her. But wouldn't be spending a Saturday night with her if we lived in the same city. I figured one of you must be visiting and this is your chance to catch up."

"Oh, right." It was a pretty solid observation that most thirty-something siblings didn't go out on the town on a weekend night, and she bumped the guy up a half notch, even though his smile was a little practiced and bland. And he wasn't putting off creepy serial-killer vibes, which was a very big bonus.

"I live a few blocks south of here," she said vaguely, deliberately trying to steer the conversation away from her "brother."

"Yeah? I'm around the corner. Just moved from FiDi, still getting used to the neighborhood."

"You like it so far?" She took a sip of her wine.

He smiled, his teeth straight and perfectly even. She tried to remind herself that it was simply a measure of good orthodontic work and not a sign of lack of character.

"I like this bar," he said in response. Leaned in slightly. "Like the people in it."

She met his eyes, a startling shade of blue, and realized that he was, without a doubt, flirting. Claire felt a surge of pleasure. Not at the guy so much, he was a dime a dozen in the finance game in this city. But at the sheer victory of doing something about her own life, instead of letting life merely happen *to* her.

She shot another glance at Scott. A brunette had joined the mix, leaning slightly on her pool cue in a way that showed off her ample cleavage.

"I'm Jesse," her companion said, extending a hand with a smile.

"Claire." She smiled back.

Jesse held her hand just a beat too long, and Claire realized comfortably that Scott had been right on target with this approach—and that if she wanted a one-night stand with this guy, it was hers for the taking.

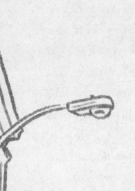

## Chapter Nine

*B*loody Mary?"

Scott glanced up from his friend's couch where they'd been watching the Yankees day game. "You make brunch cocktails now?"

Oliver Cunningham held up a glass bottle. "I buy premade Bloody Mary mix from the fancy grocery store across the street and add vodka."

"Sure, pour me one of those," Scott said, leaning back on the couch. "Don't put a garnish on it though. Keep it manly."

"Not even bacon? A brunch place up the street puts bacon in their Bloodies."

Scott glanced back toward the kitchen. "You got any bacon?"

Oliver held up a plate piled high with an obscene amount of bacon for two people.

Scott gave an affirmative nod. *Yes, on the bacon.*

"For the record," Oliver said, as he mixed the drinks, "it was between Bloody Marys and an elderflower Prosecco cocktail with an edible flower garnish that Naomi tried to tell me was 'delish.'"

"I'm suddenly not so disappointed that she bailed on us."

Earlier in the week, Naomi and Oliver had invited Scott over for brunch, but at the last minute, Naomi had flown to Chicago to fill in as a keynote speaker at some entrepreneur event. Had it been anyone else, Scott probably would have suggested they re-schedule. A brunch date between two guys was a little out of his usual social routine. The idea of brunch in general annoyed him. What was wrong with a cup of coffee for breakfast and a ham sandwich for lunch?

But he made an exception for Oliver. They went way back, and the guy felt more like a brother he could sit in silence with than someone he had to make small talk with over mimosas and baked eggs.

He glanced at his friend, who'd plopped down on the couch and was munching a piece of bacon. "We're not having baked eggs, are we?"

Oliver held up his bacon platter. "I have a pile of this, and I was going to scramble some eggs. Maybe."

Scott nodded his agreement with this plan. They ate their bacon and drank their drinks in companionable silence as the Yankee pitcher loaded the bases, and then struck out three bat-ters in a row.

At the commercial break, Scott crunched an ice cube and sat up and looked at Oliver. His friend had annoying Hollywood good looks with thick brown hair—politician hair, Scott thought—and light blue eyes that had made the girls crazy when they'd been in architecture school together. Scott had ultimately dropped out, realizing he liked *building* buildings better than he did designing them. Truth be told, he'd assumed at the time that he and Oliver would drift apart. That Oliver would go back to his prep school friends, and Scott would go back to his semi-loner status.

But by then, their fiancées at the time had become best friends. And since Bridget and Meredith had been big fans of double dates, Oliver and Scott had found themselves developing a friendship outside of architecture school, in spite of their different worlds.

Oliver was a pampered rich kid, who'd grown up just a couple of blocks from where Claire lived now. In fact, Claire and Oliver had moved in the same circles not so long ago. Scott, on the other hand, was a scholarship kid from Nowhere, New Hampshire, who'd barely known a soup spoon from a ladle. A natural friend pairing they were not.

Strangely enough, Scott and Oliver's friendship had lasted while their respective engagements had not. Maybe it had lasted *because* of their failed engagements. Scott didn't like to spend a lot of time thinking about that time in his life. He limited it to the facts: Bridget had bailed on Oliver when both of his parents had gotten sick and demanded all of his time and attention. And Scott had bailed on Meredith when she'd decided to sleep with her coworker. Many times. Over the course of an entire year before Scott found out.

He rubbed absently, irritatedly at his chest. "How's your dad?"

Oliver glanced over, his blue eyes dimming just slightly. "He's all right. There are fewer and fewer good days, but I can't say I didn't know it was coming."

Scott nodded in commiseration. Walter Cunningham had been diagnosed with early-onset Alzheimer's a couple of years ago. Oliver had done everything he could to keep his dad at home for as long as possible, but he'd put him in a care facility last year.

Having lost his own father a few years earlier, Scott didn't envy what his friend was going through, but he was glad Oliver had met Naomi. The woman was a damn firecracker and perfectly balanced out the more staid and conservative Oliver, who looked like he probably slept in his suit. More importantly, Scott liked knowing that Oliver had someone to lean on.

His thoughts shifted slightly, and he looked at his friend again. "Hey, did you and Claire ever date?"

"Claire?" Oliver frowned, then shook his head. "No, never. I mean, I always thought she was . . . you know. Attractive. But, no, not even close. Why?"

"No reason." Scott took a swallow of the spicy drink. "You just seem her type, is all."

"What's her type?"

"Pretty boy? A little delicate?"

Oliver lifted a single finger in response.

Scott finished off the last of his bacon and tried not to think about the fact that Claire had left the bar with *Brah* last night. He didn't care. Or at least, he didn't want to care.

It was what she'd wanted. Hell, he'd wanted that for her. Right up until the moment he'd seen that asshole sit next to her and make her laugh. Then the only thing Scott had wanted was to take the randy pup by the scruff of his chubby neck and put him on a stool far, far away from Claire. Better yet, outside.

At his insistence, Claire had agreed to text him at the end of the night, letting him know that she was okay. He supported women having the same freedoms as men, absolutely respected that a woman should be able to sleep with a man she'd just met as easily as a man could. But he wasn't immune to the fact that life was far from fair and that women were unfortunately vulnerable to the sadistic freaks of the world.

He was glad that *Brah* wasn't one of them. But it didn't mean he had to like *Brah*.

"How's that going?" Oliver asked.

It took Scott a second to register his friend was asking about the renovation, not Claire's *no-strings-attached-sex* mission.

"Good. The place is outdated as hell, but it's mostly surface fixes. The bones of the house are strong. She's pretty agreeable about everything, which is a nice change from my recent projects."

"Yeah, I like that about her," Oliver said. "She's no pushover, but she also picks her battles. Doesn't waste a lot of energy getting worked up about shit she doesn't know anything about, or doesn't care about."

"Except she's on a pink thing."

"A what?"

"Don't ask me. Best I can tell, I think it has something to do with reinventing herself? But she keeps talking about pink paint and pink wallpaper. She even texted me a picture of a pink chandelier for her bedroom."

Oliver winced. "Well, I guess it's her house. She doesn't have to worry about creating a dude-friendly zone."

"Yeah, but she will eventually."

"I don't think so." Oliver shook his head. "I ran into her the other day, and she seemed pretty dead set against any serious relationships in her future."

She'd said as much to Scott, but it still didn't seem right somehow. The more he got to know her, the more she struck him as the type of woman who belonged with someone else. Not that she needed a man, quite the opposite. But rather, the sense that some relationship-inclined man was missing out on the opportunity to have a partner in life. It pissed him off all the more that Brayden Hayes had abused that gift.

"The dead husband really did a number on her, huh?"

Oliver's mouth twisted in distaste at the mention of his fiancée's ex. "On all of them."

"Is it true none of them knew about the others until he died?" Scott asked, aware that he was prying—it was unlike him to get up in anyone else's business, or to even care, but he was damn curious about what had gone down with that.

He'd planned to fix up the pampered widow's home and move on. But then he'd met Claire, and he was intrigued. Intrigued about what sort of man could fool a woman who seemed as smart and savvy as they came. Same went for Naomi—she was nobody's fool.

"I don't know," Oliver said with a sigh. "Naomi gets sort of death to men whenever his name comes up, so I don't go there. Best I can tell, he was one hell of a con artist, only his aim was sex with as many women as possible, not money."

Scott looked down at his thumbnail, thinking about Meredith for the second time in an hour, which was more than he thought about her most months these days. Finding out about her and Jonathan had made him feel the fool, too, but at least he'd been prepared on some level. The two had always been flirtatious, and he'd asked her point-blank if something was going on. She'd sworn up and down that it was just work camaraderie. He'd been dumb enough to believe her, but at least he'd suspected. He couldn't imagine what it would have been like to be truly blindsided.

No wonder Claire didn't want to get remarried.

"Another drink?" Oliver asked, standing.

Scott held his empty glass over his head as Oliver walked around the back of the couch and took it on his way to the kitchen.

"More bacon, too," Scott said.

The game came back on, and Scott had just started to let himself get distracted when Oliver spoke up again. "You and Claire getting along?"

There was concern in Oliver's voice, and Scott looked over at his friend, trying to read him. "Sure. Yeah. She's great."

Oliver studied him for a moment, then went back to measuring the vodka. "'Kay."

Scott's eyes narrowed. "What's that about?"

Oliver put two slices of bacon into each glass. Then added one more as he looked back at Scott. "I meant it when I said she didn't want a relationship."

"I know."

"I think she could get hurt easily."

Scott felt something unpleasant curl in his stomach, because he knew what his friend was implying. Claire seemed somehow unfailingly strong and yet alarmingly fragile beneath it all.

"Ollie," Scott said, deliberately using his friend's hated nickname in an attempt to lighten the mood. "Are you warning me to stay away from her?"

Oliver brought both glasses into the living room, handed one to Scott. "I'm just saying, you seem intrigued, and I get it. There's something inherently compelling about Claire. But I care about her. Naomi *really* cares about her. And you know you can be . . ."

Scott lifted his eyebrows in question. "Dying to hear this."

"You're transient," Oliver said. "You're one of my closest friends, but I never know when I'm going to see you next or what city you'll be in two months from now. I don't know that *you* know."

"I don't," Scott snapped. "I like it that way."

"I get that and it's fine," Oliver said. "But as much as I hope

Claire enjoys life as a single woman, I'd hate for her to get used to you being around."

"Well, then I guess it's a good thing I'm just her *contractor* for a few more weeks," Scott said.

"Yeah," Oliver said, watching him closely. "Good thing."

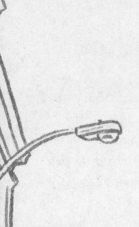

# Chapter Ten

*C*laire was adding her creamer to a fresh cup of coffee when there was an insistent pounding on her door, more of a *thunk* than an actual knock. Carrying her mug to the front of the house, she opened the door to a hyper Bob and Scott carrying an enormous box.

"Sorry." He stepped into the foyer. "Hands were full."

"What the heck is that?" She followed him down the hall toward the kitchen.

"AC unit."

"I've already got an AC unit. I've got *two* AC units."

"You want me to renovate your kitchen in the middle of August, we're putting another one in here as well," he said, setting it on the floor in the corner and then helping himself to a cup of coffee. She'd taken to making an extra-large pot since he'd been around.

"Don't worry," he snapped, even though she hadn't said a word. "Cost is on me."

She looked at the dog. "Bobsie, you're supposed to warn me when your dad wakes up on the wrong side of the bed."

"She's my dog. And her name is Bob."

"So, this is fun," she said, waving a hand in his general direction. "Are you pissed at me specifically, or just life in general?"

He gave her an irritated look, lifting his backward cap off his head and running a hand through his hair before tugging the cap back on again. "I may have had one too many Bloody Marys yesterday. I usually stick to beer."

"And pink wine," she said, hoping for a smile, or at least a good-natured eye-roll. She didn't get either. But since nobody was at their best after too much vodka, she decided to give him a break.

"You're starting the kitchen today?" she asked.

He bobbed his head. "Yeah. I wanted to hold off, since it'll be the biggest inconvenience to your routine. But it's also the biggest undertaking, so I really can't afford to wait any longer, or I won't be able to finish it before my next project."

"Oh, you've booked something else?"

"No. But I will, and it won't be local, so I won't be around to tinker with any of your last-minute whims on this house."

Okay. Enough was enough.

Claire picked her phone off the counter. "I'm ordering you a bagel sandwich and a Gatorade. Carbs and electrolytes can only help that rotten mood of yours."

"No, I'm fine," he said, pinching the bridge of his nose. "I'm sorry. It's just . . ." His hand dropped. "You know most of my jobs are abroad, right? That I have a place here, but I'm not local."

"Sure. Why?"

"Nothing. Oliver just . . . nothing."

Huh. There was something there, but she sensed pushing

would get her nowhere. Instead, she held up her phone, danced it at him. "You're sure on the bagel?"

"Sure. Just keep the coffeepot full, and I'll be good."

Claire nodded agreeably. "So, are you going to bite my head off if I ask how long I'll be without a kitchen?"

"Couple of weeks."

She couldn't help the sigh. "I'm not much of a cook, but I'm also not looking forward to eating nothing but takeout for the next month."

"Don't worry. You get used to it."

"You don't cook?"

"Toast. Cereal. Frozen dinners."

"So, that's a no." Claire went to refill her coffee, but he beat her to it, topping off her cup and his own.

"Okay, what do you need from me to get started?" she asked. "Clearing out the cabinets?"

"No, I can do that. You're on your own with cleaning out the fridge though. I don't want to be responsible for throwing away some million-dollar truffles or something."

"Yeah, because that's what I keep in there. Million-dollar truffles right next to my caviar. What about essentials? I can't be *totally* without a fridge for two weeks. I have to eat."

"You mean you need a place to store the sugar-cream goop you put in your coffee."

She batted her eyelashes. "You know me."

He rolled his eyes and pulled out his phone. "I've got a couple of guys coming over to take out the wall today. I'll have one of them pick up a mini fridge; you can keep it in another room."

"Dean?" she asked, fanning herself.

Scott gave her a dark look over the top of his phone, never pausing in his typing.

"Kidding, jeez."

Scott put his phone back in his pocket and took another swallow of coffee. "So. How'd it go?"

"How'd what go?"

He gave his first smile of the day. "Things with *Brah*."

"Oh." She laughed, remembering Saturday night's out-of-character adventure. "Not much to tell, I'm afraid."

"You left together."

"Yeah." She fiddled with her earring. "I was feeling reckless and a little . . ."

She opted not to finish the sentence since the only thing that came to mind was *hot and bothered*, and Scott wasn't one of her girlfriends. More than ever, Claire was realizing she missed the physical closeness with someone. It was intriguing to think she could have that with someone without risking her heart in the process.

Alas, Jesse had not been that guy.

"Your place or his?" Scott asked.

"His. At least that was the plan. It was around the corner, and I don't know that I'm ready to have someone in my space yet."

He nodded. "Smart."

"In theory. In reality, we didn't make it there."

Scott's eyebrows rose.

Claire laughed. "Not like *that*. We were headed back to his building, and I had second thoughts. Decided to test the waters with a kiss—wait, why am I telling you this?"

He leaned back against the counter, crossing his boots at the ankle. "As your wingman, I must know all."

She shrugged, realizing that she didn't feel as embarrassed as she'd expected. "Okay, so I stopped him and kissed him."

He was watching her carefully. "No good?"

"It was very . . . wet."

Scott winced.

"I made a polite excuse, and he let me go without much more than a vacant, drunk grin. I'm not sure he'll remember the details of the evening all that clearly."

"Idiot."

"Eh," she said with a wave of her hand, "we've all been there. And I'm glad my first attempt was with someone who was too far gone for me to embarrass myself."

Still, she'd be lying if she wasn't a little disappointed that her first kiss after being widowed was so . . . blah. She hadn't wanted it to be epic—she didn't want that kind of entanglement. But she'd at least wanted it to be hot, and Jesse's slobber all over her face definitely hadn't qualified.

Claire took another gulp of coffee, glanced at the clock, then blinked. "Crap, is that the time?"

"Yeah. Hot date?"

"Actually, sort of," she replied, putting the mug on the counter. "I mean not hot, but I have a coffee . . . thing."

Crap, now she felt awkward around Scott, especially when he was watching her with a slightly knowing grin. "You're giving *Brah* another shot even after the waterworks kiss?"

"No. Not him." She pointed at the fridge. "Can I clean that out when I get back?"

He shrugged. "Sure."

"Perfect." Claire went to the sink to rinse her mug, started to put it in the dishwasher, then paused. "You're getting rid of this, huh?"

"I'm getting rid of that piece-of-shit that insults dishwashers everywhere, yes, and that's the last question I'll answer about the kitchen renovation. Remember, you signed over complete control to me."

"Seriously?" she asked, adding soap to her mug and washing it by hand. "It's my kitchen. I at least need to be prepared. And for the record, I signed it over to you for wingman assistance, and I ended up with a slobbering dude who kissed like a dog."

He pointed at Bob. "Apologize."

"Sorry, sweetie," she said, scratching the dog behind the ears. "No offense."

"Not my fault you picked the wrong guy," Scott said. "I just told you how to reel 'em in; I didn't tell you to reel *that* one in."

"Fair enough. Better luck this time, right?"

She started for the stairs, intending to finish getting ready for the day when Scott's fingers wrapped lightly around her wrist, halting her movement.

"Who's the guy? For your coffee thing?"

Her mouth went a little dry, and it took her a full ten seconds to remember what he was talking about—where she was heading.

"I was at Citarella yesterday, waiting in line for their roast chicken, which by the way is amazing—"

He rolled his finger for her to get to the good stuff.

"Right. Anyway, there was this guy behind me in line. It was crazy crowded so we were waiting forever and got to talking. He's a widower, and we kind of hit it off. He asked me to coffee."

"You're into this guy? Coffee in the middle of the day is first-date stuff, not booty-call stuff."

"Wait, what? You mean he didn't invite me to coffee to hump in the Starbucks bathroom?!"

He laughed. "Jesus."

Claire patted his arm. "Don't worry, wingman. This guy lost

his wife fairly recently. I'm pretty sure he just wants someone to talk to, not the future Mrs. McDonald."

Claire had known the second the silver fox behind her in line had started chatting her up that he was flirting, but there'd been a sweet awkwardness to it that belied his forty-something age. She'd have bet that maybe he was doing just as Oliver had encouraged her to do. Practice.

And since she was still in need of a little practice with flirting herself, she'd agreed to meet him. Plus, who knew, maybe Carter McDonald was looking for the same thing as her—no strings. It didn't hurt that he'd been exactly her type. Clean-cut and polished. His polo shirt had been Burberry, his watch Rolex. Not that it was about labels. She wasn't *that* much of a snob. But she was allowed to have her fantasies, and she was fully okay admitting that hers was a Christian Grey–millionaire vibe, minus the whole spanking thing.

Scott shrugged and dropped her wrist. Claire's arm fell back to her side, and she was acutely aware of the coolness on her skin where his fingers had been. "But if I *do* hump him in the Starbucks bathroom," she said, "I'll be sure and tell you all about it."

"Please don't." There was a smile in his voice.

She headed toward the door, pausing in the entryway, resting her hand on the doorjamb as she turned back. "Oh, I didn't ask. Which one did you go home with?"

"What?" He was helping himself to more coffee.

"The girls at the bar on Saturday. Did you go home with the blonde or brunette? Both were super pretty."

Scott took his time putting the coffee carafe back in its place before picking up his mug once more.

His eyes flicked up to hers. "Neither. Went home alone."

"Oh. Well. I guess we both struck out then. Better luck next time."

He gave a noncommittal nod, and Claire headed upstairs. She frowned halfway up, her hand on the railing, as she tried to figure out why she felt so relieved that Scott's Saturday night had worked out as it had.

And why, suddenly, she didn't feel as excited about her up-coming "date."

---

Scott's head was under her kitchen sink when Claire got home a few hours later. Her ancient garbage disposal had been a real pain in the ass, but with a final twist of the wrench, he finally got the damn thing free, grunting in satisfaction just as he felt a slight tap at the bottom of his foot.

Placing both hands on the edge of the cupboard, he levered himself out, found Claire staring at her kitchen in bemused dismay. "How long was I gone?"

"Told you I was fast," he said, wiping his hands on a towel. "My guys do good work."

"But where'd the wall *go*?"

"It was shitty drywall. Came off in big flimsy pieces, the guys took it with 'em when they left."

"It looks so different," she said, walking gingerly around the dusty, newly opened-up floor plan.

"Well, take it all in now. It's the last view you'll get until it's done."

"How do you figure? I live here."

"Starting tomorrow, the kitchen's off-limits until I'm finished. I don't want you getting all freaked out, trying to race in here with your *raspberry ice* paint samples."

"Aha! So you've looked at my paint samples."

"Absolutely. I gave a real long look as I was tossing them in the trash. And I'm not lying. The kitchen's off-limits while I work."

"All right," she said, surprising him with her easy agreement. Then again, he didn't know why he was surprised. That seemed to be her MO. She was both unbearably complicated and bafflingly easygoing.

He thought about standing, but he wasn't quite done with his work under the sink, so instead he hauled his knees up and rested his elbows on them as he looked up at her. "So. Did we end our dry streak with a little afternoon delight?"

"None of your business." She dragged a fingertip along the counter, then wrinkled her nose when it came away covered in drywall dust.

He tossed the towel up to her, and she gingerly wiped her finger.

"Thought you were going to tell me all about it," he said, not entirely sure why he was pressing on something he didn't really want to know.

She sighed. "Okay. Fine. It was weird."

Scott looked up at her, sensing she needed to talk and finding it both strange and pleasant that he seemed to have found himself in the role of confidant for the first time in his life.

"He was *perfect*," she said, and Scott's fist clenched. He changed his mind. Nothing pleasant about being the confidant.

Claire continued. "We went to coffee and just . . . talked. There was plenty of chemistry, or at least enough. Then he asked if I wanted to go for a walk in the park, and who doesn't, right?"

Scott mimed sleeping, and Claire gently kicked his shin. "*Anyway*, we got to this secluded part of the park, no one was around, and he kissed me—"

*I definitely do not want to hear this.*

"And I was so sure it was going to be perfect. I mean, the guy looks a little like Jon Hamm. But . . ."

"Another slobberer?" he asked, sympathetic, and not in the least displeased.

"Worse," she grumbled. "He moaned."

Scott winced. "From kissing?"

"*Yes*, and it's not like we'd gotten really into it. It was like, first contact—" She made a comically disturbing groaning noise.

"This is what you get for going solo," he said, starting to go back under the sink. "I'd have told you not to take the date."

"Hindsight. How helpful." She crouched down so that they were at eye level. "How can you *tell*? How do you know when you meet a girl that she's not going to lick your face or moan?"

"Well." Scott carefully unscrewed the base of the garbage disposal. "In all honesty, a woman moaning can be kind of hot."

She pinched his calf with irritation. "You know what I mean. How do you find someone to hook up with that doesn't turn you off? Am I being too picky?"

"Maybe," he admitted. "I mean, if your goal is to get laid, you can't nitpick."

"My goal is to get laid and like it."

Scott nearly bit the inside of his cheek to keep from volunteering. He closed his eyes, and when he opened them, he found her patiently watching him. *Trusting.*

He sighed. "Give it a little time. It's been two days."

She huffed and stood, clearly not liking his response.

"Where are you going?" He called after her.

"You're useless. It's time to bring in my wing*women*."

# Chapter Eleven

*T*here's a reason I RSVPed *no* to this," Claire said, taking a sip of her champagne and trying to ignore the feeling that everyone was looking at her.

"Fate was the reason you RSVPed no," Audrey agreed happily, linking arms with her. "You RSVPed no so that you could end up being *my* plus-one."

"I thought Clarke was supposed to be your plus-one," Claire said, referring to Audrey's longtime best friend.

"Yeah, but he had his own invite to this shindig, and his flavor of the week wanted to be *his* plus-one."

Claire smiled at the idea that one of the city's most exclusive black-tie events was being described as a shindig, though it didn't surprise her in the least that Audrey and Clarke West had warranted their own respective invites. They were both Manhattan elite in the truest sense of the word, more so even than Oliver's family. The Cunninghams were old money, but in a stately Park Avenue–address sort of way.

The Tates and Wests were on a whole other level entirely.

Audrey's father was one of those people who seemed to be a majority stakeholder in every business Claire had ever heard of, and Clarke's family legacy had started with early funding of railroads and was now in honest-to-goodness space exploration.

It was no wonder Clarke and Audrey were as close as they were. Claire knew it was no hardship to have that sort of family money, but she *also* knew that it came with a massive set of pressures and stereotypes. She saw it on her friend's pretty face sometimes, the sheer exhaustion of being Audrey Tate. She suspected Clarke understood Audrey in a way that she and Naomi never could.

Claire *also* figured it was why Audrey had never let herself fall for her handsome friend—she was too afraid of losing her rock if things went south.

"Plus, I figured this was as good a time as any for you to take a step forward with *the plan*," Audrey said, lowering her voice.

Claire groaned. "I *knew* I shouldn't have told you guys about that."

After her disastrous kiss with the moaner in the park, and Scott's relative lack of helpfulness, she'd confessed everything to her girlfriends. About her embarrassment over her inability to flirt, Oliver's suggestion that she practice, and that she wanted to bend the rules of the pact just a little. That she actually maybe wanted to find a guy who didn't plan to call the next morning.

"What are we talking about?" Naomi demanded, appearing by their side, an absolute knockout in a royal blue dress, cut into a deep V in the front and the back.

"Hold on," Audrey said, circling Naomi. "It must be asked: How the heck hasn't Oliver dragged you back to his lair and had his dirty way with you? That dress is sexy."

"I know," Naomi said a little smugly. "It's killing him to have to keep his hands to himself."

She gestured with her wineglass, and all three women turned to see Oliver across the room talking to an elderly couple, and sure enough, the look on his face when he looked over at Naomi could have set her on fire.

"The suspense is delicious though," Naomi said, turning back to Claire and Audrey. "So, what are we talking about? Claire's *Under the Tuscan Sun* ambitions?"

"Oooh, yes," Audrey said with a dreamy sigh. "A hot Italian stud like in the movie would be just the thing."

"No argument here," Claire admitted. "My problem is *finding* him. I'm reminded a little more every day why we made that pact in the park. The men in this city are about ninety percent swine. They either cheat, fart, drool, moan . . ."

"Wait, where was the farter?" Naomi asked. "Did I miss a new development?"

"Hypothetical," Claire said. "But I took myself out to dinner the other night, sat at the bar, and the only guy who approached had garlic breath and nose hair."

"Everyone has nose hair."

"No, *nose hair*. Whole other level. Like it *curled*," Claire specified, making an upward curving motion along the side of her nostril.

Naomi mimed a heaving motion.

"Well, don't worry," Audrey said, patting Claire's hand. "There's this guy I want you to meet—"

"No. *No*," Claire repeated emphatically when Audrey started to protest. "This is why I didn't want to tell you guys in the first place. No setups. It's part of the rules."

"Whose rules?"

"Mine and Scott's. Or at least, those were the rules when he was my wingman. I think I'm going to fire him."

"I still don't get what this Scott guy has to do with any of this," Audrey said. "I also don't know why I haven't met him yet."

"You haven't?" Naomi asked in surprise. "We have to fix that. I'll introduce you tonight."

"Wait, tonight?" Claire interjected in surprise. "Scott's not here."

"Yes, he is," Naomi said distractedly, already scanning the crowd of sequined gowns and tuxes. "He sort of *has* to be. He's one of the top donors every year."

Claire stared at her friend, trying to figure out what was more jolting: the thought of Scott at a black-tie event at a stuffy museum or the realization that Scott was a top contributor for a charity for the homeless.

The first. Definitely the first. She had no trouble wrapping her head around the fact that he was generous—the more she'd gotten to know him these past weeks, the more she suspected a good guy was lurking beneath the crusty exterior. But, on the note of his exterior, the thought of Scott Turner wearing a tux simply did not compute.

No doubt he used his top-donor label as a chance to buck the status quo; he probably showed up in jeans and—

"There he is!" Naomi announced triumphantly, grabbing Audrey's hand. "Come on, I'll introduce you while we have a chance. Knowing that guy, he'll be in Barcelona next week, Fiji after that, and we won't see him for another year."

Claire had turned in the direction Naomi indicated but didn't see any sign of Scott. She trailed after her friends, pausing as they stopped at a guy in a tux, her gaze scanning the crowd for an out-of-place beard and too-long hair . . .

She heard Audrey chattering to someone beside her. "It's so nice to meet you! I'm dying to see what you've done to Claire's place . . ."

Claire's eyes stopped scanning the room and swung back to the man Naomi and Audrey were speaking with. Her mouth dropped open. The man in the tux *was* Scott.

Or at least a version of him. His brown eyes met hers, and the sardonic gaze was familiar, but that's where the familiarity ended.

"You shaved," she blurted out.

He gave a slight smile, revealing deep creases in his cheeks she hadn't noticed before, since they were always covered in stubble. "I've learned about these contraptions called razors—"

"You're wearing a tux," she interrupted.

Audrey gave a light laugh. "Claire. You sound angry about it."

"No," Claire said quickly, even as she registered that she *did* sound irrationally mad. "I'm surprised, is all."

"You expected me to be here in overalls?"

"I didn't expect you to be here at all," she said, no longer caring that her tone was a little testy. They spent five days a week together, and he hadn't bothered to mention that he was attending this? As a guest of honor, no less?

Granted, she hadn't mentioned that she was attending, either, but hers was a last-minute decision when Audrey had called her yesterday afternoon and begged.

Instead of explaining himself, he deliberately turned away from Claire and faced Audrey and Naomi. "You ladies look lovely."

Claire scowled and took a sip of her champagne. Sure. *Now* he has pretty manners.

She was now foolishly wishing she'd spent a little more time on her appearance. Claire used to love events like this, had loved the pampering process, selecting a new gown, getting her hair done. Brayden had often surprised her beforehand with flowers, and she'd felt like a princess. They'd been the magical types of nights where she'd wanted to pinch herself, thinking, *Is this my real life?*

But tonight's prep hadn't been like that. Audrey had insisted Claire come over to get ready, so they "could pretend it was like prom." Claire had readily agreed. She adored Audrey, and they'd had fun sipping martinis and debating Audrey's shoe options.

But Claire herself had phoned it in. She'd gone with the first gown she'd pulled out of the closet, a dark navy dress that didn't have much going for it other than it was reasonably comfortable as far as formal wear went. Same went for the shoes. Since nobody could see them beneath the gown anyway, she'd opted for silver heels that were completely forgettable compared to Audrey's sexy T-strap sandals and Naomi's new SJPs.

She regretted now not wearing the daring pink dress that she'd bought on a whim a couple of months before Brayden's death but hadn't gotten around to wearing because it hadn't seemed widow appropriate. Not that she'd had many opportunities. She'd turned down nearly every invitation in the past year, and there hadn't been many.

Even now, she couldn't escape the sense that hardly anyone noticed her, and those who did were vaguely pitying. At least one person noticed her though. A tall man appeared at her side, his hand touching lightly on her back as he kissed her cheek. "Claire, love, you look ravishing."

She rolled her eyes at Clarke West's over-the-top compliment, even though it did lift her spirits slightly. It didn't hurt that the man was the best-looking guy Claire had ever seen, and that included the entire cast of *Ocean's Eleven*.

Over six feet tall, with dark hair and friendly gold eyes that always promised an inside joke in the making, Clarke West would be downright intimidating if he wasn't so nice. His charm was so convincing, his kindness so genuine, it was easy to forget that he was the biggest player in the city.

"Where's your date?" Claire asked him.

Clarke blinked, looking confused. "My date? What— Ahhh," he said after a quick glance toward Audrey. "Um, ladies' room."

Claire narrowed her eyes. "What's her name?"

"Ruth," he said at the same time Audrey blurted out, "Arabella."

"*Ruth?*" Audrey said, turning on him outraged. "I *knew* you weren't listening when we went over the plan."

"Well, how was I supposed to remember *your* suggested name of Aquafina?" Clarke protested.

"Arabella!" Audrey looked ready to strangle him.

Claire made a scolding noise as she realized her friend had lied about needing a plus-one. "Audrey, Audrey, Audrey."

"Okay, in my defense, we have a pact," Audrey said. "You said . . ." She looked at the group and caught herself. "I was trying to help. With your *mission.*"

"Ah, yes," Scott said. "*That* mission."

"You. Shut up," Claire grumbled, earning her a surprised grin from Clarke.

"We've already got some very promising prospects," Naomi said.

"You were in on this, too?"

Naomi didn't look fazed by Claire's outrage. "It's like Audrey said. We have a pact. We take care of each other. And each other's needs."

"This is fascinating," Clarke said. "*Please* continue."

Claire covered her face with her hand. "I said I wanted your guys' help, not this."

"Well, without our help, you found yourself with guys who ended up licking your face!" Audrey said.

"Never mind," Clarke muttered. "Please stop."

Audrey whirled toward Scott with an accusing finger. "I blame you."

"I do, too, a little bit."

Claire looked at him in surprise. "You do?"

Scott rubbed the back of his neck. "I did forget how shitty we guys can be when we're horny."

"Well, whatever," Claire said. "I do not need a whole fleet of wingpeople to get laid. You're all terrible at it."

Audrey pouted. "But we haven't even introduced you to the prospects."

Claire looked at Clarke, the only one she didn't currently want to strangle. "Help."

He winked, taking pity on her, and took over changing the subject. He extended a hand to Scott. "Turner. It's good to see you again. Been a while."

"Wait, *you* know him?" Audrey asked Clarke. "How am I the last to meet Scott?"

"Best for last, definitely," Scott said, clinking his glass to Audrey's with a charming smile.

Claire stared at him in disbelief. Where had this charm been for the past two weeks when he'd been stomping around her home, complaining about "shoddy insulation"?

She turned to Clarke. "How do you know Scott?"

"We met a couple of years ago. Charity baseball game?" he asked Scott, trying to place their first meeting.

"I believe it was far worse than that. The rent-a-bachelor business downtown."

"Right." Clarke snapped his fingers in recognition. "Ian Bradley's crew set it up for the fund-raiser for foster kids. You got yourself the highest bidder, if I remember. A super-rich widow not a day under eighty-five who was obsessed with your ass."

"It was neither the first nor the last time I've been groped by someone using a walker," Scott said.

Everyone but Claire laughed. She was still too busy trying to reconcile this laughing, clean-cut, do-gooding man with her contractor. He caught her eye, and she shook her head slightly in bemusement, putting her fingers to her temple and making an exploding gesture, as all this was blowing her mind.

He smirked, then turned his attention to Oliver, who'd joined them, fresh glasses of champagne for all the women in hand, which Claire eagerly accepted.

She'd just taken a sip when the live band, who'd been playing upbeat crooner classics all night, shifted into a slow, moody version of "Ain't That a Kick in the Head."

"Ooh!" Audrey said, "I love this song!"

"Aren't you about a hundred years too young to love this song?" Clarke asked.

Audrey pointed at him. "Says the guy who knows every Bublé song by heart."

"Which is why I know that Bublé hasn't done a cover of this song yet, so don't look at me like that. You *know* I only dance to Bublé songs."

Audrey ignored his protest, handed her champagne to Claire, and dragged her friend out to the dance floor. Claire smiled as Clarke immediately spun Audrey dramatically. They really would be such a cute couple if they ever got their heads out of their asses and saw what was right in front of them.

Claire glanced over at Naomi and, slipping the stem of Audrey's champagne flute between her pinky and ring finger, extended her left hand to Naomi. "Hand your drink over and take your handsome man out there. I can hold two glasses in one hand and still have another one free for sipping."

Naomi hesitated. "You sure?"

Claire wiggled her fingers in silent command.

Naomi shrugged and handed her glass over, then smiled as Oliver whisked her onto the dance floor.

Claire smiled in contentment at seeing her two friends dancing with handsome men when she felt Scott studying her. "What?" she asked, sipping her champagne without looking at him.

"This is your role now? Frumpy wallflower who holds her friends' drinks?"

"Frumpy!" She turned toward him, a little stung.

"That's how you're thinking of yourself, isn't it? Your shoulders are down; you're all but shrinking into the wall. What happened to the woman who commanded the attention of every guy in the bar just a couple of weekends ago?"

"That was different," she snapped. "I was having a *moment*. This is real life."

"Bullshit," Scott said crossly.

She smiled a little at that, because this version of Scott was the one she knew. The one she could handle. Her smile disappeared as he deftly plucked all three glasses out of her fingers one by one and set them on a nearby table.

"Hey! What—"

He extended his hand, palm up, his eyes locking onto hers in challenge. "Dance with me."

# Chapter Twelve

*C*laire knew the dance was a mistake the moment Scott rested his left hand on the small of her back, nudging her closer as his right hand closed around hers.

"You weren't expecting to see me here," he said, easing her into the slow dance with a surprising amount of skill.

"It doesn't seem like your scene," she admitted, keeping her eyes fixed over his shoulder as she concentrated on matching her steps to his. She'd never been one of those natural dancers. It was hard for her to relax, and she was always acutely aware of her motions, certain that she probably looked as stiff as she felt.

"I choose to believe we all belong wherever we want to be in the current moment. You looked just as good sitting on a dirty bar stool at a dive bar drinking cheap wine as you do tonight in an expensive dress drinking champagne."

"Wait, that bar stool was dirty?"

He squeezed her hand in warning. "Don't think I didn't notice that you just dodged my compliment."

"I know what I look like," she said stiffly. "I lack Audrey's prettiness and Naomi's bold confidence."

He pulled back slightly so he could see her face. "What's going on with you?"

Claire glanced up briefly, then looked away again. "Sorry. I'm in a bad mood, just hate being here. I feel like everyone knows about Brayden."

"Oh, you think they noticed he's not here?"

She gave a surprised laugh. "I think they all know about his women."

"Probably."

Claire grunted. "Thanks."

"Who cares what they think. What happened to him is his problem. It doesn't have anything to do with you unless you let it have something to do with you."

She was quiet for a moment, realizing it was oddly nice to be able to talk about this with someone other than Audrey and Naomi. "Do you know he told Audrey that he and I were getting divorced? The entire time they were together, she thought we were long separated and I was completely out of the picture."

"Well, then she fell for the oldest line in the book. That's not your fault, either."

"I know. But then I start wondering who else he lied to. What other lies he told. And I go down this path of thinking everyone around me knows more about my life than I do."

Instead of replying, Scott pulled her infinitesimally closer so her chin brushed against his shoulder as they danced. She closed her eyes just for a moment, relishing the proximity to another human being. To a man, specifically.

"You know, when I was a kid, my mom disappeared," he said,

causing her eyes to pop open in surprise. "People said my dad killed her. The kids at school, mostly, but adults, too."

Claire's stomach twisted in dismay. "Scott—"

"He didn't," he interrupted. "My dad wasn't an outstanding individual by any stretch of the imagination. He was lazy, a little selfish. But he wasn't violent. Couldn't even abide hunting. My mom wasn't murdered; she left in the middle of the night. She just left. Drove away without looking back when I was eight. Sent me birthday cards every year, always a month late, but I knew at least that she was alive."

Claire tried to pull back to see his face, but he held her close, avoiding eye contact.

"The point is," he continued a little roughly, "I learned early on that we create our own narrative. It doesn't matter what other people say about us as long as we know who and what we are. And here's the other thing people don't want you to know: you don't have to be the same thing all the time. You can wear scuffed work boots one day, a bow tie the next. You can make out with an overgrown frat boy in the street one weekend and dance with a handsome contractor the next."

She smiled a little at that.

"So, what's your narrative, Claire?" His voice was husky.

"Well." She glanced at the swaying couples over his shoulder, caught one or two women whose gaze quickly darted away from hers when she made eye contact. No doubt about it, people were curious and a little puzzled that she was here. That she was dancing with someone who apparently was the guest of honor.

Claire liked that. She liked surprising them.

She told Scott that. "I have to admit, it amuses me that some of these people are wondering how we know each other. What we're talking about. Wondering if we planned this and what we are to each other. I love knowing that *they* don't know that we weren't expecting to see the other person here."

Scott's palm pressed more firmly against her back. "I knew."

Claire frowned. "What?"

He cleared his throat slightly, but his voice was still husky when he answered her question. "I knew you'd be here."

Scott slowed to a stop, and Claire realized that the song had ended. Embarrassed that she hadn't realized the dance was over, she took the slightest step back, though Scott didn't release her.

She raised her eyes to his, asking a silent question she was too scared to verbalize out loud. *Did you come* because *you knew I'd be here?*

Claire was too scared to ask it—but not too afraid to hope.

Scott's brown eyes burned into hers, and Claire wondered if she had the courage to step forward, to press her lips to his in front of a hundred people. Wondered if he'd kiss her back, wondered—

"There you are!"

The moment was shattered by an unfamiliar female voice, and Scott's hand dropped away.

Claire turned, then sucked in a breath when she came face-to-face with one of the more stunning women she'd ever seen in real life. There was little doubt in Claire's mind that the woman was a model. The wide eyes, full mouth, high cheekbones, and waifish figure were classic supermodel.

"Hello," the woman said with a friendly smile and a faint accent. "I'm Ivet Orlav."

Claire recognized the name. Definitely a model. A very famous supermodel.

"Ivet, this is Claire Hayes," Scott said. "I'm in the process of renovating her house."

"Oh, you are so lucky!" Ivet said with a beaming smile. "He does the best work. Did he tell you I first met him in Paris when he was hired to consult on some maintenance on the Louvre?"

*No, he didn't, Ivet. There's a lot he doesn't mention.*

Claire sucked in a quick breath when Ivet reached out and wrapped both skinny arms around Scott's arm and brushed her lips to the corner of his mouth. "I'm always so thrilled when Scott and I are in the same city at the same time," Ivet said, flicking a playful finger over Scott's bow tie. "He always makes the best date to these events."

Date. Here she was, stupidly wondering if he was here because of her, when all the time he'd brought a date.

*It hurt.* It hurt, and she didn't have a clue why.

"Claire," he said softly.

She held up a palm to stop his words but didn't meet his eyes. Instead, she walked off the dance floor, chin held high.

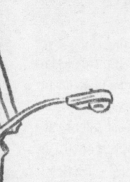

## Chapter Thirteen

There weren't many venues in Manhattan that had a proper outdoor space, but the American Museum of Natural History was one of them. And even though the late summer night was muggy, and probably wreaking havoc on her hair, Claire was grateful for the space. She needed a moment of solitude to properly chastise herself for thinking, even for a moment, that Scott Turner had been interested in her as a woman.

After all, the extent of his compliment had been, "You look good." Not beautiful. Not gorgeous. Not *you take my breath away*.

She'd never taken anyone's breath away. Even Brayden, in their early dating days, had always told her that what he liked most about her was that she was "easy to be around." She'd thought it a compliment at the time. Now she wasn't nearly so sure.

Even more galling than her mistaken assumption that Scott was interested in her romantically was that for a minute, for a silly, irrational minute, she'd wanted him to be. Being in his arms during that dance had been the most *right* thing she'd felt in a long time, and it had had nothing to do with his startling transformation from gruff contractor into tuxedo-wearing prince of the whole damn gala. It had been him. His reluctant smiles that were all the more rewarding because they were hard-earned. His subtle, wry humor. The way she suspected he felt far more deeply than he ever revealed to the world.

And while she'd been discovering that, he'd been killing time while waiting for his supermodel girlfriend to return from the ladies' room.

With a huff, she sat on a bench, not particularly caring if she got her boring dress dirty before she went back inside. *If* she went back inside. What she really wanted was to go home. She'd only come for Audrey's sake, and now that she knew the night had all been good-intentioned maneuvering by her girlfriends, she didn't feel the least bit bad about ditching.

"You all right?"

Claire's head swung around in surprise at the interruption. She'd been prepared for one of her friends to seek her out to check on her, but she was a little surprised to see *which* friend.

Clarke West slowly closed the distance between them. Looking down at her, he flicked his wrists toward himself, pointing both fingers at his tux jacket. "You want this?"

She laughed. "I know what you're trying to do. You're trying to pawn that thing off under the guise of being a gentleman, because it's eighty-something degrees."

He sighed. "Damn. See, this is why I like winter events better. We men get to be the heroes when we hand off our jackets that were damn uncomfortable in the first place, *and* don't have to sweat our asses off." Clarke gestured with his chin at the bench. "Can I sit?"

"Depends," she said, even as she scooted over to make room.

"Are you already sweating your ass off? Actually, don't answer that."

"I thought it'd be cooler out here," he grumbled, tugging off his tuxedo jacket. "I think it's actually worse."

"You can flee back to the AC. I'm fine, I promise. Just getting some fresh, if slightly swampy, air."

Instead of going back inside, Clarke sat beside her, draping his jacket over his knee and tilting his head back to look at the sky. She turned to look at him more fully, taking in the long eyelashes, thick hair, Superman-perfect jaw . . .

"You're insanely beautiful," she accused him.

"I know, right?" He gave a faint grin, but she sensed he was on autopilot, well accustomed to his good looks, to people commenting on them. And maybe even a little bored with the whole thing.

He looked down at her, and though he still smiled, his gold eyes were more serious than usual. "What's your story, Hayes? Why are we out here getting sweaty?"

She sighed and plucked at the skirt of her dress, wishing for the hundredth time that night that she'd gone not only with something prettier, but lighter.

"I don't even know where to start."

"Rumor has it, you decided to decorate your house like strawberry lemonade?"

"Heard about that, did you?" she asked with a laugh.

"I caught the gist."

"I'll have you know that I just ordered mauve chairs for my new sitting room, and I have zero regrets."

"What's Scott have to say about that?"

"Scott will be long gone before the last coat of paint is dry, so he doesn't get a say."

"Yeah. That is his MO. I think he's out of the city more often than he's in it," Clarke agreed. He studied her. "That bother you?"

"No!" The word was too emphatic, and she realized she doth protested too much. She lowered her voice to a bored tone. "He's just my contractor."

"You always sexy slow dance with your contractors?"

"Careful," she said lightly. "If we start attaching meaning to a slow dance, I'll have to ask about you and Audrey."

He barked out a surprised laugh. "Touché. Sometimes a dance is just a dance."

*Too true. Especially when the guy you're dancing with has a supermodel waiting in the wings.*

"Okay, so you're not mooning over Turner," Clarke mused. "Someone else?"

"More like the lack of someone else," she admitted. "I'm brooding. And don't tell me women can't brood. We can. We do. Or at least I do."

"Noted."

Her hands gripped the side of the bench, and she looked down at her feet. She knew Clarke, but she didn't *know* him.

She definitely wasn't at all sure they were at the point of discussing her sex life.

He nudged her arm. "I get it, you know?"

She looked up. "You do?"

Clarke nodded. "Don't forget, I knew Brayden. I saw what he did to you women, just like I know you all responded differently. Audrey . . ." He shook his head. "Somehow the whole thing made her more determined to put her head in the sand and believe that Prince Charming was coming for her. You, though, you know better."

"A fellow cynic?" she guessed.

"Let's just say my reputation as a love-'em-and-leave-'em guy isn't entirely unearned."

"Okay, so how do you do that?" she asked. "How is it you guys do that so easily, and with normal women?"

"They're not always normal," he muttered. "But I see your point. In all my years, I've never come across a face-licker."

She groaned and put her face in her hands, hunching forward. "I'm too old for this crap."

"What crap? One-night stands?"

"Finding a guy to have one with. You know it's bad when your girlfriends lure you to a black-tie gala to try and set you up for a sex date."

"You know. If it's a one-night stand you're after, you're talking to the right guy."

Claire's head snapped up. "*What?*"

He laughed, holding up his hands innocently. "I don't mean *me*. Audrey would kill me since she's declared all her friends are off-limits. Tricky, since she has a lot of friends. But I'm just saying, if you need some, ah . . . assistance, you should come to the guy who actually has one-night stands."

"I tried that with Scott," she grumbled. "It was not successful."

"Something tells me Scott was not the right man to help you hook up with somebody else," Clarke said.

"Why's that?"

"Just a hunch. But regardless, I . . . how do I put this . . . know a guy. I've got a friend. Brett. He's a good guy, Claire. I wouldn't mention him otherwise. Polite. Funny. Takes his grandma shopping once a month."

"But won't call me the next morning?"

"Better yet, he's the type of guy who's very up front about not intending to call you the next morning. He doesn't mess with people, and he's not indiscriminate. He actually likes women. As in genuinely respects them and enjoys their company. Especially the smart, pretty ones."

Claire batted her eyelashes, even as she wondered why Clarke's compliment didn't affect her the way Scott's had.

"So?" Clarke said with a grin. "I could introduce you to Brett. If you want. Or not. Aaand . . . it's official. I feel like a pimp."

"You're not," Claire reassured him, even as she intended to turn down his sweet, if slightly bizarre, offer. Hooking up with someone random was one thing. Being set up for a hookup was another. And was this really what she wanted? She missed sex, yes, but she wasn't so hard up that she couldn't wait to meet someone on her own. She wasn't so controlled by her basic instincts that she couldn't wait to meet a nice guy.

Then she remembered. She didn't want to meet a nice guy.

And she hadn't slept with someone since Brayden.

That, more than anything, gave her the courage she needed. The courage to be bold. To put her vanilla life behind her and just *live* a little.

Claire turned to Clarke. "You know what? Yeah. Sure. Why not. Introduce me."

---

A month ago, Scott wouldn't have recognized himself at this moment. Former Scott would not believe that he'd turned down a supermodel, one he knew from previous experience never wore underwear, and who'd also made it perfectly clear that she was flying out to Monaco tomorrow and wouldn't be back for several months.

In other words, he'd walked away from a woman offering one night, and one night only, of hot sex and was heading toward the home of a woman who was infinitely more complicated.

Yes, he'd told Oliver he wouldn't make a move on Claire. Yes, he'd told himself the same thing at least a dozen times. Recently, a dozen times a *day*.

And that had been *before* Scott had learned what she'd feel like in his arms. He still didn't know what compelled him to ask Claire to dance. On the rare occasions he dragged himself to one of those damn fancy parties, he made a practice of shaking a few hands, accepting thanks from whatever charity he'd written a check to, and getting out of there as soon as possible so he could swap the tux for jeans, the champagne for a beer.

He didn't dance. And he certainly didn't dance with a woman who wasn't his date. Scott ran a hand over his face, wondering why he'd agreed to accompany Ivet in the first place. He liked the beautiful woman well enough, liked even more that she didn't make any demands on his time aside from the occasional night they spent together. Saying yes had seemed harmless.

And yet, seeing Claire's face when she'd learned that he'd come with Ivet didn't *feel* harmless. And when Ivet had plastered her body against his while waiting for the elevator in her hotel, it had been Claire's body he'd been thinking about. Claire's curves, Claire's softness.

Ivet was good company, but he'd never craved being around her. Not like he did with Claire, who somehow both calmed and excited him. He didn't even know what he wanted from her, he only knew that he wanted to be near her. He couldn't escape the feeling that they had unfinished business, that tonight, for the first time, she'd been aware of him the way he was of her . . .

He turned off Lex onto Seventy-Third, a little surprised that the neighborhood he'd belittled just a few weeks ago was starting to grow on him. Hands in his pockets, feeling light in a way he couldn't remember feeling since back before he'd known his fiancée was cheating on him, Scott half jogged the last few steps to Claire's house, hoping she'd be there so they could talk—

Scott drew up short.

Claire was here all right. She was standing on her front porch, face tilted up to a blond guy who had his hands on her waist, unmistakably a prekiss pose.

Scott froze for a full ten seconds, trying to sort through the unfamiliar surge of something that ripped through him. He didn't begrudge her this. He didn't. And yet . . .

She jerked back from the blond guy, her eyes going wide as she saw him at the bottom of the steps. "Scott? What're you— Did you forget something at the house?"

Scott wasn't prone to taking shortcuts or easy outs—ever— but he took one now. "Yeah. Yeah, sorry, thought you'd still be at the gala, I was just going to grab— Never mind. It can wait until Monday. Sorry to interrupt."

"But—"

Scott didn't let her finish. He turned and headed back down the street, feeling like the world's biggest fool.

## Chapter Fourteen

*H*ow many times do I have to tell you that you can't see it until it's finished? You'll just meddle and make it worse."

Claire jumped at Scott's sharp bark and turned around, more than a little ready to bark right back.

"I wasn't going to creep on your precious kitchen, which is actually *my* kitchen," she said, gesturing to the opaque tarp that kept the under construction kitchen hidden from view. "I was just going to adjust the AC because it feels like the arctic in here."

"Don't blame the AC for that," he muttered, stomping toward the unit in the window and turning it down.

"What's *that* supposed to mean?"

He started to brush past her without replying, but she snagged his flannel sleeve, and it made her mad that she didn't dislike the fabric as much as she once had.

"What's that mean?" she repeated, tired of being ignored for the past two days. Things had been almost unbearably tense between them since Saturday night, and in true *man* fashion, he hadn't seemed to want to acknowledge it until now.

Scott sighed in annoyance. "It means that you've been putting off ice-princess vibes for days."

"Oh, *I'm* the problem? You've barely said two words to me since you stopped by on Saturday night because you *forgot* something."

"I apologized for that. For the interruption."

Claire took a breath for patience. "I don't want you to apologize; I want to know what's wrong so things can go back to normal. What the heck is wrong with you?"

"Nothing." He pulled his sleeve away.

Claire gathered her courage.

"You're being unfair," she said to his back. "And hypocritical."

Slowly he turned around, face unreadable. "Meaning?"

"Meaning that you can hook up with Ms. Supermodel whenever it suits you, but I can't bring a guy home."

"I don't give a shit who you bring home. I just stopped by—"

"To get your cooler. I know. I'm sure that *really* necessitated a one a.m. visit on a Saturday night."

"What do you want me to say, Claire? I'm sorry if I ruined your night. It wasn't my intention."

"You ruined my night far before then."

Well, crap. *That* was not supposed to have come out.

Scott frowned. "What?"

"Nothing."

This time it was she who tried to brush by without responding, but as she had with him, he grabbed her arm and held her fast. "Tell me. How did I ruin your night?"

She looked away, not wanting to have this conversation. She'd thought the way she and Scott had been circling each other, icing each other out ever since he'd seen her with Brett was bad. But this was worse.

She couldn't bring herself to answer his question. She wasn't ready to tell him that their dance on Saturday night, their conversation, and the feel of him had meant something to her. But she did have something she wanted to clear up.

Claire looked up at him. "I didn't sleep with Brett. The guy you saw."

His jaw ticked. "I didn't ask. I don't care one way or the other."

Her stomach dropped. Well, that answered the question once and for all whether the attraction on Saturday had been one-sided.

Maybe he really had come by to get his freaking cooler. She tried to pull away, but he didn't release her arm. "If you don't care, then let me go," she said firmly.

Scott's gaze dropped to his fingers on her arm, and though he eased the grip slightly, he didn't release her. "Who was he?"

"Just . . ." She swallowed, suddenly breathless. "Some guy. Clarke—"

"Clarke?"

"He thought Brett and I might hit it off."

"Looked like you did from where I was standing."

"I thought you didn't care one way or the other," she retorted.

Scott's jaw moved again. "How did I ruin your night? Before that."

"Fine," Claire said, realizing that they needed to have this out before they could move on. He was still weeks away from finishing her house, and they couldn't go on like this. "You really want to know? You made me feel *pathetic*. You danced with me, and you—it felt like maybe—I felt—"

His gaze sharpened. "What did you feel?"

"It doesn't matter! Because then your date showed up, the date you couldn't even bother to mention."

*To warn me about so I could protect myself.* Which wasn't fair. She knew it wasn't fair. Scott didn't owe her loyalty or explanation. And yet knowing that on the rational level didn't take the sting out of imagining Scott with the supermodel.

He rubbed his free hand over his face, looking tired. "Ivet and I have known each other for years. She's my go-to when I need a date, and if she's in town . . ."

"Exactly my point. It's okay for you to have someone on speed dial when you need companionship, but you shoot daggers when I try to find that for myself."

"I didn't! She was *just* a companion. I didn't sleep with her," he ground out. "I haven't slept with Ivet in months."

Claire's breath whooshed out, and she both hated and relished the relief that coursed through her. "She's very pretty," Claire said a little stiffly.

"Yes. She is."

Claire searched his face, trying to figure him out, to see if she was all alone on this precipice of confused want. "At the gala, you said you'd known I'd be there."

He nodded once.

"Why—" She licked her lips nervously, then went for it. "Did you ever think about asking me to go? Instead of Ivet?"

He flinched slightly, and it was all the confirmation Claire needed. "Got it." She jerked her arm free, but this time when he came after her, it was to move in front of her, physically blocking her path with his body, just inches separating them.

"I've told you, Claire, I don't get involved with people I consider friends. Or even friends of friends. You're not—you're not the kind of woman you mess around with and then leave."

"I never said I wanted to mess around."

"You sure?" he asked boldly, bending his knees slightly to put them at eye level. "Because I was there for that dance, too, Claire. That wasn't nothing."

"No, it wasn't!" she said angrily, shoving back at him, frustrated when he didn't budge. "But I don't want this any more than you do, Scott. I don't even *like* you. I don't like that you can't seem to figure out what you want from me. I don't like that somehow I've come to think you look just as good in this stupid farmer flannel as you did in that tux. I don't like that you go home with your model, and then get pissed when I try to kiss a guy, which I can't even seem to do by the way. They're either bad at it, or I don't feel it. Brayden got to sleep around all over the place, and yet he's been dead for a year and I can't seem to find . . ."

She broke off and Scott took a small step closer, his gaze intense. "What can't you seem to find?"

*Someone who makes me forget what he did to me. Someone who makes the hurt of Brayden's betrayal stop.*

But casual sex with a random stranger wouldn't fix that for her. She knew that now. She'd known it when Brett stood on her porch, charming and willing and likable.

She hadn't wanted him. She wanted someone who mattered. Someone who made her feel . . .

Like Scott made her feel.

The realization was surprising, unavoidable, and she didn't have the faintest clue what to do about it.

His question seemed to stretch between them in the silence. And though she didn't verbally answer, his gaze locked on her mouth as though he knew. Knew what she was thinking, knew what she wanted—

He caught her sigh with his lips, his mouth moving gently over hers in a searching, searing kiss. Scott kept his hands to himself; his lips did all the coaxing, leaving her free to step away if she wanted. She didn't want.

Scott's head lifted slowly, and she took her own time opening her eyes to meet the question in his gaze.

"Yo! Scott. Where you at, man? Where am I putting this oven?"

Claire jerked away from Scott at the unfamiliar voice coming from her front door.

Scott's eyes closed just for a moment, then he turned his head slightly to yell over his shoulder, "This way, Daryl."

His gaze came back to Claire's, the message in his eyes clear. *We're not done here.*

Except they were.

She'd kissed Scott. Her contractor. Worse than that, she'd wanted to kiss a man who was best friends with *her* best friend's boyfriend, which meant they'd likely be crossing paths at some point in the future.

She let out a sigh of relief that she'd avoided some major awkwardness for her future self. Even if her present self was still sort of . . . wanting.

Doing her best to keep it together, Claire calmly headed toward the stairs, ignoring the muttered curses as Daryl and some other guy struggled to get her new stove through the front door.

"Claire." Scott's voice was a quiet command.

She ignored it.

"Claire!" He reached out a hand, but she dodged it, all but running for the stairs, taking them two at a time. He let her go.

Claire started to head into her bedroom, but she froze in the doorway, her gaze flitting to her left, to the *room*. The ever-closed door behind which Brayden's belongings continued gathering dust. The time was rapidly approaching when she'd have to open that door and deal with it. Scott wanted to tear up the carpet, replace the drywall, add a new coat of paint. For that, she'd need to clear out the room, to do *something* with the stuff.

She walked toward the door, hand outstretched to the doorknob, only to realize . . . she couldn't do it. Her hand dropped back to her side. Apparently, she couldn't face the man from her past any more than she could the man who was rapidly becoming her present.

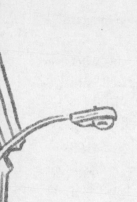

# Chapter Fifteen

*C*laire needed a friend, and she needed one *now*. She considered going over to Audrey's. Her friend's apartment was close, and Audrey usually knew the right thing to say. But then, Audrey was also more inclined to say what Claire wanted to hear.

And right now, what Claire needed was a little tough love and a gentle reality slap. For that, she turned to Naomi. Not to mention, Naomi knew Scott and would understand the magnitude of the mess Claire had gotten herself into.

Since it was the middle of the workweek, she headed to Naomi's office, which Claire always loved visiting. Her friend's company may have been started from her kitchen table years ago, but Naomi wasn't the type to be satisfied with a scrappy start-up. Eventually, Maxcessory had grown large enough to necessitate a dedicated office space, and last year the rapidly growing company had expanded yet again. The new office was modern, bright, bold, and had Naomi's touch everywhere, from the bright orange furniture to the *help yourself* table of accessories in the reception area where Maxcessory's accessory overstock was up for grabs for visitors.

Claire usually made a point of perusing the table whenever she came in, but today she sailed right past it as well as the reception desk, where a startled Laura faltered slightly in her phone conversation before waving Claire on when she recognized her.

Next line of defense was Deena, Naomi's personal assistant. Deena looked up when she saw Claire. "Hey, babe, how you doing?"

"Fantastic," Claire lied. "She available?"

"Sure, let me just—"

Claire ignored Deena and pushed open the door to Naomi's corner office, then shut it again before Deena could protest, making a mental note to apologize later.

Naomi was standing at her window, pacing as she reviewed something on her iPad. When she glanced up, her surprised expression turned to concern when she saw it was Claire. "Hey. What's wrong?"

"I kissed Scott." Might as well get right to it.

Naomi's finger was still frozen in the pointer position above the screen of her tablet, and she stayed that way for several seconds before slowly lowering her hand to lock the iPad before setting it down. "Scott Turner?"

"Yes, Naomi, what other Scott would I be talking about?" Claire said in exasperation.

"All right," Naomi said calmly, shrugging out of the dark green blazer she'd paired with jeans and a white T-shirt. She looked effortlessly chic. Claire felt a flash of relief that she'd picked today to wear her new sleeveless berry turtleneck instead of the white blouse she'd almost grabbed.

Naomi tossed the blazer onto the back of her chair.

"Was it a spontaneous one-time urge or something that's been brewing for a while?"

Claire dug her fingers into her hair. "I don't know. I thought the attraction was just something that came up out of nowhere on Saturday night at the gala, but now that I'm thinking it through, I'm wondering if it hasn't sort of been there all along. I thought he just irritated me, and then I thought he could maybe be an okay guy, and now . . . damn it, Naomi, I think I *like* him."

"Oh dear," Naomi murmured.

*Exactly.* Claire looked at her friend in desperation. "You have to help me. I don't want to like *any* guy. Especially not him."

Naomi sat in her chair and rested her elbows on the desk, face in her hands as she tapped her fingers thoughtfully against her cheeks. She stayed that way for a long while, thinking it over, before placing her hands palms down on the desk. "Okay. I'll be honest. I'm worried."

Claire hadn't been expecting that. "I thought you liked Scott. And you said it was a good idea for me to get Brayden out of my system." She didn't mention the room full of Brayden's stuff that remained untouched. Naomi had seen it, but months ago. Claire wasn't about to admit that she hadn't done a damn thing with any of it.

"It is a good idea for you to move on," Naomi said. "And I *do* like Scott. He's one of my favorite people, and I don't like many people. You get what you see with Scott, and I love that. But you're not . . ."

"His type?" Claire guessed, remembering the supermodel.

"More importantly, he's not yours," Naomi pointed out. "Remember when we watched *Gilmore Girls*, and you had the gall to suggest that Christian was better for Lorelei than Luke? Come to think of it, isn't it because Luke wore *flannel*?"

Claire winced. "You make me sound like a snob."

"No, you just know what you like, and it's not men like Scott."

*It didn't used to be.*

"Maybe it's just a proximity thing," Naomi said gently. "I mean, you guys are two attractive people spending a lot of time together in a relatively small space. Plenty of opportunity to be thinking about . . ." She made a childish sex motion with her hands.

"I don't think it'll come to . . ." She mimicked Naomi's hand gestures.

"Do you want it to?" Naomi asked.

Claire hesitated. "It's been a long time since I've felt like this."

"Horny?"

Claire laughed, trying not to feel embarrassed by the frank discussion. "I guess. But it's a little more than that, because as we've seen, not just any guy will do it for me."

Naomi sighed. "Just Scott, huh?"

"You think it's a bad idea."

Naomi tapped her fingers and considered. "Okay, here's what I know about Scott. He's hot. Crazy successful, mostly without even trying. Oliver says he's got some sort of genius thing happening. Like he sees things and does things in a way other people can't see, and won't do. He's one of the good ones, and I don't just mean that he gives a crap ton of money to charity, but that under all that gruffness, he's incredibly kind. Rescue a kitten from a highway kind."

"In other words, not the kind of guy we agreed to protect each other from when we made the pact," Claire said, feeling a surge of relief at the confirmation that Scott was one of the good ones.

Naomi lifted a single finger. "I'm not done. I also know that he got his heart broken. Badly."

Claire leaned forward. "What happened? The way he talked about Brayden, there was something in his tone that made me wonder if he'd been through what I'd been through."

Naomi made a wincing face. "Well, Scott's fiancée didn't fall off a yacht and drown after cheating on him, but she *did* cheat. It was back when Oliver and Scott were in Columbia's architecture program. From what I've gleaned from Oliver, Scott was all kinds of smitten with this woman, only to find out she'd been banging her coworker for like a solid year. All while Scott had been working two jobs in addition to school, in order to pay for the expensive wedding she insisted on."

"I hate her," Claire said automatically.

"Me, too. But the point is, you know how we all dealt with Brayden a little differently? I got mad, you got bitter and jaded—no offense—and Audrey's more determined than ever to prove that love *is* real?"

"Yeah."

"Well, of the three of us, Scott handled it a little like me, a lot like you, and Audrey's style not-at-all. That crap with his fiancée went down like a decade ago, and according to Oliver, Scott hasn't been in anything close to a serious relationship since. And yet, he hasn't been a monk, if you get what I'm saying."

"Hard to miss," Claire grumbled.

"He's not a playboy in the sense that Clarke is," Naomi continued. "With Clarke, women think it's all about the chase, believing they'll be the one to tame him. With Scott, nobody even tries to tame him. Nobody bothers."

Claire felt as though someone were pressing on her chest. "That makes me kind of sad."

Naomi gave a small sigh. "See, I was a little worried you'd say that, but I'm almost glad because now I know how to advise you." She hesitated. "That *is* why you're here, right? Or did you just want to talk it out?"

"Advice," Claire said immediately. "Please."

"I think that kiss with Scott needs to remain a one-time thing. A blip."

"But—"

"You're starting to care for him, babe. I can tell from the way you responded to everything I just told you. It wasn't an 'Oh great, booty-call perfection!' It was you hurting for him—wanting him to change, and he won't. Not even for you."

"I'm not looking for a relationship, either," Claire reminded her, even though that somehow felt less true, and she was less sure than she had been a few weeks ago.

"I know you're not *looking* for one. But I also know that your heart's enormous, and a little fragile. Do you really want to risk giving it to someone who won't want it?"

Claire sat back and thought about everything Naomi had just said, and realized her friend was right. Something about Scott had wiggled beneath her defenses, slipped beneath the jaded cynicism that had been so firmly in place since Brayden died. She desperately wanted to believe that she'd be able to separate sex and emotion, but she was no longer certain she could. Not with him.

She scrunched down farther in her chair, feeling decidedly dejected. "I don't suppose you have any junk food in here?"

"Nothing good," Naomi said, standing and grabbing her purse. "But there's a place a couple of blocks away that has onion rings served with like five types of cheese sauce."

"I can't decide if that sounds amazing or disgusting."

"Let's just say it's the second-best thing to sex. You in or out?"

"Oh, you mean since you just told me I can't have sex?" Claire said, standing. "I'm in. I'm so in."

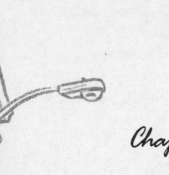

## Chapter Sixteen

*C*laire was avoiding him. Scott wasn't surprised. He'd been trying to give her the space she obviously wanted, even though he'd wanted to linger at her house last night, waiting until she returned home that evening. From wherever she'd run off to following their . . . interaction.

Today, too, he'd been patient about the fact that she pointedly walked out of any room that he entered. However, as he started packing up for the day and realized that she'd been upstairs for *hours*, he'd decided enough was enough. Scott had given her the better part of two days to think through whatever was going on between them, waiting for her to decide what would happen next. The ball was in her court, but damned if he wasn't going to try to influence which way it went.

As always, he took the time to put everything in his workspace in its proper spot before finally washing his hands and calling it a night. He was pleased with the way the kitchen was coming along. It was down to the final touches now, and he planned to put those off awhile as he started on her living room.

He had a few ideas but wanted to give himself the time and space to get it exactly right.

Scott headed to the base of the stairs, pausing and listening for any sign of her. "Claire?"

She didn't respond, but he headed up the stairs anyway. His traitor of a dog gave him an excuse to seek her out. As promised, he'd been bringing Bob to the work site each day, and he was a little amused to see that woman and dog had taken to each other so thoroughly despite their rocky start. So much for canine loyalty. He didn't mind. Scott had had years to figure out how to be alone. Claire was newer at it, and he was glad the dog gave her company.

"Claire? Bob?"

As he'd expected, his dog came bounding out of Claire's bedroom, an unfamiliar stuffed animal in her snout. "Where'd you get that?" he muttered, wrestling the toy away from Bob and stepping into the open doorway of Claire's bedroom without entering.

"Hey, Claire, I think Bob was well on her way to destroying . . ." He glanced down. "A pink baby dinosaur?"

Claire came out of the master bathroom, both hands to her earlobe as she put her earring in. "Oh, that's Tooshie," she said, nodding at the mangled ball of fluff. "I bought it for Bobsie at the pet store up the street."

*Tooshie? Bobsie?*

But Scott had bigger things to worry about than his dog turning into a delicate princess, so he didn't fight it when Bob jumped up and reclaimed the toy from Scott's hand. Instead, he focused all of his attention on Claire, who looked . . .

*Shit.*

He tried to get a grip on the warning bells going off in his head at her appearance. He'd been half prepared for her to be a little frazzled and on edge at the unfinished business between them. He knew he was. He hadn't counted on the simmer between them, couldn't deny that it made him nervous.

But Claire didn't look nervous. Or frazzled. She looked . . . hot. And very in control.

"That's a hell of a dress," he said. It was black, but nothing like the other black dress he'd seen her in. This one hit just south of mid-thigh, clung to all the right places, and was tied in bows at the shoulders in what managed to be both innocent and seductive.

"Oh. Thanks." She glanced down and gave a little smile. "Naomi and I went shopping yesterday. I was trying for something in between my usual 'funeral garb,' as you called it, and the outfit you picked out for me. Not that I didn't love the whole white shirt over the black bra look, but I think that was a onetime thing for me," she said with a smile.

"For the record, I was a big fan of that look, but this works, too," he said, his voice huskier than it had been a moment ago. What he wouldn't give to step forward and tug at the bows on her shoulders. Would it allow the dress to pool at her feet the way he wanted it to? Would she be wearing the same black bra that had tortured the hell out of him that night at the bar?

Then reality stepped in and shoved his fantasy out of the way.

He met her eyes and forced himself to ask the question, "You going out?"

Claire's expression flickered for the first time since he'd entered the room. She tried to cover it with a quick smile as she stepped back into the bathroom. "Yes, and I'm running a little late. How's my makeup?"

Blood thrumming with suspicion alongside the arousal, Scott

stepped into the bathroom doorway, watched as she applied something to her cheeks.

He didn't give a shit about her makeup. "Is it a date?"

She snapped the compact shut and met his eyes in the mirror. "Sort of. I'm still not in the market for anything serious, but I've come to accept that I'm too old-fashioned to sleep with someone I just met. Guess I want to be wined and dined before I jump in the sack, even if it is just casual."

He leaned a shoulder against the doorjamb and crossed his arms. "You want romance."

Claire looked away. "No. I mean, I guess. Maybe." She took a breath and turned toward him. "I know I don't want to get married again. I don't want a boyfriend. I don't believe in the fairy-tale ending. But apparently I need to actually like the person I'm going to sleep with."

*And I don't qualify?*

Scott managed to keep from saying it out loud, but was less successful at warding off the stab of hurt from her words.

"Anyway, I'm trying again with Brett." She began putting the makeup scattered across the counter back in the cosmetics bag.

Hurt shifted to anger. "The guy from Saturday night?"

"He seemed really nice. He called, suggested a do-over—"

Scott had heard enough.

"*Damn* it, Claire!"

She jumped at his shout, dropping the makeup bag to the counter. The contents spilled out, and she started to put everything away again, but Scott was faster. Reaching out, he snagged her elbow, pulled her gently around to face him. "What game are you playing?"

She frowned. "No game."

"Really? Because it feels a lot like you wanted me to kiss you yesterday, and now you're pretending it didn't happen so you can go on a date with some pretty boy."

She jerked her arm out of his grip and turned away. "What do you want from me, Scott? You want to take me to dinner? Make small talk? Discuss my childhood aspirations, learn my favorite color—"

"I already know your favorite color. Pink."

"No!" She spun around, her eyes a little wild. "No, it's not pink. You know why I want pink all over this house? Because *he* hated it. Brayden hated it. He was one of those typical guys who got nervous when I bought him a tie with coral stripes for Christmas, worried it was the slippery slope toward magenta. I once bought pink throw pillows and had to get rid of them because he complained nonstop about living in a bordello. My favorite color is actually green, not that anybody has ever remembered that. Not my parents, not Brayden. But anyway, that's not the point. I want what he said I couldn't have, because I need to know that this is *my* life and he's not a part of it anymore. This date," she said, waving her hand wildly, "it's not about you. It's not even about Brett. This is about Brayden, and how I need to get the hell over him even when I already hate him."

She threw her hands in the air, seemingly exasperated, but she wasn't done. "You've had time to deal with your fiancée's betrayal. You've had *years* to become hardened and practiced at cynicism. I *want* to say that I'm there, too. But I'm still new to this whole jaded-widow thing. I need some space to figure out this part of my life because I'm not going to be good at it immediately. And I don't want to stumble through it with someone who I have to sit across from at a dinner party a few months from now, or whenever you'll be back in town from your next fabulous international adventure. Can you understand that?"

Her eyes were dry but pleading all the same. Pleading with him to understand.

The hell of it was, Scott *did* understand. He didn't know how she knew about his past with Meredith—Naomi, probably—but he'd been messed up over that for years, and that's without the added trauma of his ex passing away.

Belatedly, Scott was realizing that Claire had had two hats foisted upon her at the same time: betrayed wife and widow. She had to figure out how to be mad at Brayden, how to mourn for him, and how to live without him, all at the same time.

He couldn't blame her for being a little inconsistent. A little confused. And though he wished like hell he could help, he heard loud and clear what she was telling him.

Right now, Claire needed someone completely temporary—someone she could flirt with, sleep with, and never see again if she didn't want to. Or she needed someone who would be there for the long haul and work through this with her.

Scott didn't fit into either category. He had to let her go.

"Say something," she said softly.

Scott reached out slowly and, acting on an unfamiliar tender emotion he didn't recognize, pulled her toward him gently to press a kiss to her forehead. It was a gesture he'd never made toward anyone, ever, but it was the best he could do to tell her that he was there if she needed him—in whatever way. "I'll see you tomorrow morning."

Then he turned, snapping once for his dog to follow, and thankfully Bob got the message, because the dog fell into step beside Scott as he headed down the stairs, but not toward the front door. To the in-progress kitchen.

He had some changes to make.

## Chapter Seventeen

"Shit," Scott muttered, already knowing what the exterminator was going to say.

"Termites," George Romero announced, sounding almost gleeful. George had been Scott's go-to "bug guy" for years, and Scott had learned that George seemed to take on every pest infestation as a personal challenge he loved to accept.

Scott had known the second he'd ripped up the ugly carpet and baseboards in the living room off the kitchen what he was dealing with, but the confirmation still chafed. "How bad?"

"I've seen worse, but it's not great," George said, putting his meaty hands on his hips and looking around. "And it looks like you're the first guy to do any work on this place in a while. Wouldn't be surprised if these little shits are everywhere, but I'll have to take a look."

"What are my options?" Scott asked.

"You've got two. You said the owner's been living here while you work?"

Scott nodded.

"I could use the gentle, save-the-environment stuff, and she wouldn't have to leave. That'd probably take care of it."

"Probably?"

George shrugged and pulled a pack of Nicorette gum out of his back pocket, popping a piece in his mouth. "If I've got choices, I'd rather do it right with the industrial-strength stuff, get them all the first time. But she'd have to get out of here for a day or two. Pets, too," he said, bending to give Bob a scratch behind the ears. Scott's dog had managed to leave his usual spot by Claire's side to greet her old friend George.

"I'll talk to her," Scott said, walking George to the door, even as Bob bounded upstairs to find Claire. "But for now, let's count on option two. I've got to get her out of here anyway while I redo the hardwood floors."

"Two birds," George agreed, stepping onto the porch. "Call me. I've got a cancellation for today and tomorrow. Next week's pretty booked up though."

Closing the door behind the exterminator, Scott glanced up the stairs, surprised he was a little hesitant to seek out Claire. He hadn't seen much of her since their terse, strange conversation on Thursday evening. She'd spent most of Friday upstairs in her bedroom as he'd started tearing up the downstairs living room. Scott had hated that he'd carefully listened for the sound of the front door in those early morning hours, waiting for Brett to do his walk of shame.

But when Claire had finally come downstairs for coffee on Friday morning, she'd been alone and friendly, if a little unreadable. He had no idea how her night had ended up. He hadn't gotten a good read on how her date had gone. He wasn't sure he wanted to know, and yet it continued to eat at him. So much so, that instead of spending his weekend off hanging around the city as he'd planned, he'd headed up to his mountain place for a long holiday weekend. He'd needed some fresh air and a chance to clear his head. He figured Claire could use some space as well. But as much as he'd enjoyed the spontaneous fishing trip and letting Bob chase Poconos squirrels, Scott was a little surprised how right it felt to be back in the city.

To be here, in this house, specifically. He couldn't ever remember getting so attached to a project. Bob felt it, too. His dog had lost her poor head in excitement when Scott's truck had pulled up outside Claire's house this morning after three days away.

Scott jogged up the stairs, finding her bedroom door open just a crack. He knocked lightly with a knuckle. "Claire? You decent?"

His body half hoped she wasn't. His brain reminded him that the line in the sand had been drawn, and he'd ended up on the hands-to-himself side.

"Come in."

He pushed open the door. Claire was sitting cross-legged on the bed, laptop open, though she seemed more absorbed with rubbing Bob's belly than whatever she was working on.

She smiled when she saw Scott, a little tentative, but genuine, and he felt his tension ease away, grateful they could get back to the way they'd been pre-gala.

"So, you want the bad news or the good news?" Scott asked.

"Good."

He winced. "You weren't supposed to say that. I hadn't come up with any good news yet."

"So come up with some." She made kissing noises at Bob.

He considered, came up with a positive. "I've outdone myself on this project; we're coming along at record speeds."

"Does that mean I get my kitchen back?"

"Not yet. But the rest of your downstairs will be easy going, just floors and paint and ripping out those ugly built-in bookshelves."

"Well, that's good. Okay, I'm ready for the bad news."

"You've got termites."

Like plenty of females he knew—and most males, for that matter—the mention of any kind of bugs had her face scrunching up in horror. "Eeew! Where?"

She immediately started rubbing her calves as though they were crawling on her.

"They're in the living room." They were probably everywhere, but he didn't tell her that part.

"So, what's that mean?"

"You'll need to clear out for a couple of days. My bug guy's already been here. He can work around you if he has to, but it'd mean he'd likely have to come back a couple of times for multiple treatments. Since I'm going to have to kick you out anyway when we sand the floors and get new hardwood downstairs, I suggest we get you out of the house so he can thoroughly blast the place."

"How long?"

"Two days. The floors upstairs have been protected by this ugly carpet for so long, the original wood beneath is in pretty good shape. Assuming you're okay with buffing the original instead of some fancy new bamboo shit, it's just the downstairs we'll have to overhaul."

Claire nodded and rubbed Bob's ears. "I guess I can eat takeout just as easily out of a hotel room as I can here. You know, I didn't anticipate missing my kitchen so much. I don't even love to cook, but I'm getting super sick of that little card table in the front room having to be desk, coffeepot stand, and dining table.

And I could go the rest of my life without eating another bite of fried rice."

"You realize there are delivery options other than Chinese in this city?"

"Nothing that tastes as good. Though, I think I'm turning into a dumpling. How many more sleeps until I get my stove back?" she said, with the hopeful anticipation of a little kid waiting for Christmas Eve.

"A few," he admitted, making a mental note to haul ass on the final stages of the kitchen.

"Can I see it?"

"Nope."

"But I've seen the rest of the place as you work!"

"Because those are face-lifts. The kitchen is more like open-heart surgery, and I guarantee you don't want to see what goes on on the operating table. It's not just you; it's my rule for all projects, all clients."

"Fine," she said glumly, swinging her legs over the side of the bed. "I'll look into a hotel. When's this all going down?"

"Up to you. We can do it as soon as today if you want to speed things along."

"I do," she said immediately. "I'll pack. I guess the bonus of a hotel is that at least I can get one of those little room service carts. No more card table for forty-eight hours." She glanced at him. "Can Bob come with?"

"You do realize she's *my* dog."

"I know," Claire said, kissing Bob's head. "But in a couple of weeks you'll take her away from me. These last few days are all I have."

She said it lightly in between playful cooing kisses to the top

of Bob's head, but his chest ached anyway at the thought of her
being all alone once again.

*She'll get her own dog,* he reminded himself. *Another man
around the house . . .*

*Nope.* He halted his thoughts right there.

Scott sighed. "If you find a hotel that takes big, smelly dogs,
sure. You can have her for a couple of nights."

Claire lifted Bob's paw and slapped it against her own palm
in a high five. "You hear that? Girls' night! Slumber party! You
bring the popcorn."

Scott smiled and shook his head, hoping the playful mood
wasn't the result of her ending her yearlong celibacy. Though,
even if it were, he supposed he was happy for her. It was good to
see her without any shadows, even if it was some other dude who
had helped banish them.

Actually no, screw that. He hated that it was some other guy.

Scott had already left the bedroom, but he turned back. "My
place has a kitchen."

She looked up from where she was already hauling a suitcase
out of the closet. "What?"

"My apartment on the West Side. It's got a kitchen. The
guest room bed has sheets. I think."

She set her bag on the floor. "I don't—"

"I won't be there," he was quick to interject. "I've got the
place in Brooklyn, remember? I can stay there. That'll give you
the Manhattan apartment to yourself."

"I can't kick you out of your apartment."

"I'm offering. C'mon," he added when she hesitated. "A
couple of days without takeout? My coffeepot's top-notch, too.
We can bring your nasty creamer."

"Hey. That coffee creamer is *delicious*."

He smiled, knowing he had her, even if he didn't quite know why it seemed so important that she say yes.

"I can still have Bob?" she asked.

"Yes. You can still have Bob."

*You can have me, too, if you want.*

He rejected the thought as quickly as it had popped into his head. He wasn't available, not in the way she needed. Hadn't been in a long time.

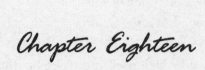

# Chapter Eighteen

*C*laire was expecting Scott's place to be a stereotypical bachelor pad. She didn't anticipate a guy who mostly lived in denim and flannel would have much beyond a lumpy sofa and huge flat-screen TV.

But she'd forgotten that she was dealing with one of the world's most in-demand contractors, not to mention a guy who wore a tux *very* nicely when he put his mind to it.

"It's *stunning*," Claire said, as Scott wheeled her suitcase through the front door. Bob was already running circles around the place, seeming adorably excited to have Claire in *her* space for once.

"Thanks," he said, not bothering to deny that his apartment was a work of art.

"No, I mean . . ." She spun around, taking in the high ceilings, the entire wall of windows. "Wow. I guess I should have known what to expect when you punched the button for the penthouse."

Scott shrugged. "I don't like having neighbors. The pent-

house means I don't have to share walls, just a floor with someone else's ceiling."

"Your apartment takes up the whole floor?" she asked, going
to the windows and taking in the unobstructed view of the
Hudson.

"Yeah. The building's one of Oliver's."

She spun around. "*Really?*"

"Yup. He designed it a couple of years ago. The management
company mostly does high-rises, but they'd bought this building
before the neighborhood was cool. It's only eighteen floors,
which, anywhere else on the island would have you staring in
your neighbor's windows, but this is far enough west that it
works."

"I'd say it more than *works*." Claire turned away from the
windows and headed to the enormous open kitchen. "If my
kitchen turns out even half as fabulous as this, I'll be one in-
debted lady."

"It will be. Smaller. But it's coming along."

"It's so bright in here," she said, turning in a full circle. "You
must think I'm nuts to be living in that little house with almost
zero natural light and nosy neighbors on all sides."

Scott shook his head. "Not really. I get the appeal of those
old brownstones. You've just got to get 'em right, and we will."

She nodded, as she ran a finger over the granite countertop,
which was completely clear of any clutter, dirty dishes, or a stack
of mail. "You're tidy."

"I am. Though I had my cleaning lady come by to make sure
about those guest sheets I promised."

"Right. Point me toward the right room. Where should I put
my bag?"

Scott gestured down the hall. "Either door. Both have beds,

though I recommend the one on the right. Better view, and the bathroom's connected."

She frowned. "Is that the master bedroom?"

"Nope, that's that way." He pointed to the left. "Though you're welcome to it—"

"No," she said quickly. She absolutely did not want to sleep in Scott's bed without him in it. Not that she wanted to sleep in his bed with him in it. She just . . .

"Your place has three bedrooms?" she blurted out, trying to steer her thoughts elsewhere.

"Four. One's an office," he said, going to the fridge and pulling out a glass carafe of water that was surprisingly fancy for a guy living alone. Or maybe not. Maybe she should learn to stop being surprised where Scott was concerned.

Per his suggestion, Claire took the guest room to the right. It was decorated simply, but *definitely* decorated. At first glance, the white bedspread and basic platform bed looked sparse, the no-nonsense nightstands like they'd been ordered online, sight unseen. But having spent a lot of time looking at home details these past few months, Claire saw beyond that to the industrial-chic lamps on the nightstand, the plush gray area rug beneath the bed, the sketches of bridges on the wall hung just so to look un-intentional and yet as though they belonged there.

She stuck her head out into the main room. "You hire a deco-rator?"

"Yeah."

"She's really good," Claire said, joining him in the kitchen.

"He. Sean went to school with Oliver and me. Unlike me, he graduated. Unlike Oliver, he didn't actually go into architecture. He and his partner, also Shawn but spelled differently, started their own interior design company last year."

"I imagine they're doing well. Your apartment could be in a catalog."

"It was."

"Really?" She perked up. "Which catalog? I subscribe to all of them."

"No idea. They asked if they could do my place for free as a showpiece, and since I'm hardly ever here, I told them to go for it."

"How much are they?" she asked, taking in every single detail, and finding fault with nothing. "Probably more than I could afford."

"Thought you were more of a do-it-yourselfer on the decorating front?"

"Well, I thought so, too, until I saw your place. My style is amateur hour compared to this. Don't worry, I promise to clean up all my drool before I leave on Thursday. The kitchen, specifically. I cannot wait to eat real food again. I'm going to work that stove over so hard . . ."

Scott had started to refill his water glass, paused a moment, then put the glass back down without drinking it. "You need anything else? I'll get out of your hair if not."

"Oh." She was a little surprised at the abrupt announcement, and maybe a little disappointed. Things had just been finally getting back to normal between them, as though the kiss had never happened, as though she hadn't come very close to breaking down on him last Thursday night before her date with Brett.

She didn't regret any of the things she'd said though. She'd needed to voice it, needed to admit that she hadn't yet healed from Brayden. And going out with Brett had been the right decision. He'd been a perfect gentleman. They'd talked about movies over dinner, debated whose pasta dish was the more decadent, even shared a dessert at the end. It had been all perfectly lovely first-date stuff, and when he'd casually asked her back to his place at the end of the night, she'd said . . .

No.

She hadn't been ready for that, but one day she would be.

Brett had smiled, thanked her for a lovely evening, and kissed her cheek before hailing her a cab. He said he'd call her again, and maybe he would, maybe he wouldn't. Claire wasn't entirely sure she cared either way, but she did know that it had been an important first step toward moving on with her life.

"Grocery store," she said, realizing she hadn't responded to his question if she needed anything. "You have one nearby you'd recommend? If not, I can check Maps on my phone."

"What are you shopping for? Basics? Meat?"

"Well, coffee creamer, for starters," she said with a smile. "I forgot to grab mine from the mini fridge at home."

Scott opened his full-size fridge. It was mostly empty, but there was the unmistakable label of her favorite coffee flavoring on the shelf.

She looked at him in surprise, and he just shrugged. "The housekeeper also keeps me stocked with a few basics, so I at least have eggs and stuff when I'm here. I asked her to pick some up."

He said it as though it were no big deal, and maybe it wasn't. The bottle only cost a few bucks. But that he'd thought of it said . . . plenty.

*He's just a nice guy*, she reminded herself. Naomi had told her as much. Thoughtful gestures did not a grand statement make, at least as far as Scott was concerned.

"Okay, so then I guess it's just dinner stuff I need," she said. "I was thinking of maybe doing a steak on the stove. With a potato. Or pasta. Just basic stuff."

"Get the steak at Esposito's. It's a longer walk, but you won't regret it." He named another store for the rest of the shopping list, then pointed at a built-in wine rack. "Help yourself to that. I'm more of a beer/whisky guy, but I've collected some decent bottles of red over the years if you're interested."

She was, although she realized for a painful moment she longed to share it with someone. For all her determination not to get her heart broken again, she was starting to realize that her decision meant a lot of nights alone in the future.

"You think of anything else, I'm a text away."

"Thanks," she said, walking with him to the front door, feeling awkward that she was the one staying behind in his house, with his dog, drinking his wine. But grateful all the same.

"Anytime." He opened the door, then shut it again when Bob made a huffing noise. "Sorry, girl." He bent down to scratch the dog's neck. Claire smiled, noting the way he pet Bob was entirely different than the way she did. She *gently* rubbed Bob's ears and softly scratched her belly. And though Bob seemed to like it well enough, it was obvious the dog relished Scott's firmer no-nonsense rubs.

"Take her with you," Claire said, noting the distraught look on Bob's face when she sensed she wouldn't be going with Scott. "I refuse to be responsible for those sad eyes."

"She'll be fine," Scott said with one last scratch of his dog's neck, standing once more. "She's overdue for a little . . . what did you call it, 'girls' night'?"

"Right, our slumber party," Claire said, smiling. "We'll probably play Truth or Dare. And you might get a prank call."

"Can't wait." He opened the door once more, looking at her as though he wanted to say something, then shook his head and stepped into the hallway, closing the door behind him.

The silence in the apartment suddenly seemed deafening. She looked down to see Bob watching her with a baleful expression. Claire told herself she did it for the dog. Knew that was a lie.

Claire jerked the door open again. "Scott!"

She caught him just as he stepped onto the elevator. He stuck out an arm to stop the closing doors, and looked at her expectantly.

She swallowed and took the leap. "Do you want to stay for dinner?"

# Chapter Nineteen

*O*kay, if you could go back to only one of the cities you've lived in, which one would it be?" Claire asked, dragging a red potato through a little pool of butter with no regrets.

"To visit? Or live?"

"Either. Both."

He took a sip of his wine. "Tokyo to visit, Paris to live."

"Paris. Really!" she said in surprise. "Is that because it's where you met Ivet?" she said coyly, waggling her eyebrows.

He smirked. "I refuse to feel guilty that one of the hottest supermodels on the planet came on to me in a hotel bar in the city of love."

He said the last word with a touch of exaggeration, and she laughed. "Okay, but really. Why Paris?"

"The Eiffel Tower."

She started to roll her eyes, then blinked when she realized he wasn't being ironic. "Seriously?"

"It's impressive. The design, the structure, the longevity, the location. I never get sick of it."

"I've only seen it once," she admitted. "I traveled through western Europe after my junior year of college, but I was more or less checking everything off my list. Venice canals, the Vatican, the Colosseum, the *Mona Lisa*, and so on. The Eiffel Tower was, of course, on the list, but I sort of just did the cursory picture and called it a day."

"Well, to be fair, not everyone gets off on it like architects and builders. But if you ever go back, do yourself a favor and get a bottle of that pink wine you like, a baguette, and some stinky cheese, and camp out at the base of the tower and just look at it."

"That sounds like a dream," she said. "With an old-fashioned picnic basket. Ooh, and a blanket. Some fresh flowers . . ."

"Flowers? You're ruining my vision." He tossed a piece of steak to the patiently waiting Bob.

"I'm enhancing the vision. You can't just sit on the wet grass, and fresh flowers add ambiance."

"Fine. Yes to the blanket, okay on the picnic basket, lose the flowers. You'll look like a dork."

"Deal." She lifted her glass, and they smiled at each other.

Claire looked away after a moment, her smile falling a little as she reminded herself that she wasn't actually going to Paris. And that if she did, it would be alone. There'd be no sipping French rosé on a picnic blanket with Scott Turner.

"Thanks for helping with dinner," she said to defuse the moment. "I've never cooked *with* someone before."

"I don't know that my putting the steaks in a pan on the stove counts as cooking, but you're welcome."

"It counts. As much as me tossing red potatoes in butter and garlic and sticking them in the oven does."

When he spoke next, he kept his gaze on Bob, but the words were clearly for her. "Was he a good husband?"

Claire froze, instinctively wanting to ask *Who?*, but of course there was only one who. Brayden.

"Why do you ask?" Still a stall, but she was also curious.

He looked up at her, his brown eyes a little irritated, though she didn't think at her. "He wouldn't let you get fucking pink pillows. Didn't like your Christmas gifts. Didn't cook with you."

"Well, hold on now," she said softly. "He didn't outright criticize anything I bought him. And as for the pillows . . . how would you take to a wife or girlfriend decorating all this with pink?" she said, waving at his blatantly masculine living space. The most color was a painting of the High Line on the wall near the front door that had a few shades of green.

"That's the difference. I don't have a wife or girlfriend. But if I did, if I had one who cared enough to pick out my clothes and make my home a *home*, I'd like to think I damn well wouldn't criticize. No, fuck that," he said with heat. "I would have bought the damn pink pillows for her myself if it made her happy."

Claire felt a little breathless at his forceful tone. The more she got to know this man, the more she realized it was a damn shame he didn't let anyone into his life. She suspected that beneath all the studied indifference there was a man who had a lot to give.

But he was determined to be alone. Just as she was. And she expected he knew, just as she did, that the more you gave, the more you lost.

"He *was* a good husband," Claire said quietly, bringing the conversation back around. "Not perfect. Maybe not a *great* husband. But he was kind. We had date nights. We were happy. I *thought* we were happy," she amended, remembering that in between date nights with her he'd had to "work late," which she'd later learned had been his nights with Naomi and Audrey, and God knew how many other women.

She laughed, a harsh, grating sound, and Scott watched her. Not prying. Just waiting.

"Did you know . . ." She pushed her plate away. "In that last year of our marriage, whenever he'd take me out to dinner, we'd always go to some little hole-in-the-wall in a different part of town. A tiny jazz club in Harlem. A pho place in Alphabet City. A Greek restaurant in Astoria. I thought it was so romantic, thinking that he was trying to change up our routine, that he'd listened when I told him I'd gotten a little weary of the whole Upper East Side scene that had dominated the first years of our marriage. I learned later that he'd been telling everyone—Audrey included— that we were separated. What I thought was romantic was just him hiding me away, playing it safe, so that we wouldn't run into anyone he knew."

She forced a smile because if she gave in to the urge to cry right now, she'd never stop. Claire was frustrated with herself. She'd thought she'd worked through this. Come to grips with the fact that her marriage was failing long before she'd realized it.

How long would it take? Another month? Another year? How long until she could do what Scott had learned to do and keep everyone at arm's length, keep things light and temporary and easy?

Claire pushed back her chair and picked up her plate. "You done?" she asked pointlessly, since there wasn't so much as a scrap left on his plate.

"Yeah. But I can clean up."

She ignored him, taking both their plates to the sink. The plates were easy—a quick rinse and into the dishwasher. The cooking pans required a bit more elbow grease, and she was grateful to have something to distract her from her thoughts— from the intimacy of the night that felt both wonderful and terrifying.

How had she forgotten, Claire wondered as she looked under his sink, found the dish soap and a sponge. How had she forgotten how nice it was to share a meal with someone?

More specifically, with someone who could cause her stomach to swoop and soar from eye contact. She hadn't had that during dinner with Brett. That had been merely pleasant, take it or leave it. This evening with Scott made her ache for more. More evenings like this, more everything. Every moment with the man seemed somehow achingly familiar and wonderfully new.

She had never felt so confused.

Claire squirted a liberal amount of soap into the pan Scott had used to cook the rib eyes, but before she could dive in with the sponge, Scott came over and nudged her aside. He plucked the sponge out of her hand and replaced it with her glass of wine.

"Drink that," he commanded as he rolled up his sleeves. No flannel tonight, but a white button-down that looked well-worn. "I'll clean."

She did as he said, mostly because he'd already gone to work scrubbing the pan, and her chances of shoving aside a man twice her size were slim. Claire leaned slightly against the counter, sipping her wine, watching the muscles of his forearm work.

"I wonder if she knows," Claire mused.

"If who knows what?" he asked without looking up.

"Meredith."

Scott froze, the water from the faucet running over his still hands.

Claire pressed forward. "I wonder if she knows what she missed out on. What she threw away."

Slowly Scott's hands began moving again, back to cleaning, but whether it was the wine or something else bringing out uncharacteristic boldness, Claire set her glass on the counter and kept talking.

"I hope that cheating wench knows that she lost out on a man who cooks, cleans, shares his dog, donates to charity, and loves the Eiffel Tower. I hope she knows that you look just as good with scruff as you do freshly shaven, that you make sure that a lonely widow not only has a place to stay, but that she has her favorite coffee creamer. I hope she knows that I've never felt like I do when you look at me, and—"

Scott tossed the sponge in the sink and turned toward her. Wet hands tunneled through her hair as his lips collided with hers.

Claire gasped a little in surprise and went still, letting herself register the moment, then she sighed, eyes fluttering closed. He caught the sigh with his lips, his mouth moving gently over hers in a searching, searing kiss. His hands in her hair were probably still soapy, but she didn't care. The kiss was perfect. It was everything she'd needed for *so long*.

A moan escaped her throat, and Scott started to pull back. Claire grabbed a handful of his shirt, pulling him closer. He groaned in gratification, one of his hands leaving her hair to wrap around her waist, pulling her all the way against him.

It wasn't just a kiss. It was *the* kiss. The one she'd been craving for months now, even if she hadn't realized it until recently. Until *him*. For the first time in a long time, she felt alive. She felt wanted. In this moment, in Scott Turner's arms, she wasn't some sad, pathetic widow. She wasn't Brayden's fool wife. She was a desirable woman who wanted to act on that desire, consequences be damned.

Her hands slid to his waist as she poured every unidentifiable emotion into the kiss, tentatively at first, then meeting his urgency, trying to convey with her kiss that she'd meant every word of what she'd been trying to tell him. Scott Turner was so much better than some woman's castaway, he was—

Special. Important. *To her.*

Overwhelmed by her sheer lack of control over what she was feeling, Claire pulled back slightly.

He searched her face, then started to slowly pull back, but she held him close, trying to sort her thoughts. "Do you remember," she asked quietly, "that first day when you came to my house? You told me that figuring things out later was half the fun?"

He frowned in confusion. "Sure?"

She fiddled with the button on his shirt, not quite able to meet his eyes for what she was about to say. "I want it to be you. I know it'll be complicated. I know we said we wouldn't complicate things, what with us having mutual friends, with you leaving as soon as the house is done, but . . . we can figure all that out later. I want it to be you," she repeated, more firmly this time.

He touched her face softly. "You want what to be me?"

She lifted her gaze to his, then she went to her toes, pressing her lips to his. He hesitated for a moment, then his arms slid down, wrapping around her as he tilted his head and deepened the kiss, and Claire gave in with a soft sigh. His arms tightened even further the second she did, until there was no distance between them, until everything drifted away, from the still-running water, to Bob scratching against the counter searching for steak scraps, to the consequences of tomorrow. There was only him, and the realization that she didn't want to be with any random guy, she didn't want meaningless sex with someone she barely knew.

She wanted this. She wanted Scott.

With a soft curse he pulled back, fumbling blindly behind him for the faucet handle, and turned the water off.

"You want me to be what, Claire? I need you to be real clear because I *really* don't want to misunderstand here," he said, his voice rough.

Claire contemplated reaching for her wine for a sip of liquid courage. But the strength she needed wouldn't come from a glass. And what she craved wouldn't come from wine. This was the moment she'd been waiting for—the man she needed to help pull her out of the shadows.

She took a deep breath. "I haven't seen the master bedroom yet. Show me?"

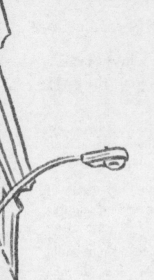

# Chapter Twenty

*C*laire woke up to the wonderfully familiar smell of coffee. Not one of those people to quickly shake off the fog of sleep, she opened one eye, then the other, her gaze immediately searching for the source of the coffee smell, even as she registered that she was in an unfamiliar place. Her sleep fog disappeared *very* quickly when she saw Scott standing beside her bed. No, *his* bed.

Claire's reality screeched to a halt.

She was in Scott Turner's bed.

And she was naked.

And she liked it.

"That's a hell of a smile," Scott said as he handed her the steaming mug. His mugs were plain white and a little boring, but as long as it was a suitable vessel for caffeine, she didn't care.

She glanced down, noted the color was exactly how she liked it. A quick sip confirmed it. "You nailed the amount of coffee creamer."

"I've been watching your morning routine for a few weeks

now. I had a good sense of the right amount of slugs of that sweet crap." She smiled, and Scott shook his head. "Again with that smile."

"They're different smiles," she clarified. "That last one was for the perfection of the coffee."

"What was the first one for?"

She looked up at him, and her expression must have said it all, because he grinned. "Ah. I see. I've had a few of those smiles myself this morning."

"A few? How long have you been awake?" she asked, belatedly noticing he was already dressed and ready for work. She felt a wave of embarrassment as she realized she'd been lounging in his bed while he'd been up making her coffee, preparing to go to work on *her* house.

"You were pretty out. I let you sleep."

"*Please* tell me snoring wasn't involved."

This time it was Scott's turn for a secret smile, but she didn't press him for an answer she didn't really want.

"I'm up," she said, already starting to move toward the side of the bed. "Is there anything I can do?"

"Stay," he said, putting a hand on her calf, sitting on the edge of the bed to block her path. "There's a reason I kicked you out of your house. Today and tomorrow will be the messiest, most intrusive of the entire renovation."

"Worse than not having a kitchen?" she fake grumbled.

"Ah, but you have *my* kitchen," he countered. "You can cook to your heart's content. I'd make something for you, but I've got to meet the guys I have coming over to help with the floors."

"Right. Of course. Um, thanks again for . . ."

*Letting me stay here? The mind-blowing orgasms, plural?*

"The coffee," she finished.

Scott winked as he gave her leg a quick squeeze, letting her know he knew exactly what she'd been too chicken to say.

"Make yourself at home." He stood. "Bob's staying with you; I don't want her underfoot today. I already took her out this morning, but she'll probably need to go out again before I get home tonight."

"Home—you're coming back here?"

He stilled for a moment, looking atypically unsure of himself. "I don't have to. I can go to my place in Brooklyn or—"

Grateful that she wasn't the only one who didn't exactly know what came next, she reached out and grabbed his hand, planting an impulsive kiss against his knuckles. "Come back here." He gave a relieved smile and bent down. Claire made a halt noise when she realized he was coming in for a kiss. She pointed at her mouth. "Not happening. Morning breath."

He made a little grunt of ascent, kissing her forehead instead, and that was almost as good. She was learning she *really* liked Scott Turner forehead kisses.

Claire took another sip of coffee, smiling as she heard him say goodbye to Bob. She laughed out loud when Bob came careening into the bedroom, leaping onto the bed the second the front door closed.

"Why do I get the impression you're not allowed up here normally?" she said as Bob nudged her hand in a blatant demand for an ear rub. Claire didn't have the heart to kick the dog off, so they compromised—she let Bob stay on the bed until her coffee cup was empty and she needed a refill.

Claire set the mug on the nightstand, immediately bending to make the bed, then straightened, wondering if that was weird.

What did one do after casual sex? She'd only had a handful of boyfriends before Brayden, and they'd always come over to *her* house, slept in *her* bed. This was new to her.

She debated for a few more seconds. Making someone else's bed seemed strangely personal and presumptuous somehow. But then she decided *not* making it was just plain sloppy and inconsiderate. It's not like she was dashing out and buying a feminine throw for the bed and squirting her perfume on the pillows.

"It was casual sex," she told Bob. "Not a big deal."

*We'll figure it out later.*

The plan to deal with the repercussions later had seemed like a great idea last night, but it felt different in the light of day. When was later anyway? And what exactly was *it*, in this case? Not a relationship. Definitely not love. Was it a one-time thing? The start of a fling?

"What are we dealing with here, Bob?" She looked at the dog. "How does this work?"

Bob wagged her tail.

"You're useless."

Claire scrambled a couple of eggs, had another cup of coffee, and showered and primped for the day. It was only after she was dressed and applying her makeup that she realized . . .

She didn't have anything to do. Not one damn thing.

It was not a pleasant feeling.

Claire knew for plenty of people having nothing on the agenda would be a blessing. There was no boss watching the clock for her arrival, no employees counting on her. No responsibilities, obligations, or demands on her time. Claire was well aware that not having to work, first because of Brayden's salary, then from the life insurance money, was a luxury.

It just wasn't a luxury she was sure she wanted.

For the first couple of years of her marriage with Brayden, Claire had worked as a brand specialist for a boutique design company. She'd enjoyed the work, but ultimately the drama of office politics had started to weigh on her. Since they hadn't needed her income, she and Brayden had agreed she'd take some time off to figure out what she wanted to do instead.

She'd initially been thinking weeks. Just a few weeks to figure out what excited her. Weeks had turned into months. But it had been easier to keep busy when Brayden had been alive, or at least to feel busy. She'd taken pride in keeping their home clean herself, rather than hiring a housekeeper like most of her friends and neighbors. She'd shopped for groceries, ensuring their fridge always had olives for her beloved, that there was always yogurt and eggs for breakfast and food for dinner on nights they didn't eat out or order in. Her social life had also been busier back then. She'd belonged to two book clubs, volunteered at charities, attended regular lunches and happy hours with friends.

Save for the charities and getting together with Audrey and Naomi when their schedules allowed for it, she had none of that now. Following Brayden's death, she'd had her renovation to keep her occupied. Planning out her vision for her house had been a way to fill the void in those endless, torturous months after the funeral. She'd spent *hours* each day planning, brainstorming, furniture shopping . . .

Now, even that was coming to a close. She'd have her dream house, and then . . .

What?

She had no job, no hobbies, few friends, minimal skills.

Claire pictured her life in a couple of months: The renovations would be done, the redecorating close to complete. Scott would be long gone. Audrey and Naomi would still be up for the spontaneous lunch or coffee, and Claire was realizing it was probably long past time to patch up some of her other friendships.

But she didn't want to go back to being a socialite. She wanted to find something that excited her, maybe even something that could bring in a little money. She'd inherited plenty from Brayden, and up until this point she hadn't felt bad in the least living off of it.

If she were going to move on—*really* move on—shouldn't she start by doing something with her life? But what? She didn't have Naomi's business sense, wasn't the least bit interested in whatever the heck Audrey did on Instagram. Her bachelor's degree was in marketing, which felt vague to her even then, and more than a decade later she didn't have the foggiest clue what to do with it. Or if she even wanted to. Not to mention, the thought of reentering the workforce at age thirty-five with what was basically an intern-level skill set was as daunting as it was unappealing.

Claire picked up her phone and started a group text to Naomi and Audrey, then remembering Naomi was in Houston for some jewelry trade show, she limited the text to just Audrey.

**Claire**

> Any chance you've got time to grab a coffee or lunch?

**Audrey**

> What happened to the Claire that suggested cupcakes? I liked that Claire.

Claire

How about doughnuts and coffee? My treat.

Audrey

Done. Any chance we can meet at the park and I can talk you into taking a few photos?

Claire agreed, having learned by now that part of being friends with Audrey meant playing amateur photographer for Audrey's Instagram feed.

An hour and a half later, she and Audrey sat side by side on a bench in Central Park, sipping pumpkin spice lattes and devouring the doughnuts Claire had picked up on her way across town.

"I half expected you to get a strawberry doughnut," Audrey said, licking the chocolate from her own doughnut off her thumb.

"They didn't have one," Claire said, biting into her maple bar flecked with little bits of bacon. "Besides, I think I'm backing off the strawberry lemonade revolution just a little."

"Oh yeah?"

Claire nodded thoughtfully. "It was good to break out of my vanilla rut, but I don't want to move from one rut to another. I'm just trying to be more . . . open, I guess." She held up her doughnut. "Case in point, maple bar with bacon instead of the usual glazed." She picked up her coffee cup. "Pumpkin spice instead of vanilla chai."

"Not me," Audrey said, polishing off the rest of her doughnut. "Chocolate is my bae for now and always. It's one rut I'm happy to be in. Does this new plan mean you're abandoning your Barbie dream house?"

"No, I still like the idea of some pink." she admitted. "But just like with food choices, I'm realizing it's more about variety. Something other than white walls, you know? I found this gorgeous marigold color for the foyer. Navy for the sitting room. Pink accents in the powder room. I'm still deciding on the upstairs, but the painting will be the final touch, so I've got another week or so to decide."

"That fast?" Audrey said in surprise.

Claire shrugged. "Apparently. Scott's true to his word that he works fast. I can't believe how quickly everything has come together. Walls have been knocked down, furniture dragged away. New sinks and toilets for all the bathrooms. He's doing the hardwood floors today, and I can't even tell you how glad I am to be done with that nasty, ancient carpet. I slept with him."

Audrey choked on her latte. "Sorry, what?"

Claire ran a finger around the lid of her cup. "I slept with Scott."

"I knew there was something going on there. Nobody dances the way you two danced at that gala without there being serious chemistry. When? How was it?"

"Last night, and . . . epic."

Audrey's eyes went wide. "*Epic*. I don't know that I've experienced epic."

Claire gave her a look. "Not with Brayden?"

Audrey wrinkled her nose. "It still skeeves me out to know we were sleeping with him at the same time."

"Same," Claire said. "But I'm taking solace in knowing that while Brayden was competent, Scott was . . ."

"Epic?" Audrey supplied. "I bet Brayden hates that from his front-row seat in hell."

"I just realized," Claire said, glancing around. "This is all very reminiscent of our first meeting."

"It is!" Audrey said. "It was a few blocks north of here, and of course there's no Naomi, but yeah. We're basically at the site of our pact."

"You know, when I agreed to Naomi's plan to help each other avoid men, I never thought that a little more than a year later, I'd be sitting in almost the same spot talking about . . . a man."

"We didn't agree to help each other avoid men," Audrey argued. "We agreed to help each other avoid the bad ones. And Scott's not one of the bad ones."

Claire smiled at the decisive note in Audrey's voice. "Says the woman who's met him once."

"I know he's one of the good ones because you think he is."

"Well, I also married Brayden."

"Still," Audrey insisted. "You wouldn't have, um, gotten back on the horse with anyone who was even remotely like Brayden."

"I love your optimism," Claire said with a smile. "Maybe you can be the one to break the news to Naomi. Help spin it so that she doesn't freak out?"

"Why would she freak out? She was all on board with you getting laid, as she phrased it."

"Yeah, but she didn't want me to with Scott," Claire said, feeling a little guilty that she'd done the exact opposite of the plan she and Naomi had devised to keep Scott at arm's length.

"Why?"

"She doesn't want me to get hurt."

"And she thinks Scott will hurt you?"

"She knows Scott is leaving."

"Right," Audrey said. "Wanderlust."

"Something like that," Claire muttered, taking a sip of her coffee.

"But at least you *know* he's leaving. You're prepared for it."

Claire nodded, even as a little knot formed in her stomach at the thought. She did know it. She'd known it all along. A couple of weeks ago, she hadn't cared. Had maybe even been a little envious of his ability to pick up and go wherever the wind blew him, to agree to whatever project appealed to him in the moment, and as he'd put it, figure out the rest later.

Now, however, the knowledge that she'd be unlikely to see him again after he was done with her renovation didn't sit quite as easily. Now, she was painfully aware that she'd come to care for the man and that she'd done what she'd promised that she'd never do after Brayden:

Set herself up to lose someone. And to hurt from that loss.

Claire groaned. "Oh damn. I think I just realized that Naomi was right. I think I'm falling for a guy who's already got one foot out the door."

"Maybe," Audrey said, putting an arm around her shoulders. "Maybe it'll hurt. But you can't shut yourself off from good opportunities just to protect yourself from risking the bad."

Claire nearly pointed out that Audrey could perhaps use some of her own advice. For all her optimism, in the year plus she'd known the other woman, she'd never seen Audrey put her heart on the line. But she always sensed that Audrey was still figuring that out for herself, and that it wasn't her place to go opening doors that weren't ready to be opened.

Audrey squeezed her shoulder. "I'm so excited you brought me here to talk about boys. And that you're having sex again. I'm kind of jealous."

Claire laughed. "Well, actually, that's not why I texted this morning. The Scott problem aside, I'm having another dilemma."

"Shoot."

"I'm bored," Claire announced without preamble. "I literally have nothing to do with my time, Audrey."

"Hmm," Audrey said, removing her arm from Claire's shoulders and sitting forward, her fingers tapping over her mouth in a thinking motion. "I admit I've been sort of wondering about that."

"Wondering what the hell I do with myself all day?"

"No, I know you've kept busy furniture shopping, antique shopping, doing whatever the heck one does in Home Depot. But I also was sort of figuring that there might be a bit of a void when the house was done."

"Void feels like an understatement."

"Well," Audrey said, "are you thinking you want to get a job? Start a club for widows of shitty husbands? Train for a marathon?"

Claire gave her a look.

"Right, not that last one. What about starting a blog? You could talk about home improvement stuff? Or, like, you could get a fancy, super-difficult cookbook and blog all about the process of trying to cook your way through it. People love that stuff. Sort of like that movie *Julie and Julia*?"

"Maybe," Claire said, not hating the blog idea, but not particularly warming to it, either.

"Any hobbies? Scrapbooking? Oh!" Audrey turned toward her, eyes wide. "I know! Calligraphy. Remember when my girlfriend was throwing that fancy baby shower, but the gal she hired to address all the envelopes broke her wrist playing tennis? You volunteered to do it, and they were amazing. My friend couldn't stop talking about it."

Claire snapped to attention. How had she not thought of that? She had taken calligraphy lessons as a teen, mostly as a way to satisfy her parents' insistence that she have some sort of extracurricular activity, and to satisfy her lifelong aversion to sports. Their neighbor at the time did professional calligraphy and offered to give her lessons. Claire had agreed, mainly because it had appealed more than the drama club and debate team, and had fallen in love with it. She'd even made some money from the hobby during college when she'd answered an ad for the alumni department looking for someone to handwrite letters to the school's biggest donors.

She was good at it, and more importantly, she loved it. Which was why it was a little embarrassing to have to admit . . .

"I don't have much of the stuff for it anymore," she told Audrey. "The paper, the nibs, I'd have to replace everything."

Audrey jumped to her feet. "Well, then I guess it's a good thing we live in a city where you can literally buy just about anything. Come on. Let's go find a craft store, or wherever they sell all that crap."

"What about your pictures?" Claire asked, standing.

Audrey waved her hand. "Please. We can do that later. This is way more important."

"Not really," Claire said, even as she let Audrey link arms with her and drag her toward the park's entrance. "Having your picture taken is your life. This is just a hobby."

"Instagram started as just a hobby for me, too, babe. Who knows? Maybe this will be the start of something amazing."

Claire felt something swell in her chest and realized it was joy. Audrey was right. This *could* be something amazing.

A small part of Claire had come back alive in Scott's arms last night.

Now it was time for the rest of Claire to start learning how to live again as well.

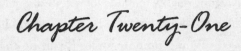

## Chapter Twenty-One

*W*ouldn't it just figure that when, for one of the first times in his life, Scott was actually excited about something other than work, work would demand more than usual of him.

Normally Scott didn't mind long hours or late nights, and he'd been prepared for a longer-than-normal workday given the demanding task of refinishing hardwoods, but he usually didn't have a woman waiting for him at home. A woman that he was very much looking forward to seeing naked again.

It was nearly eight thirty by the time Scott pulled his truck into the parking lot of his apartment building, and he was whistling.

*Whistling*. Jesus. He barely recognized himself.

Scott opened the door and was greeted immediately, first by Bob's bark, then by Claire's happy exclamation. "Hey! You're home!"

The first sound was welcome. The second even more so.

His hand tightened on the doorknob just for a minute as he

closed the door. He gave himself a firm reminder not to get used to it.

In fact, the joy he felt at coming home to Claire was the reason he hadn't let women into his house—or his life—in the first place. He didn't want to get attached to happy times that wouldn't last.

Bob, a wiggling eighty pounds of excited energy, greeted Scott at the door. He didn't have the heart to remind her that she wasn't supposed to jump up on people. Realizing that the time was rapidly approaching where he'd once more have to leave her with a pet sitter, or load the poor girl into cargo for a long flight, he hunched down and gave the dog some extra love, even as he scanned the apartment for Claire. She was sitting at his kitchen table, her back to him, head hunched over whatever she was working on.

"Just give me one second," she said, more to herself than to him.

Curious, he wandered to the table, looking over her shoulder. His kitchen table wasn't small, but nearly every inch of the wood was covered in . . . stuff.

"What am I looking at here?" he asked curiously.

Her right hand finished what it was doing with a flourish, and she turned toward him. Scott blinked a little in surprise at the expression on her face. She looked happy. No, that wasn't it. Claire was elated.

He didn't think he'd ever seen her look so full of life, though his masculine pride liked to think that had the lights been on last night, she'd have looked the same when he'd had his hands and mouth all over her. At the memory, Scott's body tightened, every fiber of his being wanting her again. It wasn't a familiar sensation. He was accustomed to sex being more of a means to an end—a release he could get just as easily from one woman as the next. But he didn't want any other woman. Just her.

The sentiment was new. And it was annoying.

"What are these, wedding invitations?" he asked to distract himself, gingerly picking up the white card on the table.

"Oh, no. Just practice cards. I'm rustier than I'd realized."

"At . . . handwriting?"

"Calligraphy," she said. "Well, that one is. This one here's more modern calligraphy, with a brush-tip marker rather than a traditional nib, see?"

She held up two cards side by side. Both looked like fancy handwriting to him. "Okay."

Claire laughed. "They're different, I promise."

She set the cards back on the table and absently massaged her right hand with her left as she perused the mess on his table. "I'd forgotten how gratifying this can be."

"Yeah?" He went to the fridge and pulled out a beer, held one up in silent invitation. Claire shook her head, but then stood and went to the wine bottle sitting on the counter from last night. She pulled a wineglass out of his cabinet—also courtesy of Sean and Shawn's influence—and poured herself a glass as he popped the top on his beer.

The easy intimacy of the moment left his mouth a little dry. He took a sip of beer before gesturing with the bottle toward the table. "Tell me about this."

"Well, for starters, I spent far too much on supplies," she said a little guiltily. "I forgot how much damage I can do in a craft store."

"So, not a new hobby?"

She smiled as she sipped the wine. She was dressed in tight black pants and an oversize black shirt, fuzzy socks pulled up to her calves. She looked comfortable. She looked at home. He took a gulp of the beer.

"You're sweet to think I could pick that up in a day," she replied. "I actually started back when I was in high school. I hated sports, but my parents insisted I cultivate some sort of hobby, and for whatever reason, I got fixated on this. They put me in classes."

"They have handwriting classes?" Scott asked skeptically.

"Calligraphy classes," Claire corrected. "Anyway, I fell away from it after college, but I dabbled a little in my mid-twenties, even contemplated doing it professionally. You'd be shocked at how much people will pay for a good calligrapher."

"When's the last time you did it?" he asked, watching the way she lit up as she talked about this.

"Last year, I guess? I did some invitations for a friend of Audrey's. Then Audrey signed Naomi and me up for some wine and lettering party in her apartment building. That's where the brush lettering comes in, it's sort of a faux-calligraphy style that newbies can pick up a little easier."

"Which do you like better?"

"Traditional calligraphy will always have my heart," she said with a grin. "It's been around for centuries. But I see the benefits of knowing both. A formal black-tie wedding, I'd stick with the classic for the invitations. But place cards at a bridal shower? I might do the brush lettering with a nice bounce script."

"A bounce what?"

"A slightly more casual, friendly lettering style." She sighed happily and took another sip of her wine. "Anyway, thanks for letting me talk it out."

"What inspired this?"

"Well, actually, it was Audrey's idea. But boredom, mostly. Or rather, the expectation of impending boredom," she said. "I realized once the house is done, I won't have much to fill my days. Plus, while I don't miss my corporate days, I do miss the satisfaction of good, old-fashioned work, you know? Of putting in the time, getting good at something, and getting paid for it."

"I can understand that."

"Yeah, well. I don't even know if I can build a business out of this," she said, gesturing with her glass at the table. "And if I do, it certainly won't bring in the gazillions that you make building skyscrapers. But it'd be a start. Actually, before I forget, I'm having second thoughts about making the two spare rooms at my place one big room. I might want to keep one as an office after all."

Scott tensed a little, the mention of her upstairs bedrooms causing a feeling of dread he'd been warding off for a few days, but she kept talking before he could put his finger on why.

"I don't suppose you know anything about websites?" she mused.

"Zero," he admitted.

"That's all right. Naomi's plugged in to the whole entrepreneur network; I'll hit her up for some guidance. Audrey, too, for that matter."

"Yeah, what is it exactly that Audrey does?" Scott asked curiously. "Clarke mentioned something about Instagram at the gala."

"She's an influencer," Claire said. "It's sort of . . . How to explain? Basically, she has a couple of hundred *thousand* people who follow her on Instagram just to see what she wears, how she styles her home, what makeup she's wearing. She gets paid to promote some of it, but mostly I just think she likes sharing a part of herself with the world."

"Sounds awful."

She laughed. "Yeah, I can't say I'd be much for it, either, but she loves it, and she's good at it. In fact, I think she has just as much business acumen as Naomi; it just comes in a different format."

"The Instagram model, the jewelry queen, and the calligraphy ninja," he said. "You ladies make a hell of a trio."

"*Will* make," Claire corrected. "I haven't earned my stripes yet. But maybe . . ."

"You will," Scott said with confidence. And not just to make her feel better. He suspected Claire was a lot more driven than anyone gave her credit for. And granted, he didn't know much about calligraphy, but he knew that what he was seeing on his dining table wasn't run-of-the-mill cursive. There was obviously some skill involved, and Claire had it.

"Oh my gosh, I can't believe I didn't even ask," she said, turning toward him. "How was work?"

Scott rolled his shoulders, her question giving him the same sense of unease as her welcome had.

*Welcome home! How was work?* Next it would be, *What do you want for dinner?*

All domestic questions signaled a lifestyle he didn't want. He liked Claire, a lot. But the last thing he wanted was for her to think this would become some sort of routine.

Needing to remind her—and himself—that he was not that kind of guy, his response was deliberately terse. "It was fine."

"Oh. Well. Good," she said, clearly taken aback at his shortness. "Are you hungry? I can clear the table."

The hurt in her voice rubbed him wrong, even as he knew his behavior was irrational. *He'd* asked about *her* day; she was just being polite and returning the favor. And yet he hated that there was a part of him that wished tonight wasn't just a one-time thing. That a part of him wished sharing a drink and talking about his day with someone he cared about could be something he could count on.

But that wasn't his life. Next month he'd be God knew where, and then what? She'd have found some other guy to talk to about her new business. Some other man would be the one to take her to bed at night.

Some other man already had.

That, he realized, was what was bothering him more than anything. The fear that this—all of it, the companionship, even the sex—wasn't about Scott. That he was a stand-in for a husband she hadn't expected to lose.

"I didn't make it to the grocery store," she was saying as she stacked up the assorted cards and papers on the table. "I'm sorry. I can run out real quick or—"

Scott's temper snapped. "Don't."

She flinched at the sound of his bottle clinking firmly as he set it on the counter, and that made him even more pissed. "Don't apologize. I don't expect some cozy little domestic scene when I get home; I don't expect dinner on the table."

"I didn't—"

"I'm not him, Claire!"

He hadn't meant to say it, hadn't even realized it had been on his mind. And he regretted it the second the words echoed in the kitchen like a bullet. Her face went pale as she straightened, before she slowly—too slowly, as though she were fighting for control.

He expected anger, dreaded seeing hurt, but he saw something far worse. *Flatness*. As though all that life that she'd been radiating just minutes before had been sucked from her. By him.

"You're not who, Scott?" she asked coldly.

He didn't answer. They both knew who he'd meant.

It was a dick move, throwing her dead husband in her face, but damned if it hadn't clawed at him to think that he'd stepped into the man's shadow, even for a moment. First with the couple routine, a glimpse into a lifestyle he didn't want, then with her apology, which had rolled off her tongue far easier than he would have liked.

Claire might like to think her marriage had been fine—even happy—aside from Brayden's infidelity, but Scott was putting together a different picture of a man who'd taken advantage of her kindness and strength. He'd bet anything Brayden had used Claire to lever himself up, not caring that he'd pushed her down in the process.

Even the dog sensed the tension in the room, and Bob slunk away as though she'd been scolded, even though it was Scott who deserved the reprimand.

"I'm sorry," he said roughly.

She didn't respond. Didn't move. She just stared at him with cool hazel eyes.

"I just . . ." Scott scratched his cheek, feeling atypically uncomfortable. He didn't do this; he didn't get flustered. And yet now that Brayden's presence was in the room, Scott realized there was something he needed to say. Realized why the thought of her upstairs bedrooms made him tense up every time.

"I'm nearly done with the downstairs," he said. "I mean, there's still all the finishing. But the old floors, the old shelves, all the ugly is gone. I'll be starting on the upstairs soon. You're still good to move back in tomorrow night, but assuming you still want that overhaul of the master bed and bath, you'll have to sleep in whichever room we're not working on, and I'll need a temporary place to put your master bedroom furniture . . ."

"Get to the point."

Scott took a deep breath and laid it all on the table. "You've got an entire room full of his stuff."

He thought she'd been frozen before, but now she seemed to go entirely brittle.

"That is none of your business." Her voice was like ice.

"Well now, it sort of is," he said, trying to keep his voice easy. "I don't have enough room to work."

"Work around it," she said, taking her wineglass to the sink, where she dumped the entire thing.

"I can't, Claire. Where am I supposed to put your bed when I pull up the carpet in your bedroom? The other room's too small."

"Figure it out. Isn't that why they pay you the big bucks?"

He didn't reply to her snide tone, waiting until she finished washing the glass and looked back at him. "Even if I could work around it, don't you think it's . . . time?"

She let out a harsh laugh. "Time to what? Move on? To put him behind me? You tell me, Scott. How's moving on going for you?"

"How the hell are you possibly turning this around on me?" he asked. "I'm not the one—"

"Whose best friend is a dog? You can't even commit to a *house*, Scott—you have two. And that's when you're in your home state, which is never, because you can't stay in the same place for two months, much less sleep with the same woman twice in a row, am I right? Is that what this is about? Last night when I said we'd figure it out later, did you think I meant we'd figure out how to blow it up? Because you're doing a damn good job."

"This isn't about me."

"Like hell it isn't. It's about both of us. I'm not going to pretend I'm not dealing with a ghost, but I'm not the only one. I don't know if it was your fiancée cheating, your mom leaving—"

Scott's blood turned to ice, then turned hot just as quick. "Overstepping, Claire."

"Right." She put up her hands. "My life, my demons are an open book, but yours are off-limits, right?"

"I don't have demons."

"Sure you don't." Claire's voice was tired as she dried her hands and headed in the direction of the guest room.

"Where are you going?"

His only answer was the door slam. He winced, even as he felt a little relief that she was pissed rather than wooden.

Scott snatched his beer off the counter, took two swallows as he tried to sort his thoughts, and tried to figure out how to fix this without having to lay himself bare. He didn't even have anything to lay bare, for God's sake. She was wrong. She thought he was some broken soul with mommy issues? That he was pining over a faithless woman from a decade ago.

Screw that. His life was exactly as he wanted. He didn't have a whole room full of a dead person's crap . . .

His thoughts scattered as Claire opened the guest room door again, his relief fleeing when he saw her wheeling her suitcase.

She marched to the front door, head held high, and he frowned. "Where are you going?"

"I don't know. Audrey's. Naomi's. A hotel. Even bunking with the termite carcasses at my house would be better than staying here with you."

His fingers clenched around the beer bottle, but he remained silent. What could he possibly say? *Stay for another night, but please be gone by tomorrow? Sleep with me once more, but just the one time because more than that is a complication I don't want?*

"Not begging me to stay?" she said sweetly, her gaze derisive as her eyes flicked over him like he was pathetic. "Now, there's a surprise."

"Bob," she called to the dog as she opened the door. "Enjoy your last few nights with Scott. I'm sure it's only a matter of time before he bails on you again."

The door slammed shut behind her.

# Chapter Twenty-Two

*W*elp, this is a real mess," Naomi said, kicking at an over-stuffed cardboard box just inside Claire's guest room.

"I know," she said a little dejectedly. "Somehow I walk by this room every single day, but in my head I didn't think it was this bad."

Naomi wrinkled her nose as she peered into the far corner of the room. "Are those skis? I didn't know Brayden skied."

"He loved it," Audrey said, coming up between them with a tray of carefully balanced cocktails. She flinched and glanced at Claire. "Sorry. I guess she was talking to you."

"No, by all means," Claire murmured. "I think you two knew him as well as I did. Better, probably."

"Not me," Naomi said, lifting two glasses off the tray and handing one to Claire. "He and I mostly just boned."

"Naomi!" Audrey sounded appalled.

"No, it's all right," Claire said. "Keep all this stuff coming. I think it'll make the whole process easier. I can't tell you how grateful I am not to have to go through this alone."

"Anytime," Naomi said. "Though can I ask what prompted it?"

Claire's stomach dropped as she remembered yesterday's epic showdown with Scott. She'd said plenty she regretted, suspected that he had, too, but he'd been right about one thing. It was long past time she got rid of Brayden's stuff. The moral support from her girlfriends helped. As did the cocktail at . . . she checked her watch . . . 3:30 p.m.

"Scott's starting on the upstairs in a few days. All this needs to be gone before then."

Naomi gave her a sharp look at the mention of Scott's name, but Claire avoided her friend's prying eyes. She still hadn't told Naomi that she'd slept with him, and she wasn't about to now knowing how right her friend had been. Naomi had been worried Scott would hurt Claire. She'd been right.

"Where is Scott?" Audrey asked Claire carefully.

"Took a day off. Had something to take care of."

It was a twist on the truth. Claire was the one who had something to take care of—this. She'd texted him earlier in the morning saying she needed a day's break from the renovation chaos.

They hadn't had any more contact following his terse *OK* response.

"Hey," Audrey said. "Someone grab my drink so I can ditch the tray."

"Where'd you even *get* the tray?" Naomi asked, picking up the third cocktail glass so Audrey could put the tray on Claire's hallway table.

"I found it in the kitchen."

"You went in," Claire said, whirling around. "How does it look?"

"Still messy, but oh my gosh, I can tell it's going to be fabulous. You haven't seen it?"

"Scott's being rigid and weird about it. It was the biggest overhaul, and he doesn't want me to see it before it's done. Apparently clients freak out."

"And you *listened*?" Naomi was incredulous. "I would have been creeping under that big sheet thing so quickly . . ."

"Don't," Audrey instructed. "I think Scott's right about this. You're better off seeing it when it's done. It's sort of war zone–ish right now."

"I won't hate it though, will I?" Claire took a sip of her drink.

"Nope. The guy is good. You were smart to hire him."

"Hey, where's my credit?" Naomi said. "I suggested him."

Audrey gave her a look. "You or your lover?"

"Well, okay. It was Oliver's idea initially. But I pushed for it. Although, had I known she was going to be kissing the guy . . ."

Audrey opened her mouth, then shut it, giving Claire a curious look, clearly wondering why Claire hadn't yet told Naomi things had gone much further than a kiss.

Claire sighed, realizing it wasn't fair to leave Naomi in the dark, or to ask Audrey to keep it a secret. "I slept with Scott."

"*What?*" Naomi scowled dramatically at Claire. "What's the point of having a pact to protect each other if we don't listen to each other! I thought we agreed it was a bad idea!"

"Naomi," Audrey scolded.

"What! I'm right on this. We agreed to be each other's lookout, to pinpoint the guys who have bad news written all over them. And Scott, as far as relationships go, is one of those guys. Claire agreed!"

"I did agree. And turns out we were right," Claire said. "It was an *awful* idea. And by the way, Naomi, I've spent the past twenty-four hours berating myself, so your lecture would be superfluous."

"What happened?" Audrey asked gently, as Naomi's expression transitioned from scolding to concern.

Claire looked down at the olives in her cocktail and swallowed. "I'm not ready to talk about it. I don't know that I can deal with that *and* this," she said, nodding toward the mess of her guest bedroom.

"Okay, we'll handle one guy problem at a time," Naomi said. "Brayden first."

Audrey squeezed Claire's arm, but then followed Naomi's lead and changed the subject. "Okay, so I actually think this will be sort of easy. When my grandma passed a couple of years ago, we hired this service that came and cleaned out her place. All we have to do . . ." She reached behind her and pulled a stack of stickers out of her back pocket. ". . . is put blue stickers on the things to be donated, orange on the stuff that goes to the dump. I've already called the guy, and he'll be here tomorrow to haul it all away to the appropriate place."

"How much will that cost?" Claire asked skeptically, knowing that hauling away a room full of crap in crowded Manhattan was no small feat.

"My treat. I'd pay a zillion dollars to get Brayden out of your life completely," Audrey said. "All you have to do is decide what of the bastard's stuff goes to Goodwill and what is trash."

Claire took a deep breath and a fortifying sip of her cocktail before setting it on a shelf near the door. "Okay. I can do that. You guys take some stickers, too. Use your best judgment."

"All right, but how do we know what stuff you want to keep?" Naomi asked cautiously.

It was an innocent question, but it rocked Claire to the core, as she realized that right there was the reason she'd been putting this task off for so long. This room, this stuff, was the last of

Brayden. All that she had. Letting go of his stuff meant letting go of him, once and for all.

And she hadn't been ready, she'd realized. She'd been mad. She'd been determined. But anger and determination alone were not a reason to move on.

She'd needed a *reason*.

She'd found that reason but was pretty sure that reason wasn't ready to move on with her. Or just was not interested.

Claire looked around, suddenly so *sick* of men. "All of it goes," she said firmly.

"All of it?"

"Everything in this room," Claire said, knowing there was one thing she'd keep that was hidden safely in her underwear drawer. "Do you think they'll take the ugly bed?"

"There's a bed in here?"

Claire pointed to a mound in the center of the room. "Under the clothes. The mattress is awful, older than I am. I want to get rid of it and put the master bed in here so I can get a *new* bed in my room."

"A bed you didn't share with him," Naomi said astutely.

"Bingo."

"They'll take it away," Audrey said, gingerly wading into the room. "And can I just point out that Brayden apparently had more clothes than me? And that is really saying something."

"His stuff took up about eighty percent of the closet," Claire agreed, annoyed that even the mention of male clothes made her think of Scott.

She'd snooped in his closet, finding the expected small assortment of T-shirts and flannel, but also a handful of suits, dress shirts, and slacks. Not to mention the tux. And that was just in one of his houses. It made her realize there were facets of Scott she hadn't met. Probably never would.

The three of them got to work, chatting as they went, thankfully *not* about men.

"What do you guys think, donate or dump?" Claire held up Brayden's briefcase.

"Donate," they both said.

"It's Hermès," Naomi said. "*Someone* needs to get in on that action. I'd take it to Oliver if it weren't the creepiest thing in the world to give my dead lover's briefcase to the man I'm living with."

Claire flipped it around to look at it more closely. She'd thought she knew her way around luxury goods, but it looked like a boring black men's briefcase to her. "How the heck can you name the designer in four seconds?" she asked, setting the bag down and placing a blue sticker on its side.

"Practice. You don't become an accessory billionaire without knowing your designers," Naomi said, standing and stretching as she perused the room. "Is it just me or is this very unsatisfying?"

"Very," Claire enthused, glad she wasn't the only one. "I mean, don't get me wrong, I'm glad it's getting done, but I was thinking it was going to be a little more therapeutic. You know, like a big moment."

"Yeah, the stickers are convenient, but they do lack a certain panache, especially for some of the more personal items," Audrey agreed. "I don't have anything like this at my place, but I confess I've got a tie and shirt of Brayden's that I've just been holding on to. I always mean to put them in the trash, but it feels so insignificant. I keep envisioning burning them."

"Yes!" Naomi agreed, pointing her cocktail at Audrey. "A *burn* pile. Now that is a gesture and a fitting *fuck you, buddy.*"

"You mean a fitting goodbye," Audrey amended.

"Nope, I do not mean that." Naomi took a sip of her cocktail. "I want his stuff to burn the way he is burning." She pointed dramatically at the floor.

Claire pressed her lips together to keep from chuckling and looked around the room. "This is one of the very few times I've regretted we all live in Manhattan. It's not exactly firepit friendly."

"No," Audrey said slowly. "It's not." She gave a small, slow smile. "I think I have the beginnings of an epic idea."

"Ooh. Does it involve fire?" Naomi asked hopefully.

"Actually, it does," Audrey said, pulling out her iPhone. "I just need to make one quick phone call . . ."

# Chapter Twenty-Three

*I* know you ate my cheese, Clarke. So put your dimples away," Audrey said accusingly as the group filed into the enormous Southampton kitchen.

"What exactly do you think happened, Dree?" Clarke asked, setting a box of wine and other booze bottles on the counter. "That in the five-minute drive between the store and here, I unwrapped a wedge of Saint-André and took a big bite, without anyone noticing I was eating stinky cheese straight from the plastic wrap?"

"Well then, where is it?" Audrey grumbled, rummaging through the grocery bags. "I've unpacked everything."

"I think we might have *bought* everything," Oliver said, taking in the spread on the kitchen table. "Aren't we just here until Monday?"

"Yep. Which means we have two and a half days to drink wine, eat carbs, and set stuff on fire," Naomi said.

"But not eat a very delicious cheese," Audrey said, "thanks to Clarke."

"Thank you so much, Clarke, for the use of your beach house," Clarke said in an impressive imitation of Audrey. "Me and my friends are so grateful, Clarke, that you're letting us set up an enormous bonfire on your beach so we can burn a dead man's stuff."

"Hey," Naomi said, fishing a celery stick out of a veggie tray. "It's not just burning stuff. It's therapy."

"*And*," Claire said, joining in on the defense, "we didn't bring everything. Just the symbolic stuff."

"And not the Hermès bag," Naomi cut in, with a panicked look. "Right?"

Claire gave her a thumbs-up as she helped herself to a carrot, realizing that she felt the lightest she had in a while. Audrey's grand idea from yesterday afternoon had happened quickly. A single phone call to Clarke, followed by orders for them to pack their bags because they were headed to the Hamptons, went down in the span of five minutes.

Manhattan might not have much in the way of fire opportunities, but a beach in September on Long Island certainly did. Even more importantly, it gave Claire a much-needed weekend away with friends.

Now, if only girl time and the bonfire could make a dent in her complicated feelings about Scott. Because she was pretty sure whatever was happening there wasn't something a bonfire could cure.

"Hello?"

Claire sighed around her carrot stick. Wonderful. Now she was straight up imagining his voice.

"Scott! You made it!"

Claire paused mid-chew, whirling toward the sound of the male voice. Sure enough, there was Scott. Had it been just a month ago that she'd thought boots, jeans, and a flannel layered over a white T-shirt was unattractive? Just a few weeks ago that the sight of a backward cap and scruffy jawline hadn't made her a little breathless?

She was staring. She knew it, but she couldn't look away.

He, on the other hand, didn't glance her way once, instead hoisting two grocery bags onto the counter. "The trunk of someone's Land Rover was open, and I saw these. Looks like one of them had perishables, so I brought 'em in."

Audrey stood on her toes to look into the paper bag, her eyes widening in delight. "My cheese!"

Clarke made an irritated noise. "I'll accept my apology now."

"I *specifically* asked if there were any bags left in the car, and you said you got them all," Audrey accused.

Clarke lifted his palm in high-five pose. "Truce?"

Audrey slapped his palm on her way to the fridge. "Truce."

Claire smiled in spite of her jittery nerves. If only all relationships could be so easy.

Naomi caught her eye from across the kitchen. "Oliver's idea," she mouthed.

Claire nodded in acknowledgment just as Oliver himself came over, lowering his voice so only Claire could hear.

"You know, it's strange," Oliver murmured, looking across the room to where his friend talked with Clarke. "I've known Scott a long time. Never known him to readily agree to a social anything. I usually have to bribe him just to grab a beer, and yet here he is, spending a weekend with five people. It's interesting."

He glanced back at Claire, and she responded with only a slight raise of her eyebrows. "Is it?"

"Yes," Oliver said pointedly. "It is."

Scott was gesturing in the direction of the driveway, still

talking to Clarke. "Audrey mentioned it was cool if I brought my dog, but since it's your place, I wanted to check. If there's a garage or something, I can have her sleep in there . . ."

"Hell no," Clarke said. "I love dogs. Better yet, this is my family's house, and my mom hates dogs, so bring her in."

"Uh . . ."

"Don't mind Clarke," Audrey said. "His parents are a bit uptight, and Clarke's made it his life's mission to do everything they don't want him to. But seriously. Bring the dog in, I want to meet her."

Scott disappeared, and a minute later Bob came bounding into the kitchen. Claire couldn't help but grin at the sight of the dog, and then her stupid heart went and melted all over her, because Bob made a beeline straight toward her.

"Hey, Bobsie," she said, crouching and kissing the side of the dog's head, squeezing her eyes shut for a moment at the realization that she no longer wanted a dog. She wanted *this* dog.

But the dog wasn't hers any more than the man was.

"Claire, I didn't know you were a dog person," Audrey said.

"I didn't know I was, either. In fact, the first time I met this little lady, I thought she was a dinosaur. We've come a long way since then."

She met Scott's eyes across the room, letting him know with her gaze that she wasn't just talking about the dog. She and Scott had come a long way, too.

"Scott, it's so great you were able to join on late notice," Audrey was saying as she put the rest of the groceries away.

*Very late notice*, Claire realized. Audrey had had this idea yesterday. She understood why Clarke was here. It was his house. And Oliver, obviously, came as a package deal with Naomi.

But why had Scott come? She understood why Oliver had

asked him. But why had he come? Oliver was right in that Scott hardly seemed like the type to willingly spend a weekend with other people. And the two of them had barely spoken since their argument, aside from terse exchanges about the renovation.

*So why was he here?*

"Okay," Clarke was saying, as he began unwrapping the foil from a bottle of champagne. "The house is only five bedrooms, so—"

"Only five?" Naomi broke in, gesturing at the lavish home that undoubtedly was worth several million dollars. "It's practically a shack."

"Luckily," Clarke continued as he twisted the champagne cork with a pop, "two of our six-some is making sexy bacon in the bedroom—"

"Wait, what?" Audrey interrupted.

Clarke gave her an exasperated look. "Your friends Oliver and Naomi are having sex, Audrey. Keep up."

"What's that have to do with bacon?"

Clarke glanced around at the guys. "Bacon is the only thing that comes close to being as good as sex. Am I right?"

"I can think of at least ten other things," Naomi mused. "A really good dinner roll dripping with butter, dark chocolate with sea salt. Homemade macaroni and cheese, especially if it has bread crumbs on top. Tacos—"

"Tacos!" Oliver sounded outraged. "You'd choose tacos over sex?"

"Clarke was talking about food *almost* as good as sex," Naomi said. "And don't think I haven't seen the look on your face when you eat that pizza from Don Antonio's. It's awfully close to your sex face."

Claire raised her hand. "Do I have to be around for this conversation?"

"No kidding," Clarke said, pouring the champagne into the flutes Audrey had located and was holding up for him one by one. "You two are the only ones getting laid this weekend, so quit rubbing it in."

"We'd *better* be the only ones having sex," Naomi muttered with a dark look in Scott's direction.

Scott didn't look back at Naomi.

All of his attention was on Claire.

## Chapter Twenty-Four

Strange, all this time I thought Claire was the quiet one of the group," Clarke said, lifting the bottle of expensive bourbon he'd brought to the beach and topping off his glass.

"Maybe the wine brings out another side of her?" Oliver said, reaching over and taking the bourbon from Clarke, topping off his own glass.

Oliver passed the bottle toward Scott who shook his head.

He was already feeling the effects, though he didn't know if it was from the whisky or from watching Claire.

Sure, there were three women standing around the bonfire, throwing Brayden Hayes's belongings in one by one.

But he only had eyes for one of them.

The other guys were right about her being exceptionally vocal tonight, but they were wrong about the wine being the cause. Claire hadn't had a drink since dinner, and that had been hours ago.

It was close to midnight, and the bonfire that had inspired this trip seemed to light up the entire sky. The three men sat a healthy distance away in beach chairs Clarke had dug out of the garage, but the women danced barefoot around it in some sort of feminine bonding ritual that both fascinated and terrified Scott.

"And that," Claire was shouting, heaving what looked like a tennis racket into the fire, "is for all the times you made me go to freaking *Queens* for dinner so that Audrey wouldn't see us together."

Oliver looked at Clarke. "Should we be worried about the neighbors?"

"Nah," Clarke said, digging bare feet into the sand, looking perfectly relaxed. "It's off-season; we're good."

"And this," Naomi yelled, throwing in an article of clothing, "is because you were *not* better than bacon in the sack."

"I'll drink to that," Oliver muttered, taking a sip of bourbon.

"I don't know about you guys, but I'm so ready to be done with that guy. I hope this is the end of it," Clarke said.

Scott glanced over. "You knew him?"

Clarke shrugged, his usual easygoing face a little shadowed as he watched the women—Audrey, specifically, Scott was guessing. "Audrey wanted him and me to be friends, so I tried. And damn. I wish I could say I saw him for what he was, but I didn't. Still, I knew he wasn't good enough for her. He wasn't good enough for any of them."

"Agreed," Oliver said. "Though, do we know why now? What trigged the Ya-Ya Sisterhood moment?"

"Seriously. These women are on a mission."

"I did," Scott said, abruptly answering Oliver's question. "I triggered it."

Both men looked his way. "How?"

"Claire's guest bedroom was like a mausoleum dedicated to

the asshole. I guess it wasn't my place to say so, as her contractor, but—"

"*Just* her contractor?" Oliver interrupted.

Scott gave his friend a look out of the corner of his eye and winced when he saw from Oliver's expression that his friend already knew about him and Claire.

"I was going to tell you."

Oliver laughed. "Sure you were. Because you always spill about your personal life."

"Wait, what am I missing?" Clarke asked.

Oliver tilted his head toward Scott. "He slept with Claire."

"Holy shit, really?" Clarke said, glancing back toward the fire as the women linked arms, and then sat cross-legged in unison in the sand. "I thought there were some vibes at the fund-raiser thing, but she always seems so—"

"Watch it," Scott snapped automatically, earning a surprised look from both of them.

"*Careful*," Clarke finished. "I was going to say she seems careful, very deliberate about who she gets involved with. Or rather who she *doesn't* get involved with, because now that I think about it, didn't I set her up with Brett?"

"You did, and thanks for that," Scott said irritably. He felt Oliver studying him. "What?"

"Holy shit," Oliver said with a slow grin. "It finally happened."

"What?"

"You're jealous. You don't get jealous. Not even with Meredith. Not even when you learned she was sleeping with another guy—then you were just mad."

"Who's Meredith?"

"My ex," Scott growled at Clarke. "And not relevant to this

conversation. Seriously, why do people keep thinking a woman from forever ago has any bearing on my current life?"

"People? Who else thought that?" Oliver pressed.

Scott sipped his whisky, rethinking that refill if the conversation kept going in this direction.

"Ah. Let me guess. Claire called you out on your baggage after you told her to throw out her ex's crap," Clarke said, settling back into his chair. "This is getting exciting. Real soap opera stuff. I haven't seen anything this good since I got to watch Oliver and Naomi at a dinner party when he was paired up with Claire."

"The hell?" Scott swung his gaze around to his friend. "You dated Claire?"

Oliver laughed and shook his head. "No, but Clarke's right. This *is* fun."

"I'm sure as hell not having any fun. Quit acting like Claire and I are a thing. We hooked up. *Once*. And I told her to get rid of Brayden's shit because it was interfering with my job. That's the end of our story."

"Riiight," Clarke said. "And when Oliver called and invited you, did you know Claire would be here or . . ."

Hell yes, he knew Claire would be here. It was why he'd come.

Scott had thought about nothing in the two days she'd been icing him out except that he missed her. And when Oliver had told him it was a Brayden send-off, he'd known he had to be here.

For her. With her. To tell her that she could count on him for this, right now, if not for always. He wanted to do that much for her at least.

Of course, that wasn't *exactly* going as planned so far. She'd done a bang-up job of avoiding him all afternoon and throughout dinner. Still, he could at least keep an eye on her. For now, that was enough.

"Incoming," Oliver said, nodding as the three women approached.

Clarke had only been able to find four beach chairs, and a laughing Audrey flung herself into the last available one, throwing her legs over Clarke's lap. "Holy crap. That was the most fun I've had all summer. *Any* summer. We should burn people's stuff more often!"

Clarke patted her shin. "Let's maybe not say that outside of this group, hmm? I don't want to have to go bailing you out of jail."

Naomi dropped onto Oliver's lap, wrapping both arms around his neck and pulling him in for a kiss that was definitely not group appropriate. She pulled back and whispered something in his ear that made Oliver smile and pull her closer. Scott looked away, both to give them privacy and because the person he really wanted to see right now was Claire.

She hovered on the fringe of the chairs, and at first he thought she was embarrassed, maybe feeling left out. But he looked closer, saw he couldn't be more wrong. She was glowing. She had the same happy confidence as when she'd been talking about her calligraphy, but tenfold.

No doubt about it, Claire Hayes was finally coming out of mourning.

*This* was the real reason he'd needed to be here, Scott realized. He'd needed to see this. Needed to know that when he moved on, she'd be okay. She'd be more than okay. She'd thrive.

He was a little surprised when she met his gaze head-on, even more so when she walked right to him and dropped down, kneeling beside his chair. For a moment Scott's entire world tilted with something that felt a lot like joy at being part of a couple. With her. There was Clarke and Audrey affectionately bickering, Oliver and Naomi with the full-on making out, and he and Claire with . . . something. He didn't need a name for it. For now, it was enough that she'd come to him.

"Here," he said, starting to stand. "You take the chair."

Claire put a hand on his knee. "Stay. I'll sit on the ground. I can't get any sandier than I already am."

Before Scott realized what he was doing, he reached out and pulled a strand of hair from where it was stuck to her lips and tucked it behind her ear. Her gaze flickered in confusion for a moment, then she looked away, reaching for his cup. Claire turned her attention toward the rest of the group, lifted his drink. "Cheers, ladies. We did it."

"Hear, hear," Naomi said, taking Oliver's glass and lifting it. "To moving on."

"Hold up." Oliver pinched Naomi's side playfully. "Didn't you already move on?"

She patted his cheek, as Audrey made a wobbly grab for Clarke's cup and lifted that. "Goodbye, Brayden. May you never ruin another life."

"Oh, he didn't ruin us," Claire said quietly. "Tripped us up for a while. But never ruined."

The other women nodded, then the three of them drank some bourbon before they all, in some sort of silent female communion, stood up and walked away, chatting about Claire's calligraphy, the topic of Brayden closed. Scott got the sense maybe forever.

"Did they just take our whisky?" Oliver mused.

"Seriously," Clarke said, aghast. "What the hell just happened?"

Scott merely smiled. He knew exactly what had happened: Claire Hayes had just taken her life back.

His smile disappeared when he realized he wouldn't have much of a part in it.

## Chapter Twenty-Five

*T*he bonfire had left Claire feeling clean and light inside, and she let a long, hot shower do the rest of the work on the outside. By the time she toweled off her hair and pulled on sweatpants and a T-shirt, she knew this night would go down as one of the most pivotal in her life.

She looked at herself in the mirror, and though her thirty-something skin wasn't as smooth as her twenty-something skin, her hair looked closer to muddy brown than blond in its wet state, and her figure was more soft than it was taut, she felt beautiful. More importantly, she felt *whole*. The beige that she'd thought was simply her personality had really just been a layer of film over who she really was. It was gone now.

*This* was strawberry lemonade Claire. The cupcake worth looking twice at.

Grinning at her reflection, she brushed her teeth and spit, then bundling up her sandy clothes to be dealt with tomorrow, she headed back to her room.

She knocked softly on Audrey's door. "Aud?" she whispered. "I'm done in the bathroom."

Audrey made a sleepy murmur of acknowledgment from the other side. Claire smiled, guessing that singing most of the Taylor Swift repertoire and drinking a healthy portion of Clarke's bourbon had taken its toll. Her friend would probably feel it tomorrow, but Claire hoped it was worth it.

She knew it was for her, though she didn't think she was headed toward a hangover. She'd drunk just enough to celebrate without having so much as to dull the moment.

In fact, she felt as clearheaded as ever. At least about Brayden and being done.

As for Scott, on the other hand, she didn't have a clue.

Claire wanted to know why he came.

But for now, maybe it was simply enough that he had. Maybe he was working through his emotions just as she was.

Claire had felt the way he'd looked at her. Like he wanted her. And she'd noticed the small gestures. Brushing the hair out of her face. Refilling her water glass when it was empty, almost absently, as though he were instinctively aware of her.

She was at a loss for what any of it meant though.

The house was quiet as she walked toward her room. Naomi and Oliver had claimed the master bedroom with its king bed on the first floor, while the others had taken the four bedrooms on the fourth floor. Claire's and Audrey's rooms shared a bath on one side of the house, Clarke's and Scott's on the other.

Claire had been a little disappointed when, at the end of the night, Bob had followed Scott to his room, instead of her to hers, but she supposed she should get used to it. The dog would be out of her life as soon as the man was.

She opened the door to her room, then slapped a hand over her mouth to stifle the startled shriek.

"*Jesus*, Scott. You do realize that having a man surprise you in your bedroom at two a.m. is pretty much every woman's worst nightmare, right?"

He glanced up from where he sat at the foot of her bed, hands clasped between his knees, feet bare beneath plaid pajama pants, a white undershirt hugging what she now knew firsthand was a firm, unyielding torso. "Sorry."

She dropped her dirty clothes by her suitcase. "Where's Bob?" she asked, turning to face him.

He stood up. "Snoring in the middle of my bed."

"Oh."

She said nothing more, as they seemed to face off, the intimacy of the evening feeling hopelessly tangled with the antagonism of their last encounter at his apartment, as well as his imminent departure from her life.

"I came to see if you were okay," he said quietly. "But I see that I've wasted a trip. You're more than okay."

She sucked in a breath, a little surprised he could read her so clearly. "Yeah. I really am."

"Claire, about that night. When I told you to get rid of his stuff—"

"No." She held up a hand. "You were right. I mean, yes, it was overstepping. And you sort of delivered it with the delicate touch of a massive earthquake. But it needed to be said, and I'm grateful."

He gave a half smile. "That's generous. I was an ass."

"Well." She crossed her arms. "Yeah."

"Forgiven?" he asked, searching her face.

Claire nodded. "Forgiven."

His smile widened. "Was that a tennis racket I saw get hurled into the fire?"

"Eh. Yeah. I felt a *little* bad about that one. It was a good racket. But then I remembered that I used to beg Brayden to play doubles, but he never had the time. Turns out he and Audrey played at her club once a week."

"I think it's fitting that it went into the fire. Now it's burning just like he is."

"You sound like Naomi."

Scott shrugged. "Smart lady."

Claire fiddled with her earlobe, needing to confess something to someone and a little surprised that she wanted it to be him. "Scott."

His head snapped up.

"I didn't burn everything."

"No?"

"I kept my wedding ring."

His gaze dropped to her left hand.

"I'm not *wearing* it," she said. "I'm not that messed up. But yesterday morning I took it to get appraised, thinking maybe I'd trade it and get a bracelet or something new, and I . . . just couldn't. I guess it's the one part of my marriage I want to keep with me. Even knowing how things worked out, I can't deny that on my wedding day, I loved Brayden, and I'm pretty sure he loved me. The ring symbolizes all that. Is that lame?"

Scott shook his head.

"The weirdest part is I don't even *like* the ring. I've never said that out loud. Who doesn't like their wedding ring? But I never did."

"Let me guess. Ostentatious as hell?"

"No!" she exclaimed. "That's just it. When he gave it to me, he made this pretty speech about how he wanted something classic and timeless and elegant, just like me. And it was all those things, but . . ."

Scott gave a crooked smile. "You *wanted* ostentatious."

"Maybe." She burst out with a laugh, grateful she could finally say it. "Okay, yes, I wanted gaudy, damn it. I wanted a guy to put a huge tacky rock on my finger because he wanted everyone to know I was his." Claire shrugged. "Maybe that's the problem. I was never his any more than he was mine. *Damn,* that fire felt good."

"It was a hell of a thing to watch," he said, tilting his head in the direction of the beach. "All of you were in your element, but you, in particular, you were . . . you were . . ." He swallowed but couldn't finish the sentence.

"It was euphoric," she admitted, putting one bare foot on top of the other and looking down. "I knew I was mad, but I didn't realize how much I'd been holding on to it, letting it fuel me. And my decisions."

"Anger can be a good distraction from pain."

Claire looked up again. "Speaking from experience?"

He opened his mouth, and for one hopeful moment she thought he was going to let her in, but instead he shrugged.

*So that's how it's going to be.* She'd let him in, but obviously it was destined to be a one-way street. And the new Claire, the one she'd just found, deserved better than this. Better than someone who wouldn't even meet her halfway.

"It's late," she said softly.

He nodded, and she saw from the resignation in his eyes that he recognized the dismissal.

Still, his presence here tonight, this weekend, wasn't nothing. He cared about her, even if he didn't know what the hell to do with it, or what to call it. On that front at least she understood. She didn't know what to call what she felt for him, either.

"Thanks for checking on me," she said. "You've become a close friend in a short amount of time, and it really . . . it means a lot."

"A friend," he repeated softly.

"Who hooked up that one time," she said, smiling in an attempt to cut the tension that seemed to increase every time their eyes met.

He smiled back, his eyes crinkling at the corners. "Right. The one time."

The silence stretched on for another minute, until he finally nodded. "Good night, Claire."

"Good night."

He headed toward the door, but stopped when they were shoulder to shoulder and slowly reached down until his fingers brushed hers in a whisper of a touch.

Scott shuddered out a long breath, then taking her hand in his, he lifted it, his other hand unfurling her fingers to expose a palm. He placed his lips to the center of her palm without meeting her eyes before walking away.

## Chapter Twenty-Six

*A* little more than a week after the weekend at the beach, Claire hit Send on her email, waited impatiently for it to move from her outbox to her sent folder.

The second it did, she closed her laptop and let out a little squeal, hardly believing the moment was real. It was happening! She was in business. Well, sort of. Booking one client did not a career make.

But still, she was intensely proud of herself. Sylvia Zepada had just booked Claire to do the calligraphy on her daughter's wedding invitations.

With an invite list of over four hundred people, it would be a beast of a task, and though she'd been terrified when she'd stated the rate that Naomi had insisted Claire was worth, Sylvia had written back immediately asking for a contract to make it official.

Biting her lip, even as she grinned, Claire stood and glanced around her tiny office where she'd already begun organizing her ink pots and nibs. She was grateful that Scott had insisted they start the upstairs renovation with her office instead of the bedroom as she'd suggested. Claire had nervously shown him her "dream office" board on Pinterest, and Scott had looked at everything in detail and promptly banned her from the office for two days.

The end result hadn't just been close to her dream office—it had gone above and beyond. The walls and desk were painted bright white, which, as he reminded her, was different from meh white. And the built-in shelf along one wall had so clearly been designed with calligraphy supplies in mind, there was no doubt that he'd done careful research on what she'd need. Even the lighting was perfect, a dozen tiny bright bulbs carefully positioned to give her the light she'd need to work.

Claire picked up her phone, intending to text Naomi and Audrey the good news, but she put it down without typing the message. Instead, she left her office, walked past the newly renovated second guest room where she was temporarily sleeping, and into the master where Scott was finishing up. Following the sound of a drill, Claire found Scott in the bathroom sitting on the closed toilet seat, drilling something into the wall.

He gave her an exasperated look, the drill going silent as he pulled a screw from between his lips. "Really? You can't walk in and see me while I'm single-handedly maneuvering the new tub into place or installing an enormous new mirror? It has to be when I'm drilling in the new toilet paper holder? A fix a six-year-old could do?"

"Very manly," she teased. "And I'm *loving* that." She pointed at the holder. "No more stupid spring."

"No more stupid spring," he said, standing.

She stood grinning at him, and then, because she wanted to, she flung her arms around his neck. He caught her with one arm and a laugh, just as she tugged his head down for a kiss.

She felt him freeze in surprise, but she kissed him insistently. Things had been friendlier between them since the beach house, even easy, but strictly platonic. And she knew this was foolhardy, knew that if she even had a chance to keep her heart intact when he left, she needed to keep her hands to herself, but she wanted to celebrate the moment the way that she wanted to.

Apparently, that was kissing Scott.

He got over his surprise quickly, kissing her back with gratifying enthusiasm.

He kissed her for a long while, then pulled back slightly. Claire jumped when he swatted her butt and all but shoved her out into the more spacious bedroom. "What are you doing in here? You know I've got one rule."

"I know, I know. I'm supposed to let you finish a room before I see it, but guess what," she said, tapping his chest excitedly.

"What?" he asked with a smile, as though her enthusiasm was contagious.

"I got a client."

"Holy shit," he said with a laugh, setting his drill on the nearby workbench before lifting her in a hug. "Congrats. You do fast work."

"I know!" she said, her arms going around his neck and squeezing. "It's a big one, too. I'll probably get carpal tunnel. But it's worth it. The client is well-connected. If she likes what I do, I've got a good feeling about referrals."

"She'll love what she sees," he said confidently. "When do you start?"

"Tomorrow, probably," she said. "I mean, I have plenty of time, but I'm new to this. I'm not exactly sure how long each envelope will take or how many breaks I'll need. You were so right about me needing that office sooner than I expected."

"Glad it worked out," he said, his smile warm, revealing that maybe he was a little bit proud of her.

"I'm just lucky you do such fast work. Speaking of." Claire pulled back and looked around, taking in the freshly painted walls—she'd decided to go with dove gray, which she'd read was soothing for bedrooms—as well as the newly finished floor. "Oh my gosh. You're almost done in here."

"Told you the upstairs would be easy, especially since we opted not to tear the wall down."

"How much longer?" she asked, unabashedly looking around, poking her head into the bathroom, since she'd already violated his *no peeking* rule.

"Another day or two. Then it's just getting the fridge into the kitchen, a day of cleaning up all the construction mess, and you've got yourself a brand-new house."

Claire was checking out the bathroom, her back to him as he spoke, and she was glad for it. Another day or two. Plus one for cleanup.

And then . . . *done*.

He was done with her house. And done with her?

When she turned back around, he didn't quite meet her eyes, and she knew he was thinking the same thing. Thinking that for all their talk about figuring it out later, later was just about here. But they weren't ready. Or at least she wasn't.

"Does that mean I finally get to see my kitchen?" she asked, fighting for levity.

His smile, too, was a little forced. "Thursday. Let's make it a date."

"Thursday," she agreed with a nod.

Their eyes locked, and without saying a word, they came together, his mouth crashing over hers, her lips hungry under his.

*Later*, the kiss said. *We'll figure it out later.*

Even as Claire knew they were running out of *laters*. And she suspected Scott knew it, too. It was evident in the searing nature of the kiss, the greediness of his hands. Claire's hands fumbled with his buckle, and his fingers trembled a little as they found the hook of her bra. "Other bedroom has the bed," he murmured against her lips.

Claire shook her head, winding her arms around his neck as she kissed him with everything she had. Here. She wanted him here in her bedroom, just once. She wanted the most recent man in her bedroom not to be a ghost from her past life, but the memory of a man from this life. Not just *a* man. *This* man.

He backed her up against the wall, and she knew he understood.

It was enough, Claire told herself, as their clothes fell to the floor. *Enough*, she thought, when he slid into her with a groan. *Enough*, she thought, as they coaxed each other over the edge with practiced touches and heated words.

But after, when he held her as their heart rates slowed, she knew there was no more running from the truth, no more pretending she could let him go easily. She knew that whenever *later* came, she'd be left wanting so much more.

# Chapter Twenty-Seven

Scott opened the door, a little surprised to find an irritated-looking Oliver standing there. "Hey, man. Come in."

Oliver hesitated. "Claire here?"

"No, one of her college friends is in town; they went out to dinner. What's up?"

Oliver stepped inside, giving an absent pet to Bob. "Thought I'd stop by, see if perchance you wanted to run by the Apple Store, since apparently you've lost your phone."

Scott winced with guilt at the sarcasm, knowing he deserved his friend's ire. "I should have texted back."

"Or called. Emailed. Sent a telegram. I'd have taken any of the above," Oliver said, shrugging out of his suit jacket and helping himself to a beer from the fridge. That his usually polite friend didn't offer one to Scott spoke volumes about Oliver's mood. *Pissed*.

"It's been busy," Scott said truthfully. He'd been hauling ass on Claire's house, wanting to see her face when it was done, wanting to give her the perfect canvas for her fresh start.

He realized yesterday, when he'd all but devoured her against the wall of her bedroom, that it had been a shortsighted plan. Because finishing her house meant he'd be out of a reason to see her every day.

And finishing her house left him without a reason why he couldn't start on any of the other projects waiting in the wings, and there were several.

He knew that was why Oliver was here. For the first time in their friendship, Scott hated that their careers were so closely aligned, that Oliver, having an architecture firm that was in-demand in its own right, would know exactly just how in-demand Scott was.

"Ellis called you," Scott said. Not a question.

Oliver nodded.

Ellis Burke was one of the top real estate investors in the country—in the world. Every architect took his or her project to Burke first, because he had the biggest budget, the biggest vision. And every contractor hoped he or she was on Burke's short list. Not only because of the money, but because of the sheer challenge of the projects he took on.

"The project's not one of yours."

"Nope." Oliver took a sip of beer. "It's Marshall Briggs's out of Dogma."

Scott grimaced, even though he already knew that. "Prick."

"Yeah," Oliver said. "He's also one of the best, and yes, that pains me to say as a competitor. A Burke/Briggs collaboration's a damn good opportunity."

A month and a half ago, Scott wouldn't have hesitated. A month and a half ago, Scott would already be on his way to China, eager to dive in.

A month and a half ago, Scott didn't have anyone to leave behind except Bob.

"Why'd he call you?" Scott asked.

"Because he couldn't get ahold of you," Oliver said bluntly. "You want to give Burke the runaround, have at it. I know these are big decisions. But why cut *me* out?"

"I'm sorry," Scott said, looking Oliver straight in the eye even though he hated to see the hurt and frustration there.

Oliver stared back, then sighed. "It's fine. I guess. You've disappeared on me before. It's just not usually when you're still in town."

Scott knew the other man was simply speaking plainly and didn't intend to guilt-trip him, but Scott felt the guilt all the same. He was realizing, embarrassingly for the first time, that his fly-by-the-seat-of-his-pants lifestyle had made him a pretty shitty friend.

"So, you taking the job?" Oliver asked, his tone a little less curt now.

"It's in Shanghai," Scott said.

Oliver shrugged. "I know. But isn't that sort of your thing? The farther away the gig, the better, right?"

Usually, yes. That was absolutely "his thing."

Now, though . . .

"Yeah," he forced himself to say. "I'm taking it. Just haven't gotten around to getting back to Burke. It's been busy at Claire's, and he's been working out of London, so the time difference . . ."

"The time difference?" Oliver didn't bother to hide his incredulity. "They're offering you a chance to build the biggest hotel in the world, and a five-hour time difference is what's getting in your way of accepting?"

Even Bob was looking at Scott with disdain.

"Scott," Oliver said, sounding slightly awed.

Scott looked up. Oliver rarely called him by his first name. Usually it was *Turner* or *dude*, or any other variety of guy speak. As a rule, Oliver didn't use his first name, and he definitely didn't have that surprised, sympathetic note to his voice.

"Is this about Claire?" Oliver asked, when Scott said nothing.

Hearing her name alongside the Shanghai conversation hit Scott hard. He looked away, and his friend swore.

"Damn it, man. I don't love admitting it, but I think Naomi was right. You two hooking up *was* a bad idea."

"If it was a bad idea, it was the best mistake I've ever made," Scott said sharply.

Oliver's eyebrows went up. "So it's not just sex. You're dating."

"No," Scott said quickly. "We're not . . . we haven't. We've just been enjoying each other."

"Not a horrible idea," Oliver said. "Unless one of them is a commitment phobe, the other a fragile widow who's overdue for a little stability. Oh, wait . . ."

"She's not fragile," Scott snapped.

"No. You're right," Oliver backtracked quickly. "And normally, I'd be all for two consenting adults having sex for as long as it worked out, and then moving on with their lives. But I'm getting the impression that's not what this is."

"I don't know what the hell this is," Scott said, deciding he needed a beer after all and going to the fridge. "I only know that every time I went to call Burke back, to tell him I'm in, I just . . . couldn't."

"Because you were contemplating turning it down? For her?"

"No. This is my life, you know that. I follow the job, not the woman."

"Lives change. You and Claire know that better than anyone."

"Because we picked the wrong people to marry when we were twenty-something idiots?"

"Because you know circumstances change," Oliver reframed. "Maybe this is one of those times. One of those circumstances."

Scott was already shaking his head. "I'm not some wild young buck biding my time until I'm tamed. This isn't a phase; this is who I am. I don't settle down; I don't stay."

"Why not?"

Scott glared at him. "I swear you weren't this annoying before you and Naomi got together."

Oliver shrugged, picked up his suit jacket, and set his beer on the counter. "That's because I didn't know how good it could be before I met Naomi."

Scott wasn't sure he wanted to know, and Oliver was all the way to the door before he could bring himself to ask: "Didn't know how good what could be?"

Oliver opened the door and pinned Scott with a level look. "Loving someone."

# Chapter Twenty-Eight

*I*s this really necessary?" Claire asked, fumbling along the hall with her right hand as Scott held her left. "I could have looked at the kitchen a million times before now."

"But you haven't," Scott replied.

"How do you know?"

"I just know."

Had her eyes not been forced to stay closed with one of her winter scarves that Scott had commandeered as a blindfold, she'd have rolled them. Still, she was glad there was a hint of playfulness in him. He'd been downright brooding all morning.

Claire understood. She'd been feeling a little surly herself, exceedingly aware that the clock was ticking down, even as she didn't fully know why it felt that way.

They'd slept together a handful of times since that spontaneous moment in her bedroom. Couldn't keep their hands off each other, really. And though she'd relished every minute, she was also aware that for all her talk about wanting to have no-strings-attached sex, she apparently wasn't cut out for that. Because there were strings now. And Claire was all tangled up in them.

"All right," he murmured, halting her and moving in front of her. His fingers slid beneath the scarf, lifting it gently. Scott balled it into one fist, but his other hand lingered near her face, his fingertips drifting lightly over her cheek.

Claire's heart flickered in surprise at the tender touch, and she searched his face, looking for explanation, but the guarded look in his eyes was at direct odds with the sweetness of his action.

His hand dropped, and he smiled slightly, the moment over. "You ready?"

"What if I hate it?" she teased.

"Everyone's entitled to their opinion."

Claire gave him a knowing look. "Bullshit. How do you really feel?"

His grin widened, amused at being called out. "If you hate it, then you have none of the taste I thought you have, and I'll wish I'd given you laminate cabinets and linoleum counters. Beige."

She mock gasped. "You wouldn't do that to me."

"Never." His kiss caught her off guard; it was a little firmer than usual, a touch desperate. As though he were nervous.

Then he stepped back, and Claire got her first glance at her new kitchen.

She didn't move. Couldn't. When she finally forced her feet forward, it was only a couple of steps before she stopped and stared again.

The cabinets were dark brown, nearly black, with modern silver handles. The counter was enormous, made of stunning black marble. The appliances were a dark graphite she hadn't seen before in all her Pinterest stalking, and they were perfect. None of that's what had her feeling a little breathless.

It was the backsplash behind the six-burner stove, the pillar she'd joked about painting magenta, the walls of the kitchen . . .

They were all green.

A gorgeous, rich shade of sage green that managed to be vivid without being *loud*.

She walked slowly around the kitchen, taking it all in before coming back to his side, realizing that he'd been looking at her the entire time she'd been looking at the kitchen.

"It's green," she whispered. "You made my kitchen my favorite color."

"Do you like it?" The touch of vulnerability in his voice squeezed her heart, hard. It also told her that this was no coincidence. He'd listened to what she'd wanted. Not to what she thought she'd wanted. There was no pink. But he'd listened when she'd told him her favorite color. That she'd mentioned it in passing and he remembered, felt . . . it felt like something.

Her eyes watered as she nodded. "Like it" was an understatement. She didn't like it. She loved it.

She loved him.

She bit back the sob, tried to cover it with enthusiasm over the finished kitchen.

"It is perfect. I never thought—I didn't expect," she babbled. "Why?"

He stared at the newly installed refrigerator, avoiding her eyes. "You might have mentioned earlier that pink wasn't actually your favorite color, you know. I had to redo the damn thing, but I'm glad I did. You said you wanted the pink because you wanted to be reminded that your life was yours, to remember that he couldn't tell you what to do anymore. I didn't want to build you the anti-Brayden kitchen. I wanted to build you the *Claire* kitchen. It makes no sense, now that I'm saying it out loud."

Her heart squeezed again, harder this time. "No, it does."

He cleared his throat, clearly embarrassed. "I want you to be happy. I guess . . . that matters to me."

"Ah. Always leave the client satisfied," she said lightly.

He didn't move his head, but his eyes darted back to hers. "No. That's not what I meant."

"Scott." Claire swallowed and forged ahead, heart in her throat.

This was hard. And a little awful. But Claire pressed ahead anyway. She'd been in love once and lost it. And it had sucked. She was in love again, and she knew that loving and not even *trying* would be so much worse.

"Scott." Her voice broke. "I think I—"

"I'm going to Shanghai," he interrupted shortly.

Claire's breath whooshed out. "Shanghai? China? Why?" Then it clicked into place. "Your next job."

He took a step forward, his motions a little jerky, his eyes pleading. "It's a big one. A new hotel. The plans have it being the tallest in the world when it's done. It's got an indoor waterfall, rooftop infinity pool—it's a demanding as hell challenge."

"Well, of course you have to do it," Claire said, her voice a little shaky with shock.

He exhaled. "Yeah?"

"Of course," she said with a smile that she knew wobbled. "You have to know—I'd never expect you not to chase your dreams. I know you'd never tell me not to chase mine."

"Never," he agreed.

*What if you're my dream?*

Even as Claire's thoughts spiraled, she still clung to hope. He was leaving, yes, but not forever. He still lived here; people did long distance all the time.

"So, how long?" she asked.

"A year. Maybe a little longer."

Claire's heart dropped to her feet. "A year? That's— Do you come back at all? Like . . . weekends?" she finished, hating how lame and pathetic this was making her feel.

He shoved his hands into his pockets. "It doesn't really work that way. I can get a weekend off here and there . . ."

Her heart couldn't take it anymore. She couldn't handle the not knowing.

"Scott. Just tell me," she said, her voice surprisingly calm. "If you tell me to wait, I will. But you have to tell me. You have to ask. That's all you have to do. We can figure everything else out. Later."

Scott made a harsh exhaling noise, as though she'd knocked the wind out of him.

"Just ask," she whispered; this time it was a plea. *I'm not your mom. I'm not Meredith any more than you are Brayden. You can count on me.*

He closed his eyes for a moment, and when he opened them, she knew. She knew and felt as though her heart had been cleaved in half.

"Don't wait," he said hoarsely. "Don't wait, Claire."

She stood still, even as she felt a little dizzy with the pain of it. Somehow though, she held herself upright, kept her eyes dry. Claire had learned she was a survivor.

She'd survive this, too.

"Got it," she said, her voice light but sure. "Understood."

"Claire—"

"What about Bob?" she broke in. "Can I at least have her?"

She smiled a little, and Scott blinked, clearly surprised at the abrupt shift in conversation. Probably a little relieved, too. He looked tired, almost boyish, his shoulders hunched forward. "In hindsight, it was selfish to get a dog with my job. I don't know why I did it with my schedule . . ."

*It's because you wanted somebody to love—and somebody to love you back, you big oaf.*

But that wasn't the type of thing you could teach someone. They had to figure it out on their own, and Scott wasn't there. At least not with her.

He glanced up, looking like himself once more, a little distant and completely in control. "I can't ask you to watch my dog."

"You didn't," she argued. "I asked you. I want to. Really. Please."

Scott searched her face for a long minute, then finally nodded. "Thank you. I'd rather leave Bob with you than anyone else."

Any other time, Claire might have warmed to the compliment. In light of the fact that she'd just handed over her heart only to have it handed right back, her responding smile felt a little plastic.

"When do you leave? How much time do I have to find Bobsie a proper dog bed? That ugly yellow one you have is all wrong for her fur. Pink would work so much better. Or green." She expected a smile, but she didn't get one.

"Tuesday," he replied.

"Tuesday," she repeated. "As in five days from today?"

He nodded. "It may not be much of a consolation, but I just found that out this morning. In fact, I just committed this morning. But these things move fast."

He was right. It wasn't much of a consolation.

She inhaled. "All right. Keep me in the loop about logistics. I can come pick Bob up Monday night if it's easier. And don't worry about Bob forgetting you. Dogs never do, but just in case, we'll Skype or FaceTime or whatever so she can see you."

Scott looked stunned. "You want to FaceTime with me?"

*Yes, because unlike you I don't just cut people out of my life the second I'm done with them.*

"I want you to FaceTime with Bob," she corrected.

"With Bob," he repeated a little robotically. "How often?"

Claire smiled with false brightness. "Whatever. We'll figure it out."

## Chapter Twenty-Nine

Scott peered more closely at the slightly pixelated video of Claire and about half of Bob's head.

"Is that fried chicken?" he asked incredulously.

"Yup," Claire said around a bite of drumstick. "Don't forget it's eight p.m. here. Dinner."

"Yeah, I've mastered the twelve-hour time difference," he said. "I guess what I'm a little confused about is why *Bob's* eating the fried chicken."

"Just the occasional piece," she said, breaking off a piece and giving it to an enraptured Bob. "No bones."

Scott shook his head with a smile. "Glad I'm not the one who has to take her out tomorrow morning."

"I'll have you know that Bob's morning constitutional lately has been supremely healthy."

"You know, when you mentioned FaceTime with my dog, this isn't what I imagined."

Claire took her time wiping her mouth of chicken grease

with a paper napkin, and Scott felt the strangest sense of elation that they were at that level of comfort with each other.

"What did you imagine?" she asked.

Scott realized he didn't have an answer, because he hadn't imagined any of it. He hadn't imagined that Claire would even be willing to speak to him after the way he'd left. Certainly hadn't imagined that she'd offer to watch his dog.

Least of all that she'd not only want to keep in touch about Bob, but like this.

But the biggest surprise of all was how much Scott enjoyed it. How, in the two weeks since he'd been in Shanghai, had this become the highlight of his day? They didn't talk every day, mainly because he couldn't bring himself to ask her for that, much as he longed to. He was the one who'd left; he definitely didn't get to make demands.

Thus far though, it had worked out to be *nearly* every day. Unless he had an early meeting or she had evening plans, they had a standing "date" at 8:00 a.m. Shanghai/8:00 p.m. New York time.

If someone had told Scott a few months ago that his day would feel incomplete until he could talk to a woman, he'd have laughed in disbelief. And yet here he was, every morning, impatiently clock-watching through his breakfast of coffee and cereal, counting the minutes until he could see her again.

*Them*, he corrected. Until he could see *them*.

The calls always began with Bob and Claire's faces greeting him on the screen, usually while sharing dinner. Bob, shockingly, lost interest in the whole thing once the food was gone. Scott and Claire both pretended not to notice when their supposed reason for the call inevitably bailed, and it was just Claire and Scott. Talking about everything. Or nothing. It didn't matter. Scott had always loathed small talk, but there was no such thing with

Claire. Even when he ended the call without a clear sense of what the hell they'd talked about for the better part of an hour, he never felt restless. Never bored.

What he felt was *lonely*.

The very same feelings that had once been his impetus to live the way he did, to leap at the most exotic locations, the longest projects, now seemed bigger than ever because he'd accepted this job.

"How's the hand?" he asked.

Claire lifted her right hand, curled comically into a claw shape. "Basically useless after six straight hours of writing, which Bob loves. She hasn't lost a single tug-of-war game since I started the invitations."

"How're they coming?" he asked as he refilled his coffee.

"Great. Did I tell you that my client's daughter loved the sample I sent over at the end of last week? The bride already asked me to do the invitations for her best friend's baby shower next month. Naomi thinks I should charge more, since they didn't balk at the last price, but I think I'll keep my prices consistent until I feel more confident in the whole process."

"That's great," he said, fighting a surge of frustration that he wasn't the first to hear about these wins for her fledgling business. Why would he be? He'd forgone that right when he'd walked away.

"Oh, crap," Claire muttered, glancing away from the screen. "Is that the time? Hey, sorry, I have to cut this short tonight. Though I guess Bob already did that, huh?"

Scott loved his dog, but he did not care for one second where Bob was at the moment. It was the woman he was here for.

"Where are you headed?" he asked, sipping his coffee with feigned casualness.

"It's Clarke's birthday. He's rented out a whole cocktail bar for something like two hundred people."

In that moment, Scott firmly believed that he deserved a gold medal for not asking whether or not Brett would be there. And he deserved a blue ribbon for not asking what she was planning on wearing, and suggesting the ugliest, frumpiest dress in her wardrobe so other men wouldn't know her shape like he did. And he deserved a round of applause for not begging her to stay on the call with him just a bit longer so he could hear her voice . . .

Oblivious to the ache in Scott's chest, Claire turned away and shouted for the dog. "Bob! Come say goodbye to your dad! There's a good girl," she cooed, as Scott saw the uppermost part of the dog come back into view.

Claire hoisted Bob onto the couch beside her and pointed toward the screen, trying to get the dog to look toward Scott. She was only half successful. Bob was clearly convinced she was pointing to a rogue piece of fried chicken that needed to be eaten.

Claire lifted Bob's paw and waved at Scott. "Say 'Bye, Dad! See you tomorrow!' Scott, your turn," Claire said, glancing at the camera. "Say bye to your girl."

He rolled his eyes but played along. "Bye to my girl."

The second the words were out, Scott's world tilted on its axis as the truth rolled over him.

The FaceTime window went black as Claire ended the call, off to primp for her party, off to live her life, but Scott didn't move. Not when his computer stayed inactive for so long the screen went black. Not when his coffee turned cold, the mug still frozen in his hand.

*Bye to my girl.*

He hadn't been talking to the dog. He'd been talking to Claire.

Claire was his girl. His woman. And he didn't want to have to say bye to her. Not ever again.

## Chapter Thirty

*Y*ou're sure you don't mind?" Claire asked for the hundredth time, as she watched Bob do a third perimeter sniff of Audrey's apartment. It was a significant time investment, as Audrey's apartment was huge.

Claire assuaged some of her guilt, slightly, by reminding herself that Bob would like all the extra space. That she wouldn't feel ditched, first by Scott, then by Claire.

Granted, Claire's "ditch" had a one-week expiration date. As far as brownie points went, she was way ahead of Scott.

"I'm *positive*," Audrey reassured her. "I love dogs."

"Yeah, but, and I mean this with love, you've got a distinct purse dog vibe about you," Claire said, miming the size of a tiny little lap dog.

"I like all dogs," Audrey insisted. "I did my homework. I read a bunch of pet blogs and learned new tricks to teach her. Oh, and I didn't show you . . ."

She teetered away on her high heels, came back holding something small and aqua.

"See!" Audrey proclaimed, unrolling it slightly. "Tiffany blue poop bags! And look . . ." She unrolled it further. "It says *Pooping at Tiffany's*."

Claire shook her head. "That is the most *you* thing I've ever seen in my life."

"Right? I even watched a YouTube video on how to use them. You put your hand inside, and then pick up the poop, pull the bag inside out, and knot it. Voilà! Her poops aren't that big, right?"

"Not at all," Claire lied, because the truth might result in Claire missing her plane because Audrey had backed out of her offer to watch the dog.

"Okay, I have to ask," Audrey said as she walked Claire to the front door. "Does Scott know?"

"Not the details, but I told him the truth. That I came across a travel deal I couldn't resist, that I haven't gone anywhere since Brayden died and I was overdue a vacation, and that I wouldn't leave Bob with anyone I didn't trust with my life."

"Aww," Audrey said, giving her a quick hug. "But wait, I feel like you're avoiding the topic. Is this trip just for kicks or because you're trying not to think about him?"

Claire winced. "You know."

"That you're in love with Scott?" Audrey asked sympathetically. "Yeah, honey. I think we all do. In those final days before he left, you had a frequent sex glow, but it was the other stuff at the beach house that made me realize it was more than that. The way he looked at you like you were the best gift he'd ever received. The hand brushes. The food sharing."

"You and Clarke share food."

"Because Clarke can barely feed himself. It's different, and you know it."

Claire wasn't so sure it *was* different, but she wasn't exactly in a position to be lecturing anyone about romance right now. She'd *barely* recovered from the reality of her crappy marriage before getting her heart broken all over again. Hence the spontaneous trip. She'd decided that this time, she wasn't waiting an entire year to heal. She needed a shortcut to resetting her life, and a new environment seemed the way to do it.

Plus, it gave her an excuse to take a break from the FaceTime calls with Scott. They were the highlight of her entire existence, and *that* wouldn't do. At this rate, she'd have to have another bonfire next year to get over Scott.

"I'm sorry," Audrey said, her brown eyes worried. "I hate that you're hurting. Again."

"My fault," Claire said with a smile. "The guy *did* warn me from the very beginning that he wasn't sticking around. And Naomi warned me a million times. I should have trusted the pact, trusted you guys to pick out the heartbreakers when I couldn't."

"Well, actually," Audrey admitted, "I sort of feel like I let you down. Naomi knew that Scott was one of the heartbreakers. *I*, on the other hand, thought he was the one. Why do you think I insisted Oliver invite him to the beach house?"

"Audrey! That was you?"

"I know! I'm sorry. But you and I had such good luck with Naomi! Remember when she was dating Dylan, and we were like, 'Hello? Oliver?' I thought Scott was your Oliver. I was so sure . . ." She sighed. "Naomi would be a gloating terror if she ever found out that she was the one who was right."

"It'll be our secret, but maybe next time don't get so . . . involved?"

"Done," Audrey agreed.

Claire looked at her watch. "Okay, I've gotta get going. Just let me say goodbye to Bob."

Five minutes later, after an extremely emotional goodbye to the dog, Claire loaded her suitcase into the truck of a cab and climbed into the back seat. "JFK, please."

The taxi started its slow crawl through traffic, and Claire looked down at her iPhone, double-checking her boarding pass for peace of mind.

JFK to CDG. Nonstop.

She was finally off to see the Eiffel Tower properly.

## Chapter Thirty-One

*I*t was a gray day when she arrived at her hotel, but Claire didn't mind in the least. In fact, it suited her slightly melancholy, jet-lagged mood. And though she'd thought she wanted nothing more than to go straight to bed after a sleepless red-eye flight, it was morning in Paris, and as she stepped onto the small balcony of her hotel room, she realized that the excitement of being in a new city provided a surprising source of energy.

She inhaled as she scanned the Paris rooftops, then let her breath out again when she caught partial sight of the Eiffel Tower in the near distance.

As she'd known it would, it made her think of Scott. Of his fondness for the city, his obsession with the structure. It had occurred to Claire when she booked the trip that there were other destinations where it'd be easier to get over him. Places that he hadn't mentioned, where she wouldn't be thinking of him every time she passed his beloved Eiffel Tower.

But she didn't want to do what she'd done with Brayden. To lock all of her feelings in a room with a closed door. She wanted to face the emotions, knowing that even though there'd be pain, there'd also be memories. The good kind.

Claire needed to figure out how to be okay with how she and Scott had ended up—her being in love, him not so much. Paris had seemed like a good compromise. To be reminded of him without having to see him. By the end of the trip, her goal was to be able to think of the man without her chest aching.

It was a tall order, but she was determined.

Claire sent a text to her parents and Naomi, letting them know she'd arrived safely. Then another to Audrey, thanking her for the twelve—yes, twelve—pictures of Bob.

Then . . .

Then, she had nothing planned other than to roam and, hopefully, acquaint herself with the city. Armed with her purse and an umbrella, Claire left the hotel to begin exploring.

She got why the city was so beloved almost immediately. Not in a way her early-twenty-something self had grasped. She'd liked it well enough then, but as she'd told Scott, that had been more about checking sights off a list.

Claire saw Paris through a different lens now. Saw the way the city had both elegance and grit, noise and quiet, crowds and solitude. She caught a whiff of fresh bread, saw a bakery line out the door, and made a mental note to stop by tomorrow for what she'd been calling her "Eiffel Tower Day."

She was determined to do it right, as she had promised Scott she would. Wine, bread, the blanket, the picnic basket. And yes, she'd be bringing the fresh flowers he'd vetoed since he wouldn't be around to know one way or the other.

For now though, she just wandered, not taking pictures, not walking anywhere in particular, and yet somehow she ended up at the Eiffel Tower anyway. She stood for a long time, staring up at it, trying to see it through Scott's eyes.

She imagined he saw a whole boatload of stuff she didn't see. The engineering, the metal, the geometry of it. Even to her untrained eye, she had to admit it was pretty fantastic.

So fantastic that even without her picnic supplies, she scanned the grass area for a place to sit, comforted to see that she wasn't the only person alone. There were plenty of couples, a handful of families, but there was also an older lady in a yellow dress. A guy with his sketchbook. A teen on her cell phone. A man in flannel . . .

Claire's gaze had already flitted on to the next person, but slowly, as though in a dream, she dragged her eyes back to the guy wearing flannel. His back had been to her before, but he'd turned his head. And was now looking right at her.

*Scott.*

No, it couldn't be.

She looked closer. It was him. Heart pounding, she started walking toward him.

His gaze was unreadable, even when she stood directly in front of him, looking down at his face, half-terrified he'd disappear if she said a word.

He spoke first, looking pointedly at both her empty hands. "Was I not clear in the proper way to do this?"

"What?" Her voice was breathy, nothing like how she was used to hearing it.

"I distinctly remembering mentioning wine. Baguette. A blanket. Flowers."

"You nixed the flowers," Claire interjected.

He smiled slightly, reaching to his left and holding up a bouquet of mixed flowers in shades of pink and yellow. "I decided you were right."

Slowly coming out of her daze, Claire took it all in. The flowers. The wine. Two glasses. The baguette poking out of the picnic basket.

The fact that *he was here*.

He shifted to the side in silent invitation, and Claire slowly lowered beside him, mostly because her legs were shaky and she still wasn't sure this was real. She looked back at him, found his gaze moving hungrily over her face as though relearning her every feature and committing them to memory.

"What are you doing here?" she whispered.

He nodded toward the tower. "Best view in the house from right here."

"No, I meant—"

"I know what you meant." Scott took a deep breath, and she realized that he wasn't quite as calm and unaffected as he wanted to seem. "Ask me how Shanghai is," he said.

"Um, okay," Claire said slowly. "How's Shanghai?"

"Fascinating."

*Wonderful.*

"Ask me how the job is," he said.

"I already know how the job is; I just talked to you—"

"Ask me, Claire."

The urgency in his voice gave her pause. "All right. How's the job?"

"As interesting as promised."

"Good, I'm glad—"

"Ask me again why I'm here." He was closer now, his eyes intent on hers.

"Well, it's hard when you keep interrupting me."

He didn't look away. "Ask me."

"Why are you here?"

Scott lifted a hand, pressing the backs of his fingers to her cheek, then cupped her face. "I'm here because apparently an interesting city and a fascinating job don't do it for me anymore. So I quit."

Claire shook her head, not believing what she was hearing. "You can't quit. That's your life."

"No, Claire." He moved closer. "*You're* my life. You, Bob. New York."

"But you *left*," she said, unable to keep the accusation out of her voice. "You left me. And Bob. Rather easily, too."

"Not easily," he said roughly, moving even closer, his expression pleading. "Not even close. I know I made a mistake. And I know I haven't earned a second chance, but damn it, Claire, I want one more than I've ever wanted anything."

"A chance for what?"

"Anything. Whatever you'll give me." Both his hands were on her face now. "Please—" Claire cut off his words with a kiss, feeling the way he froze in surprise, then relaxed with relief before kissing her back. "I love you," he whispered softly against her mouth.

Claire couldn't remember ever feeling so happy. She rested her hand against his cheek, smiling at the familiar stubble, then she pulled back slightly. "Wait. How did you find me?"

"It's Paris. Everyone comes to the Eiffel Tower on their first day. But if you hadn't, my plan was to show up every day until you did."

"No, how did you know I was in Paris at all?"

"Two guesses. And let's just say it wasn't Naomi, who hung up after delivering a blistering assessment of my character."

She laughed. "Audrey, then. So much for her promise not to get involved anymore."

He smiled. "Turns out she had a good feeling about me."

"Actually, more like she was trying to soften you up so you didn't get mad."

He frowned. "About what?"

"I take it you don't follow her on Instagram."

He shook his head, and Claire pulled out her phone and brought up Audrey's feed.

"Holy hell," he muttered. "Is my dog dressed up as Chewbacca?"

"Audrey wanted to get her Halloween on early. She decided ages ago on sexy Princess Leia but wanted a Yoda. Clarke said no, so she decided on Bob."

He glanced again at the picture in confusion. "So what happened to the Yoda plan?"

"This was her plan B after Bob ate Yoda's ears."

Scott nodded. "Sounds about right." He looked up. "How much longer do we have to talk about my dog and Audrey and *Star Wars* before you tell me how you feel about me?"

"Well now, see," she said, plucking grass, "I tried to tell you when I saw my kitchen. That's when I knew. But you cut me off."

"I know," he said in a rough voice. "I won't cut you off now."

Claire lifted his hand with both of hers, pressed a kiss to his knuckles. His eyes closed, only to open when she spoke. "I love you, Scott."

He swallowed, then cleared his throat with a jerky nod, before pulling the picnic basket toward them.

"You hungry?"

"Um, sure," she said, surprised and a little disappointed at the unceremonious reaction to her telling him how she felt, but then this was Scott. She hadn't fallen in love with the guy because he was one for romantic words.

She lifted the lid and peeked inside. The baguette, as expected. Cheese. Strawberries. Champagne. She looked at him with a smile, but he didn't smile back, his expression strangely intense.

When she glanced into the basket once more, she saw why. Nestled among the picnic supplies was a small white box that didn't look like it belonged. Baffled, she reached for the box and opened it.

Claire gasped. Sparkling up at her was the biggest, most extravagant ring she'd ever seen. The center diamond was large in its own right. The diamonds surrounding it were *each* bigger than the stone on her old ring. And the little pink diamonds that formed a border around the bigger diamonds? Those were perfect.

"Don't you dare tell me it's too much," he said, reaching out and pulling the ring from the box. "Because I want everyone who sees this, and that includes the astronauts on the International Space Station, to know that you're taken."

His eyes searched hers. "You want me to do the knee thing? I'll do the knee thing."

She laughed, a little breathless, still staring at the ring. "Isn't this all kind of soon? We have time."

He reached for her left hand, rubbed his finger along the base of her fourth finger. "It's not too soon for me. You're it for me, Claire. But if you need time, I'll wait as long as it takes."

Claire gave the only answer she could, the one that had been lodged in her heart the second she saw him sitting on the picnic blanket watching her. "I don't need time," she said, looking at him with a bright smile. "Yes. Yes!"

She laughed as he enthusiastically slid the ring on her finger, as though fearing she'd change her mind.

"Oh, that's heavy," she said in surprise.

"Good heavy?"

"*Great* heavy," she said, kissing him softly.

"How soon until I get to marry you?" he asked, lowering her to the blanket beneath the Eiffel Tower.

Claire smiled. "We'll figure it out. Later."

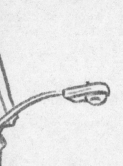

# Epilogue

*A*nd you thought *I'd* be insufferable," Naomi protested. "Audrey hasn't stopped gloating since you got back from Paris. Also, Claire, hon, please make sure you take a water break. Lugging that ring around has got to be dehydrating."

Claire grinned, lifting her left hand and wiggling her ring, the light bouncing around Audrey's sunny kitchen. "It never gets old."

"Bob, sweetie, put the Louboutin down," Audrey said as she handed them each a champagne flute. "I swear, they say dogs are color-blind, but Bob only seems to go for the red soles."

"Don't judge her," Naomi said. "She has excellent taste. Who is that poor dog even living with these days?"

"Claire and Scott, but I get regular visitation rights," Audrey explained.

"Ah. And where are you living?" Naomi asked Claire. "Since you have, what? *Three* places to choose from?"

"Mine. Are you kidding? That sucker took months of planning. I want to enjoy the fruits of my labor," Claire replied.

"And Scott's labor?" Naomi nudged.

"Eh. Maybe a little. I guess he did some stuff. Built the kitchen, redid the bathrooms, changed all the flooring, painted all the walls . . ."

"But you Pinterested *hard*," Audrey pointed out.

"I did. I really did. Thank you for noticing."

Naomi had picked up Claire's left hand and was tilting it in every direction. "I still can't believe you're married. I haven't even found my dress yet."

"Second wedding prerogative," Claire pointed out. "I've already done the big white wedding. This time around, I just wanted Scott."

"Don't cry," Naomi said, pointing a warning finger at an already blubbering Audrey without looking away from Claire. "But it is pretty damn sweet the way you guys are doing things your way, all out of order."

Scott and Claire had spent the week in Paris on what they'd called their honeymoon. Then they'd come home and gotten married at city hall on the way back from the airport. Then they'd moved into the home they'd built together.

Scott had started work almost immediately on a new building in the city, one he swore he liked even better than the Shanghai project. It didn't hurt that the architect of this one was none other than Oliver Cunningham.

Life was just about perfect.

Naomi set Claire's hand aside and turned her attention toward Audrey. "All right, Tate. Two of us in the pact down, one to go."

"Well, actually," Claire pointed out. "The pact was to help each other *avoid* the Manhattan womanizers, not necessarily to help each other find the right guy."

Naomi gave her a look. "Really? Says the one who's been

looking like the personification of the heart-eyes emoji for the past few weeks?"

"I do want that," Audrey admitted. "But I'll also point out that I'm the only one with a perfect record on picking out the good ones. Naomi couldn't see Oliver when he was right under her nose, and she misjudged Scott. Claire saw Oliver's potential, but kissed way too many frogs before realizing Scott was the one."

"Your point?" Naomi said.

"Just that the record proves that I am the best judge of male character. I love your intentions, but at this rate, I'll have *married* my dream guy before you two have even spotted him. Bob, no! Drop the Louboutin!"

Claire and Naomi exchanged a knowing look as Audrey bent to wrestle a shoe from the dog. They'd both already spotted Audrey's perfect guy.

And he was sitting right under her nose.

# *Acknowledgments*

Thank you so much for letting me share Claire and Scott's love story with you! I hope you enjoyed watching these two stubborn souls journey to happily ever after!

I *loved* writing this story, but as always, it didn't make it from my imagination to the bookshelf without the help of a fantastic team who deserve my heartfelt thanks:

My agent, Nicole Resciniti, always deserves a shout-out, but she was instrumental in this book in particular for helping me navigate some tricky rewrites.

Marla Daniels, my lovely editor, for throwing your entire heart into making sure we got this one exactly right. And to Sara Quaranta for stepping in and taking this book under your wing to help get it out into the world.

To the entire Simon & Schuster team, thank you for your amazing marketing, design, and production support. Especially Hannah Payne for making sure this book got into all the right hands!

Kristi Yanta—I hope you know that I absolutely could not have made this story sparkle without your thoughtful notes.

Lisa Filipe, you're a freaking treasure.

Jennifer Probst and Rachel Van Dyken, your email assistance on this book was absolutely pivotal, and Jessica Lemmon, you always know when I need to be reminded to take a breath and step away when I feel stuck.

And last, but never least, to Anth. For the coffee, and for the wine.